'This is my dear wife, Cry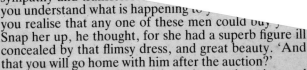
all the appearance of a st
'We've fallen on 'ard tin
bring 'er 'ere. But I got
before I signs up and go

It was a familiar stor
sympathy and transferre
you understand what is happening to y
you realise that any one of these men could buy y
Snap her up, he thought, for she had a superb figure ill
concealed by that flimsy dress, and great beauty. 'And
that you will go home with him after the auction?'

For answer, she stepped into the auction ring and
stood there without moving or smiling; the wind lifted
her hair and skirts. She held the flimsy tatters of her
dress across her bosom, and looked into the distance as
though she saw neither the men nor the cattle . . .

After graduating from Bristol University in 1973, Una Power travelled and lived on the Continent, enjoyed reporting and interviewing for BBC Radio Bristol, and lectured in Social Sciences in England and Southern Ireland. Her art student son Robert encouraged her to write, which she now does all the time in her Irish country home. For recreation she abandons her garden and typewriter and samples Dublin theatre.

THE BRIDE SALE

Una Power

MILLS & BOON LIMITED
ETON HOUSE 18–24 PARADISE ROAD
RICHMOND SURREY TW9 1SR

First published in Great Britain 1988
by Mills & Boon Limited

© Una Power 1988

Australian copyright 1988
Philippine copyright 1988
This edition 1988

ISBN 0 263 76107 X

Set in 10 on 10 pt Linotron Times
04–0688–83,050

Photoset by Rowland Phototypesetting Limited
Bury St Edmunds, Suffolk
Made and printed in Great Britain

For Maurice and Mamie Power

PROLOGUE

THE DISTANT thunder of many horses moving swiftly over the sun-baked land held an ominous quality that sent ripples of disturbance through the quiet of the great hacienda. The child stilled her faltering hands and allowed them to rest on the keys of the pianoforte. Surely Papa would never drive his men and horses so quickly in the heat of the noonday sun? She sent a questioning glance at her mother, but the smooth head of Dona Margaret was bent upon a piece of embroidery and her slender white hands continued as calmly as ever. 'Pray continue that piece, Maria. I should like you to master it,' Dona Margaret commanded gently.

But as the relentless pounding drew closer and closer to the great walled house the atmosphere in the room became imperceptibly tense and the child saw that her nurse, Pepita, was uneasy and restless. There was a clamouring at the gates and the air rang with the coarse shouts of alien horsemen. Even then the child felt no stirring of the fear which showed plainly in the eyes of her elders, for her father had left the strictest instructions that the iron gates were to be opened to none but himself, and in the ordered world in which Maria existed nobody would dare to disobey Papa, for he was lord and master of all the lands beyond the massive white walls that circled the house.

Then the incredible and unbelievable happened: the unmistakable sound of the gates swinging wide open and the clatter of hooves upon the cobbled courtyard. Setting aside her embroidery, Dona Margaret rose from her seat, tall and graceful, but the uncertainty in her face filled the child with more terror than the urgent clamouring at the front door and the sounds of servants running in all directions, their voices filled with fearful dismay.

'Take Maria to her room. Bolt the door, and do not come out until I send for you.' It was the altered state of voice and face of her dignified and authoritative Mama that signalled the collapse of Maria's small safe world, for she barely understood the significance of the battering against the doors and the sharp splintering of wood.

Pepita, running down the long corridor that led to the rooms at the back of the house, pulled the sobbing child with her. 'We must make the greatest of haste,' she whispered urgently. 'Dry your tears and be silent.' She pushed Maria into the dim cool bedroom; with trembling hands she dragged the bolts across the door, and flattening herself against it, began to listen.

'What is happening, Pepita?' Maria tugged at the coarse wool skirt of her maid. 'Why is Mama afraid? Where is Papa?'

The colour drained from Pepita's rosy cheeks and her eyes darkened with some new terror; her full bosom began to heave and her nostrils dilated; her thick dark curls clung to a damp brow. 'They are invading everywhere!' Her voice was hardly more than a whisper, but the child knew instantly that 'they' were not good people.

Many booted feet tramped everywhere, and glass shattered and wood splintered. The child dimly comprehended the meaning of the sharp agonised screams, abruptly stilled, to be followed by more and yet more hideous noises of carnage.

'Will Papa come?' Fear began to suffocate her, and her breathing was as laboured as that of her nurse.

'I do not know.'

Maria felt suddenly stifled in her many petticoats and stiff red damask dress, and experienced a primitive urge to flee—to flee that room that was no longer safe, and the great house itself, and escape across the sun-baked plain. She ran to the window. It was shuttered, but a slight opening afforded some light and a narrow view across the back courtyard to where the stables lay, as yet untouched by the intruders. Beckoning to Pepita, she pointed to a small wooden door beside the stable. 'Look, it is open!' She was excited and hopeful, for the glorious prospect of freedom was revealed in the vast empty plains beyond the house.

Pepita was transfixed with naked fear, for the booted feet had begun to run down their corridor and drew closer and closer. There must be many men, and their excited shouting and guttural laughter seemed to immobilise her.

Grasping her hand, Maria pulled her nurse forward. 'We can escape! There are horses in the stable.'

A spark of hope showed in Pepita's sombre eyes and she sprang into action as a thunderous assault began upon the door of the room. She lifted the bar from the shutters, opened the window, and throwing the child out, clambered after her. Stout as the door was, it could not long withstand that assault.

They ran to the stable, and even here the horses stirred and fidgeted as though they knew that their privileged life was over. Choosing a small sturdy mare, Pepita flung a saddle over her back and with inexpert hands made clumsy with fear, began to fasten the girths. Maria pulled a halter from the wall, and thrust it at her. As they led the mare out, the child breathed in the familiar warm tang of the place and longed to remain there, hidden and safe, but the shattering of wood and the angry shouts of a mob robbed of its prey made her dart after Pepita. She did not protest when she was thrown up into the saddle, but the sudden movement caused the mare to sidle about and whinny in amazement at such unexpected treatment. Sprawled upon the ground before her, the child saw her father's body-servant, João, his white shirt and trousers stained with blood. She knew instantly that he was dead. Beside him was his small son, his face a bloodied pulp, and she cried out involuntarily. This cry was their undoing, for it revealed their existence and position.

With exultant whoops, the men who had battered down her bedroom door leapt into the courtyard. They were soldiers in red and silver uniforms, their swarthy faces alight with some emotion that Maria could not identify, but feared. Some primitive instinct told her that they were more deadly than the great swords they carried, which flashed in bright arcs against the clear blue sky. Frantically she tried to pull her nurse up behind

her, but her small hands were no match for those of the
men, who pulled Pepita to the ground. The mare bolted
for the gate, and the soldiers, bent upon a different
sport, were not able to stop that headlong gallop of the
panic-stricken animal as she carried her small rider to
freedom.

Above the drumming of the hooves, Maria heard
again and again the screams of her nurse as the soldiers
pushed her to the ground. She did not see the clouds of
dust raised by the animal, but saw over and over again
the swirl of Pepita's white frilled petticoats and the
hopeless anguish in her dark eyes. Her small fingers
clung tenaciously to the mane, and she dug in her knees
as far as her stiff red skirts would allow. She was too
numbed by the shocking events of the past hour to allow
herself to contemplate what had happened to her
mother. At the back of her thoughts a fresh terror
assailed her, for she could not comprehend the fact that
her tall, godly Papa had not come, had allowed this
dreadful thing to happen; her awareness shied away
from the only explanation.

The weary animal had slowed to a walking pace as she
began to climb towards the high country. The house
servants had always spoken contemptuously of these
high plains and their inhabitants; they would shrug a
shoulder and jerk a chin towards them and speak of the
savages who lived there. Could they be the soldiers who
had invaded her home and her life? Maria shuddered
with fear, but could not turn back. It was colder up here,
and the land had a desolate lonely air. The light was
fading quickly, but she could discern the few bare shrubs
that jutted out of the dry earth. There seemed to be no
shelter anywhere, and in utter exhaustion, she slipped
from the saddle and lay upon the hard cold ground, and
slept.

The sun warmed her face and body, and she stayed quite
still without opening her eyes. For a moment, Maria
could hear quiet murmurings in a strange tongue. She
felt soothed and safe, and the events of the day before
seemed far away and unreal. Cautiously she opened her

eyes and sat up, staring about her in great astonishment.

A number of pointed tents were grouped in a wide circle, and beyond the tents, horses were coralled within a rough wooden circular fence. Curiously-dressed people with flat copper-coloured faces moved placidly about the encampment. They seemed undisturbed by her presence, and more interested in the assortment of cooking-pots outside each tent than anything else. A group of giggling children regarded her shyly and kept pointing at her clothes. They seemed to find her many petticoats and stiff damask dress exquisitely amusing. She turned her head away, for little covered their gleaming copper bodies. What manner of people were they? Even the poorest of their servants at the hacienda gave their children shoes, but these seemed content to run barefoot. Everyone had long dark hair, the women's braided, the men's confined by a stitched headband.

The fragrant aroma arising from the pot close to her made her realise how very hungry she was. She had no idea how she came to be lying on a soft striped rug outside one of these pointed tents, but was suddenly too hungry to care. Imperiously she clapped her hands, and immediately a short middle-aged woman pushed aside the tent-flap and came out to sit beside her. She stroked Maria's face and hands and crooned in a strange tongue. Instinctively the child moved away, for she had experienced close contact only with her nurse and very occasionally with Mama. Papa would throw her high into the air, calling her his little princess. The servants would never presume to touch a daughter of the house!

'I want some food. I am hungry. Bring me something to eat!' Maria demanded. But the woman did not understand. Angrily Maria leapt to her feet, and pointing to the cooking-pot from which issued those tantalising smells, she again demanded food. 'Food! I want some food.'

The woman roared with laughter, her round face crinkling so much that her black eyes almost disappeared. She got up and went back into the tent, to emerge with a small wooden bowl into which she ladled some of the food from the pot, which seemed to be a sort of stew. She handed it to Maria with a piece of hard flat bread; nodding and smiling encouragingly, she was clearly urging her to eat.

Maria was outraged: she could not eat like these savages, with no spoon or fork! The tribe seemed to have divided themselves into groups of adults and children, and were sitting cross-legged upon the ground outside the tents, absorbed in the business of eating. Mama would never have permitted her to conduct herself in such a way, to eat food with her hands, as though she were an animal. A terrible sorrow welled up in her, and the realisation that her former way of life had gone, and that this strange woman with her now perplexed face and these strange half-dressed people were a replacement, was more than she could bear. 'I want a spoon,' she said, as clearly as she could, for she was desperate to make this woman understand.

She shook her head, and Maria, thinking she had been denied, burst into an angry torrent of sobbing and flung the bowl and its contents to the ground. The flat bread she threw to one of the many dogs that rummaged ceaselessly around the circle of tents.

All eating stopped and conversation was suspended, and Maria became aware that people were staring at her with disapproval and condemnation: the children looked shocked and embarrassed, and glanced uneasily at their parents. Only the woman seemed to understand, for there was a look of compassion in her eyes as she folded the unhappy, tearful child to her warm soft bosom. There was a soothing magic in her words and touch, for Maria's fears and sorrows melted away and she was filled with warm love for this woman, who seemed to understand what was in her heart and mind and knew how to ease and protect her.

CHAPTER ONE

'TELL ME the story again: the story of my coming here.' Crystal had heard it every year for the past eight summers and never tired of hearing how her foster-mother Widela, the wise-woman of the tribe, had had a vision.

'I had felt for several days that the gods would send me a child, for you know that the cruel winter had robbed me of my man and my sons. I was very sad and lonely, and near to despair.' Widela looked dreamily into the fire then up at the star-studded sky, and fleetingly the old sadness was on her again when she thought of a good man and three strong sons who never saw another summer. Their way of life was harsh: always moving from place to place, always at the mercy of the ravages of winter and the drought of summer, stoically accepting whatever fate had for them but always sustained by a deep and abiding love of family and family life. 'I saw in my vision that soldiers would ride across the plain; that there would be much death and bloodshed; and that the only survivor would be a little girl whom I would care for, for a short while.'

'For ever, my mother! For ever,' entreated the girl. 'Tell me about the hunters finding me. I love that part of the story.'

'How surprised they were!' reminisced the woman, chuckling. 'They were hunting for our dinner and had had a good day. They were returning across the high plateau and found you curled up on the ground, fast asleep. They remembered my vision, for I had told many others about it, and they carried you here, to me.'

'I can still remember how very strange everything was—the language, the food, the clothes. But I have been so happy, so far.' She smiled tremulously. 'And when I marry Fleetfoot, I shall be even happier. I am so lucky that the gods favour me.'

Widela hesitated, as though seeking words for her

troubled thoughts, her face shadowed. 'I have always told you, Crystal, that I was to care for you for a short time only.'

'That is right, my mother, and now I shall care for you.' Crystal smiled the confident smile of youth, and her lovely face glowed with pleasure and anticipation. 'I shall marry Fleetfoot! He looks at me all the time now, and he is good and kind and the best hunter in the tribe.' She thought of Fleetfoot, his lithe strong body, bold dark eyes, and courage and daring in the hunt. 'We shall have many fine children, and care for you in your old age.'

There was a grave reserve about Widela's face. 'There will be no old age for me, Crystal. My time to depart has almost come. There was more to my vision than I have told you before, and the time has come for you to hear the rest.'

'The rest?' Crystal's green eyes widened in astonishment. 'But can there be more? I needed a mother, and you needed a daughter; the gods arranged it that way. I am to look after you, as you have always cared for me.'

'No, child, it is not to be so. I have the gift of prophecy, and I saw that you would cross a great stretch of water in a fine ship. Your marriage will not take place here, but in a country far away, the land of your mother's people. You will survive great dangers and find greater happiness than you have ever known here.'

'No, mother, no!' the girl cried out. 'This is my home, my family. These are my people.' She waved a slender hand to indicate the families who sat talking quietly in the peace and contentment of the warm evening.

'We are not your people. I have cared for you, as it was my destiny to do, and you have brought joy into my life, but it is almost over and now I must take you to the place where your new life will begin. Tomorrow we shall begin our journey to the low plains. I am taking you to the mission at São Paulo.'

Crystal did not argue, for she knew well that her loving foster-mother could be qute implacable, once her mind was made up. She knew that tone of decision and finality. Argument would be useless. She had to leave the tribe, *her* tribe, said her rebellious heart. She had quite forgotten that she had ever thought of these courageous, gently loving people as savages. She had shared their meat and respected their lodges, mourned the death of their loved ones, felt joy at each new birth and joined in each wedding feast in the happy belief that she would marry within their society.

As she carried out the usual morning duties in their lodge, her heart was heavy as she looked about the home she had taken such pride in keeping neat and wholesome. Across her bed-roll lay a lovely soft white doeskin tunic delicately embroidered with fine bead-work. Whenever she had seen Widela working upon it, she had smiled with tender love and secret anticipation, for she had imagined that it was to be her wedding dress. Her great friend Chattering Bird had married in the spring, and was already expecting her first child. Now she had learned that the dress was for her journey and not her wedding. Her foster-mother must have known for some while that they would be leaving. With a sudden pang of guilty remorse, she realised that Widela must be very ill. It was true that she did not seem to have her usual tireless energy or laugh as much, but this was not uncommon in women of her age.

'We shall take only enough food for our journey, and your own clothes,' said Widela. She could see the grief and unhappiness in Crystal's eyes but would not comment upon it, for it was not the way of her people to question the inevitable.

'Do you mean the clothes I was wearing when I came here?' Anxiety and hurt made Crystal's voice sharp.

'Yes, we shall need them.'

'Of what use are the clothes of a child to me? I am a grown woman of fifteen summers. Burn them with the other things in the lodge.' She turned away to hide her tears. The burning of the lodge took place only when a person died, and it was to be their own final task before departure.

'I know what I am doing! Do not question me. You have not yet earned the right to criticise my actions.' The little damask dress and petticoats that Crystal had worn on that day many years ago were carefully wrapped up. Widela also included the small leather slippers and the gold cross and chain in the parcel. 'Now it is time to depart.'

Silent impassive faces watched with them as their lodge was reduced to ashes and the smoke was carried away in the clear morning air. They mounted on stout ponies, and acknowledging the grave salutes of the tribe, began to move forward.

Crystal could not resist a last look at Fleetfoot. She had seen the sudden unguarded blaze of admiration in his eyes when she stepped out wearing her white doeskin dress and new boots. She had braided her hair, and wore her finest headband low on her brow. Her heart ached, for she would never look with pride upon him as he rode back from the hunt, or keep his lodge, or bear his children. There was sadness in his eyes, for his heart must be as heavy as her own.

She wondered about the low plains, for Widela had always spoken of those lands as bad lands, a place where their lives were in danger. The hunters spoke of the men with pale skins who would kill them if given the chance; only the bravest and strongest ever ventured to the low plains. She always felt a pricking of discomfort when they spoke of the men with pale skin, for her own skin was so much lighter in colour than that of the rest of them. She longed for the golden honey of her skin to darken to the glorious copper of Chattering Bird's. She had long given up the attempt to force her thick unruly brown curls into the sleek smoothness usual among her people, and had long accepted that her green eyes would never darken like Chattering Bird's. They had given her the name of Crystal because of her eyes, she believed. She was taller than the other girls, her legs were longer, and her immature frame showed voluptuous promise, but how she longed for a short body and full hips! It was not to be. She did not like being different from the others and worked harder to gather better kindling, weave softer blankets, mix brighter dyes, cook skilfully and become a good healer. She became used to walking great distances without tiring or complaint.

The weather was sultry as they made camp, and the smell of a great herd of cattle, some miles distant, wafted to them. Crystal felt stifled: she longed to return to the high plateau and breathe the cold clean air.

'This is our last camp, for by another nightfall we shall have reached your destination,' said Widela.

Crystal was surprised by this announcement in the act of making a small fire. They seemed to have journeyed endlessly, and in the enforced act of bidding goodbye to her old way of life she had given little thought to the beginning of a new one.

'And you, my mother, what of you?' Crystal had seen that, with each day, her foster-mother had grown weaker. She seemed smaller, and the much loved face was lined and drawn with pain.

'I shall be glad for both of us. Do not fret for me. I shall be happy, for very soon I shall be with my man again. He is waiting for me, and I long to see him.' There was such quiet happiness in Widela's voice that Crystal rejoiced for her.

'What shall I do without you?' she whispered.

'Live your life, silly child!' A brief return of Widela's old spirit and humour brought a smile to Crystal's face. 'Now let us sleep, for tomorrow is an important day for both of us.'

By the following evening Widela was very weak, and they were both thirsty. 'It is not much further,' murmured the sick woman. 'We are almost there. We are going to the mission station that lies on the plain outside São Paulo, and soon we shall be safe.'

Crystal had heard of the mission station many times, although she had never been there. It was the only place on the low plains that the tribe spoke of with any respect or admiration. Sometimes, if the winter had been exceptionally unyielding, the mission had given them food; once, when the chief's son had been very sick and the tribal medicine was not powerful enough to save him, he had been taken there to be cured.

The tolling of a single bell in the distance was the most welcome sound that Crystal had heard for days. When the squat, white-walled building came into view, it evoked a dim memory of her former home, except that here there were no massive iron gates and gracious cobbled courtyard with a lovely fountain. A great wooden door was firmly shut to the outside world. A bell-rope hung beside the door, and helping Widela from the pony, she tugged vigorously at it. The grille was pulled back, and the girl found herself being scrutinised by a pair of shrewd dark eyes set in a narrow ascetic face.

Brother Francis, who had joined the mission in Brazil as a young man, was devoted to his work and rejoiced constantly that God had given them such a rewarding task. The pastoral care of the poor was often intermingled with assisting Indians from the high plateau with the many difficulties they encountered when they journeyed to the low plains. Instantly he could see that the woman was beyond whatever medical help they could render. The girl was very beautiful, and although Brother Francis was long inured to the temptations of the flesh, it was several seconds before he could take his eyes from her face. With a slight start of puzzlement he realised that the girl was not Indian. She was tall and well-shaped; her wide-set eyes were green and flecked with amber, fringed by long dark lashes. Although her skin was tanned, it was not dark, and in a temperate climate would probably be much lighter. A thick mass of curly dark hair sprang away from a high round brow and fell in soft waves about her shoulders. Quickly supressing the urge to banish the anxiety and strain from those lovely eyes and make her smile, he recollected his duties and opened the gate.

Widela was barely able to walk, and Brother Francis, pushing back the hood of his coarse habit, helped her into the small courtyard. The tolling bell was still, and an atmosphere of deep calm and peace reigned in the courtyard and the buildings that flanked it on all sides.

'I must bring you refreshment.' It was a relief to hear that he spoke their tongue. 'Please sit here, on this bench in the shade.'

Crossing the courtyard, he removed the slab of wood over a well, and dipping a small metal cup into the water, offered it to the sick woman.

'I am in my last sickness,' Widela gasped as she sipped the water. 'You must bring me immediately to your Father Superior. I have spoken with him once before.'

'First, you must rest,' he insisted.

'There . . . is . . . no . . . time.' Widela's drawn face and laboured breathing bore out the truth of her words.

'I know that.' The man was infinitely kind and gentle as he looked at the sick woman. 'I shall fetch the Father Superior to you.'

'No.' Widela was firm, and seemed to gather new strength from a source deep within herself. 'Stay here, Crystal. I shall see Father Superior alone.'

Crystal watched as he helped Widela towards a door at the far end of the courtyard, and knew for certain that she had reached her journey's end. She wondered what would become of herself.

After a brief interval, the man came out of the Father Superior's room, and hurrying down the courtyard, went to Widela's pony and removed the bundle tied to the saddle. It contained Crystal's early childhood clothes, those she had worn on that desperate flight from her home. What interest could they be to anyone but herself?

Vernon Marshall had renounced title and wealth to enter the religious life. His aristocratic face and bearing were a trifle daunting until one saw the engaging twinkle in his eyes and felt the warmth of his love for his fellow man. 'It seems that your foster-mother brought you here, Crystal, so that we could take care of you and, in time, send you abroad.' He smiled, and raised his eyebrows. 'She did not have any idea just where we should send you.' He paused, and picked up the gold cross and chain and examined them carefully. 'You are probably a Christian, so we have a double duty to protect you. It is likely that your parents were among that group of landowners who sadly perished in the revolution here in Brazil in 1820, and that we shall never known your true identity.'

'Does that matter?' Crystal was impatient. 'What of my foster-mother? Where have you taken her?'

'She is being well cared for in a cubicle in our infirmary,' the Father Superior admonished her gently. 'You may go to her soon; she would like that.' He leaned forward and lightly clasped his hands. Crystal sensed that he was a good man whose delicate appearance belied a hardy spirit and iron determination. 'I have promised her that you will be prepared here, at this mission, and sent to England.'

'England?' Crystal was perplexed. 'What a strange, cold sound that has.'

'Not at all.' He smiled, and his eyes twinkled engagingly. 'It is very different from this country, but I am sure you will like it. We have connections there, so naturally that is where we shall send you. But, first, you must learn to speak English.'

A cold chill ran through Crystal's body as she became aware of how drastically her life was going to change. Leaving her tribe had been a hard experience, Widela's approaching death she could barely contemplate without anguish, and now she must learn a new language and go far away to a land with a cold, hard name. She schooled her features into passive acceptance of the inevitable and hoped that none of her feelings showed.

'Your foster-mother has given me a quantity of precious stones, which are more than enough to pay for your passage, so that there will be some money left for you.'

After Widela's death, the Father Superior insisted that Crystal should begin to learn English. He taught her a little of the history of England and the names of the large cities.

Frequently she detected a note of pride and love in his voice, and was curious. 'If you loved England so much, why did you come to Brazil?' She hoped that her question did not sound impertinent.

'I loved God more,' he replied with simplicity.

She learned a great deal about manners and customs, and mastered English so rapidly that he suspected it might have been her original tongue. The brothers at the mission, she discovered, were as industrious as they were dedicated, and worked ceaselessly among the poor.

The school which opened for a few hours every morning was well attended, and Crystal was delighted when she was allowed to help with the smaller children. Brother Michael ran it, and she was pleased when he taught her to read and write. His pupil was quick and apt, and his scholarly soul revelled in her ready intelligence and endless questions.

He was a young man, and despite his vow of celibacy, his grey eyes lit up when the tall beautiful girl entered his austere schoolroom. The doeskin dress clung to the budding curves of her body and revealed the long line of her shapely legs. He looked away, aware that he had been staring.

'Where are the children this morning, Brother Michael?'

There was music in her slightly husky voice, and he found her accented English enchanting. 'They will be here later.' He spoke gruffly, for he was ashamed of the longing he felt for her.

'Are you angry with me?' She was surprised, for she had grown fond of Brother Michael in the two months she had spent in the mission. 'Have I neglected some task?'

He looked into her green, amber-flecked eyes and understood how she had been called Crystal for the sake of their magnificence and for the quality of purity that radiated from her. 'No, it is nothing to do with you,' he managed to say in as normal a voice as he could muster. 'You never neglect a task. Indeed,' he strove to make his voice sound as usual, 'I shall be sorry to lose you.'

'Lose me?' She was puzzled, for although she knew she would be going to England, she had imagined it would be in the following spring. She had learned enough to know that a sea voyage in winter would be hazardous. 'I had not thought I was to go so soon. Father Superior has said nothing.'

'He will. The sooner the better.' Brother Michael spoke more sharply than he intended. He was angry with himself, and her closeness disturbed him deeply. Her thick hair brushed against his shoulder as her head drooped forward, and he was almost overcome with a desire to take her in his arms and tell her that he longed to keep her at his side for ever. He toyed wildly with the idea of going to Father Superior and admitting that he loved this girl and would take her back to England himself. The violence of his own tormented feelings shocked him, but he had come to Brazil as a missionary, and as such he must leave. Squaring his shoulders and breathing deeply, he attempted to call to order his disruptive feelings. He turned back to the forlorn girl, and said gently, 'I want you to stay with the children, for I must speak urgently with Father Superior.'

Crystal stared unhappily after him as he left the room. Had she offended him in some way?

The twinkle was pronounced in the Father Superior's eyes as he regarded with affection the troubled face of the young priest who sat at the opposite side of his desk. He was fond of Brother Michael, and recognised in him the burgeoning of an exceptional talent that this troubled, revolution-torn country would value highly in the future. 'You have experienced your first temptation, my son, but it is not the end of the world, you know!'

'But you gave her into my care, and I have harboured feelings for her that are . . . that should be . . . forbidden.' Brother Michael flushed painfully, and looked so wretched that the Father Superior was moved on his behalf.

'We must all suffer temptation, and you have discovered that you have the feelings of an ordinary man. The cloth you wear will not protect you against them, but it is the manner in which you choose to deal with these feelings that will protect you. Crystal is a beautiful girl, and I believe she will always have this effect on men.'

'She is hardly more than a child. I feel as though I have betrayed her!' blurted out Brother Michael.

'She is fifteen or so; hardly a child, but without a woman's experience or emotions. Many of the girls here in São Paulo are mothers at that age! Be patient with yourself in your future dealings with Crystal.'

'Do you mean that she is to remain with me?' Brother Michael was aghast.

'Certainly I do!' retorted the Father Superior with asperity. 'I can hardly send her to Rio de Janeiro immediately because you suffer temptations you find difficult to master!'

'Has she no family left? I thought you were trying to establish her identity.'

'Without much success, I fear. Widela died before she was able to tell me more precisely where the child was discovered. It would seem, from the little that Crystal has been able to tell me, that her mother was possibly English, and her father was certainly a wealthy landowner. She cannot recall her original name, which is a pity, as it would have been a great help. As it is,' he spread wide his hands, in a gesture of despair, 'there is not enough information. Possibly relatives in England or in some other European country might have come here to seek her, but with insurrectionists still roaming the country, they decided that the entire family was dead.'

'What is to become of her?'

'I intend that she shall sail to England with Sir James Allenwood, who has already promised to convey one of the boys. As our plans have changed, I am confident that he will have no objection to taking Crystal instead.'

'Allenwood!' Brother Michael frowned. 'I sailed out here with him. He is stern and, I fear, not altogether kind. I hope he does not make her unhappy.'

There was a good deal of amused comprehension in the eyes of the Father Superior. 'Sir James is an autocratic man, but just. His Captain has the greatest respect and admiration for him.'

'Captain Hastings? I remember him well. At first I thought he was the father of Sir James.'

'Dear me, no. Sir James's father was quite different! A quick-tempered man, very difficult to please, who always managed his estates with admirable sense, but was wholly devoid of humour or charm. I have often thought that his son might not have embraced the sea quite so fervently if the relationship between the two had been more loving.'

'The description of the father sounds exactly like the son, for I observed that he was dour and harsh. I hope he realises that Crystal is a girl and will not deal unpleasantly with her.'

'He has a ready intelligence, Brother Michael, so I am sure he will realise, very quickly, that Crystal is a girl,' said the Father Superior, smiling.

Despite the easy manner with which he had conducted the interview, the Father Superior was gravely disturbed. As soon as he had dismissed Brother Michael, he summoned a messenger and, giving him very precise instruction, sent him to Rio de Janeiro with a message that required an urgent answer.

CHAPTER TWO

'AM I TO leave you?' Crystal enquired with deepest anxiety as soon as the children had left the room, their lessons finished for the day.

'Not yet.' Brother Michael fiddled about with some slates on his desk, absently wiping them clean again and again. He said briskly, 'I wish you to work harder, and to study more on your own. I believe you are capable of being independent of me.'

'So I am to stay?' She breathed a great sigh of relief.

'Yes.'

'I am so happy, for I could not bear to leave you yet.' The radiant smile that accompanied these words was almost his undoing, but he remained in his seat and regarded her as steadily as he could. 'I am so happy here, Brother Michael. I have loved every minute of it. I know I must go to England soon, but I want to stay with you as long as possible.' She looked so innocently trusting that he stilled the agonised voice in his heart and determined to put away all thoughts of her.

In the weeks that followed, she could sense that he had withdrawn to some remote area of his mind that she could not reach. She was maturing, and had developed an awareness of other people; she knew that he was not angry with her, only with himself, and longed to help him. That he might feel for her as Fleetfoot had felt never occurred to her for a moment, for she understood that these holy men were father to all people who came to them, and desired no wife or child to call their own.

The first bitter winds of winter had begun to sweep across the plains when the Father Superior sent for her. 'I have great news for you, my child . . . You are to leave us. I have received word from Sir James Allenwood that one of his ships is presently docked at Rio de Janeiro and will leave for England in one week's time. You are to sail on her, and will be in England in a few months.'

'I do not think I wish to go,' Crystal said unhappily. 'Could I not remain here? I could help with the school, and I know that Brother Michael likes me.'

'I have given much thought to your future, Crystal, and I believe that the plan I have for you is in your best interests.' He placed the tips of his fingers together and regarded them steadily. 'Soon you will be a woman, a woman who will wish to marry and have children of her own. That would not be possible here.' A smile glimmered for an instant. 'Society in Brazil is divided into those who are rich and powerful, and those who are very poor. Even if we could discover who you are, your life with the Indians would preclude, absolutely, the possibility that the rich would ever accept you into their ranks. The life of the poor is crude and, frequently, degrading. I fear that you would find it impossible to live with them.'

Crystal felt chilled, but was forced to acknowledge the truth of his words. In her heart, she knew quite well that this period at the mission was only an interlude.

'I am connected, somewhat remotely by marriage, to the Allenwoods. Miss Vera Allenwood, a very good woman, I hold in the highest esteem. She has considerable means of her own, never married, and turned her home into an orphanage. I shall send you to her. I have written her a letter.' He tapped a lengthy missive which lay before him. 'It asks her to keep you at her home until such time as you are of marriageable age. Then, I trust, she will find a suitable husband for you.'

'Can she not find me a husband immediately? My friend, Chattering Bird, is married, and her baby will have been born by now.' Crystal disliked the sound of Miss Allenwood's orphanage, and could not imagine herself living there.

There was a shade of reserve about the open countenance of the Father Superior. 'It is not as simple as that. You are very beautiful, have a quick intelligence, and would adapt to English ways without any difficulty. Although society in England is more liberal than here, you will need the help and protection of someone like Miss Allenwood if you are to be accepted and established. Your residence with that lady is vital to your future success.'

'Is Sir James Allenwood, with whom I am to sail, related to Miss Allenwood?'

'They are cousins. She is a good deal older than Sir James, and has had a considerable influence over him.'

'Then they are alike!' Crystal exclaimed eagerly. 'Could he not find me a husband? Then I need not trouble Miss Allenwood.'

'Certainly not! Sir James is betrothed to Miss Sophia Jackson, and it is possible that she may exert herself on your behalf. She is much engaged in charitable works and is an estimable young woman. Single young men,' Father Superior said repressively, 'do not find husbands for young women. It is unthinkable!'

'Is Sir James a nice person? Shall I like him?'

'He is extremely reserved and lacks an openness of manner, which makes many people regard him with awe, but I believe that you will like him.'

'Do you like him?' ventured Crystal boldly, for she detected a constraint about the manner of the Father Superior.

'I respect his judgment and his ability to command the men who crew his ships.'

'But you do not like him!'

'I do not believe I expressed such an opinion.' The Father Superior sounded austere, and Crystal felt rebuked. 'There were, let us say, certain difficulties in his childhood and upbringing. He would have been quite different had his mother,' he paused, 'lived. I fear that he does not altogether care for women, and is generally more at ease with the men he commands. But I dare say that marriage will have an altogether desirable effect upon his somewhat reserved nature. He is merely the person who will convey you to your new life, so please do not worry about him.'

'I shall be sorry to leave you all, Father Superior, but you have helped me to feel more ready to go now.' She was flushed and eager for the adventure.

'I shall arrange for Brother Michael to accompany you to the city, as the country is still far from safe. He is, I

know, your special friend here, and for that reason I am
confident that he is the best person to ensure your safety
and well-being.' He looked down at the writing im-
plements on his desk and gently moved aside a small pile
of papers. 'It will be a little test of his character and
vocation, and I trust that he will survive it.'

Crystal was startled by the seriousness of his tone,
since it was she who had to make the voyage across the
ocean in a great ship with billowing sails, not Brother
Michael, and she could not understand why a ride of a
couple of days at Rio de Janeiro should be a test of his
character. Surely his vocation could never be in doubt?

She carefully cleaned and brushed her dress and
boots, and braided her hair before setting out. She was
to wear a habit for warmth and protection, because the
marauding soldiers who roamed the countryside still
respected the cloth. The Father Superior felt a momen-
tary qualm of doubt as the girl dimpled mischievously at
him from beneath her hood. 'I should have made a good
friar, Father Superior! You will be sorry to see me
go.'

'God go with you, my children,' he said to the girl and
the stern-faced young man beside her. 'We shall look for
you soon, Brother Michael, and my thoughts and
prayers will be with you.'

They rode out of the mission at a steady pace, for it
was not wise to tire the horses. Crystal's heart was glad
and her spirits rose, for although she had been very
happy at the mission of São Paolo, she had been a
member of a hunting and gathering tribe for eight years
and had begun to feel its close confinement as stifling as
the heat of the low plains. The unvarying routine of each
day had begun to irk her healthy young spirit. Quickly
banishing these thoughts, she recalled instead the great
kindness she had received from the community when her
foster-mother died. Her ignorance of their ways was
never commented upon, and she received tactful guidance for which she must always be truly grateful. But
now she longed for new sights and sounds, and with a
sudden joyous laugh urged her horse to trot, and began
to sing at the top of her voice.

Swiftly overtaking her, Brother Michael laid a re-
straining hand upon her rein. 'Are you so eager to leave
us that you would overpace your horse before the first
stage of the journey?'

'No, I am just glad to be free and back on horseback,
and—and going somewhere,' she cried out gaily. She
was not aware that, once free of the mission, she was
regarding him no longer as the withdrawn Brother
Michael of recent weeks, but as her first friend and
confidant at the mission. She longed for a return of their
easy comradeship.

'Of course you are!' His face softened, and he grinned
at her, looking younger and more relaxed.

Crystal was glad to have shed the stern and silent
companion of the last few hours and to have regained
her old friend. The next few miles were passed in easy
friendship and pleasant conversation. They were to
spend the night at a small village which marked the very
edge of the plain, and the next day they would reach Rio
de Janeiro.

'Brother Michael, surely that is the village ahead of
us? Look!' She indicated a huddle of adobe houses
ahead.

'Yes, it is.' He narrowed his eyes, and looked in the
direction she indicated. His voice and manner were
uneasy.

'Then why are there no lights?'

'I do not know. Perhaps the villagers are saving their
lamps.' He tried to sound casual, but dared not voice the
fear that had been growing in him for some time. The
lack of lights and sounds was ominous, and he had no
idea of what danger they might be riding into. They
could not turn back, for it would be dark soon, and both
riders and animals would need water and shelter for the
night.

The complete silence of the deserted village was more
frightening than anything Crystal had ever experienced.
The villagers must have left in a great hurry, for everywhere was evidence of sudden departure: an overturned
stool, cupboards standing wide open and empty, the
absence of animals and carts. Mercifully there were no

dead, but the scene evoked memories of childhood that
she had long thought to have forgotten.

'They must have fled to the city,' said Brother
Michael, when they had completed a thorough search of
the few small houses and sheds that comprised the
village.

'I wonder what made them flee,' said Crystal, looking
about in trepidation.

'It would be hard to say. Perhaps they were afraid of
something or someone, but don't worry,' he replied
quickly when he saw the fear shadowing her eyes. 'I am
sure that whoever frightened them away is far distant by
now.'

While Crystal built a fire on the cold hearth of the first
house they had seen, Brother Michael went in search of
a well for water. Soon a big fire was blazing comfortable,
shedding light and warmth about the small room. She
spread their provisions on the wooden table and went in
search of cups for their coffee. There were none, but
when she entered the house next door, she found one
mug lying on the floor. As she turned to leave, she
gasped with fright when the small doorway darkened.

'It is only me! Please calm yourself.' It was Brother
Michael. 'I saw you here, and wondered what you were
doing.'

'I came for this cup,' she faltered, on the verge of
tears. Past memories of bloodshed and violence experienced by a sheltered and over-protected child of seven
rushed upon her with sickening clarity. She heard again
the screams of her nurse, recalled the sight of a small
dead boy, saw the lust-crazed faces of the soldiers. Had
such people come here? Were they lying out there
somewhere waiting to attack? She swayed forward and
was caught against the broad firm chest of Brother
Michael. His arm circled her waist, and he was murmuring against her hair. 'It reminds me of when I was a
child,' she whispered. 'I am so afraid . . . Please do not
leave me!'

He had intended that she would sleep by the fire of the
cottage in which they were eating their supper, and that
he would occupy the one next door. But as he watched

her fear-haunted face in the flickering firelight, he knew that he would have to stay with her. He was appalled by the story she told him, and while she did not need his love, she did need his confidence and protection, and those she should have in full measure.

He soothed and petted her to sleep, promising that nothing should hurt or disturb her. As she slept now within the circle of his arm, he felt only an overwhelming tenderness, and could not resist gently kissing her mouth. Her eyelids fluttered open, and she smiled sleepily up at him before nestling her face on his chest and going back to sleep. Thus they remained until morning.

Crystal had never seen so many people engaged in so many diverse activities as she now witnessed in that great sea-port. After stabling the horses and procuring food, Brother Michael had ascertained the location of the ship that was to take Crystal to England. They walked quickly along the waterfront, constantly obliged to side-step workers unloading and loading the many ships that were tied up. They were men of all colours and nationalities, shouting and calling to each other in foreign languages.

'Keep that hood about your head and face, Crystal,' Brother Michael reminded her several times, for she was uncomfortable in the intensely humid atmosphere and pushed the hood away from her face as she stopped to gaze in fascinated amazement at the wares on the quay. There were great mountains of fruit, vegetables and carcasses. She thought of the Indians on the high plateau, and what rejoicing and feasting there would be if they could bring back just a fraction of this food.

'Thank God, I have found your ship!' Brother Michael gave a sigh of relief as he spotted the *Bristol Flyer* bobbing gently up and down. 'There are Sir James Allenwood and Captain Hastings, on the deck.'

A tall broad-shouldered man was listening deferentially to his companion, a ruddy-faced, square-built man in middle age. Sir James Allenwood radiated power and

authority; clearly he was used to the command and
respect of many men. Crystal stared at him with deepen-
ing interest for he was not much older than Brother
Michael, yet a world of difference lay between them.
Where Brother Michael was humble and anxious to
please, Sir James Allenwood was the very opposite. The
sun glinted upon his black hair; his features were firm
and uncompromising; a thin white shirt, open at the
front, revealed a muscular, deeply tanned body. Suddenly he threw back his head to laugh at something
Captain Hastings had said to him, and the transform-
ation took Crystal's breath away. The harsh lines of his
face disappeared, and she thought he was the most
attractive man she had ever seen.

Brother Michael advanced up the ramp from the quay
to the ship. Crystal, following, kept her hood about her
face.

Both men stopped talking and turned to the young
man with smiles of welcome. 'How do you do, Brother
Michael?' Sir James Allenwood extended a firm shapely
hand.

'I am very pleased to meet you, Sir James. How do
you do?' He smiled at Captain Hastings. 'Here is a letter
from my Father Superior.'

'How is Vernon Marshall? Does his mission succeed?'
Sir James had a deep voice with a pleasant timbre.

'Success is hard to measure,' returned Brother
Michael with some restraint. 'But we have succeeded in
alleviating the plight of the very poor.'

Sir James Allenwood read through the letter while
Brother Michael talked to Captain Hastings. Crystal
observed Sir James closely. His eyes were very blue, but
there were small lines of impatience about them. She
guessed that he could be intolerant of folly, and recalled
Father Superior telling her that he did not much care for
females. Momentarily, she experienced a qualm that he
might dislike taking her to England. The wind that
ruffled his hair and white shirt whipped the coarse hood
from her head, and she saw that he was staring at her,
a frown drawing his brows together, his blue eyes
darkening.

'Is this a joke at my expense?' His voice was harsh, the accents clipped and precise.

'Joke?' she stammered. 'Of course not! Father Superior sent me to you so that you could convey me to England, to your cousin, Miss Vera Allenwood.'

'I do not sail with women.' He looked her over, his eyes cold and hard. 'Even if I did, I would never consent to transport a young squaw to my cousin. It is unthinkable!'

There was such determination in his face that Crystal felt it would be difficult for him to change his mind once he had decided upon a course of action. For her, there were no options: she had to get to England. Moreover, she had to reach Miss Vera Allenwood, and only Sir James could help her to achieve this.

'Show Sir James the stones, Brother Michael,' she said eagerly. Brother Michael delved once more into his capacious pockets and produced a small leather pouch. Crystal took it and tipped the stones into her palm. They were dull and unpolished, but obviously of good quality. 'Look! You see, I can pay for my passage, and pay well.'

'Do you think I can be bought?' The contempt in Sir James's voice made her flinch. 'I have said that I will not take you, and that is that. I cannot think how I came to misunderstand Marshall's letter. He requested that I convey one of his orphans to England, a child of English origin.' He looked with distaste at Crystal. 'This young woman,' he said to Brother Michael, 'is clearly neither a child nor English. You will have to make other arrangements for her.'

'Please, Sir James, I entreat you,' Brother Michael said earnestly. 'Do not abandon Crystal; she is hardly more than a child.'

'This says that you have lived for eight years with the Indians,' Sir James said to her, holding up the Father Superior's letter. 'I am quite sure that a young woman who has enjoyed the society of savages for so long has no need of my protection.'

Anger welled up in Crystal. She had endured the pain of parting from those who had sheltered and loved her for so long, and had laboured over learning the English language and customs. She could not and would not accept defeat. 'Do not grovel to him!' she rounded on the wretched Brother Michael. 'He has given his word to the Father Superior and is obliged to keep that word.'

'I was mistaken.' Sir James was white with anger, for he was quite unused to being attacked. 'I have never failed to keep my word! But I understood that I was to convey a child, not a—a lady.'

He had paused slightly before saying 'a lady', and the effect of that pause was unpleasant. Brother Michael looked embarrassed, and the Captain coughed and looked away.

Only Crystal continued to face him. Drawing herself up to her full height, she was still obliged to look up at him. A flush stained her cheeks and her magnificent eyes flashed with deep green fire. 'Those who fail to keep their word must deceive themselves, and the Father Superior is your own kin. You will take me, because you have promised and because I desire to go to England. Please show me to my room.'

'Cabin,' he corrected automatically. 'Your cabin.'

Misinterpreting his words, she thought that he had changed his mind and was agreeing to take her. A smile trembled about her full curved mouth and then radiated over her face. 'Thank you, thank you!' she breathed. 'You have made me so very, very happy.'

'No! That is, I meant . . . Damn!' He pushed a hand exasperatedly through his dark thatch of hair.

'If I might make a suggestion, Sir James?' Captain Hastings intervened tactfully. 'Perhaps we could convey the young person as far as Port-of-Spain. There is sure to be a family there who would be glad of such a servant.'

'Good idea!' Sir James was curt and ungracious. 'I do not believe we need detain you longer, Brother Michael. Convey my respects to your Father Superior, and inform him that his protégée will be escorted to Port-of-Spain in Trinidad. There are always families, respectable tradespeople, who value and treat their servants kindly. I shall endeavour to find such a family for the young person.'

Brother Michael had no alternative but to withdraw.

He much disliked the plan for Crystal, but realised that it would be better than a return to the mission. She was looking so triumphant and mischievous that he almost laughed aloud.

Taking both his hands in hers, she kissed him on the cheek. 'Dear, dear Brother Michael, best of friends, I thank you with all my heart, and I shall never forget you.'

'Nor I, you.' He was very serious, for his heart had contracted painfully.

'Your attire makes you spectacle enough,' cut in Sir James. 'Try not to make a greater spectacle of yourself by this affected leave-taking.'

'The habit was necessary for Crystal's safety.' Brother Michael told him, and released Crystal's hands, reddening.

'She will be in no danger in this ship, since she will spend her time below deck,' responded Sir James coldly.

'You misunderstand me,' Brother Michael said.

'Believe this, my worthy young man; I have not misunderstood you at all. You had better return to São Paulo without delay.'

Life on board ship was a novel experience for Crystal. The crew, of whom there seemed a great number, never seemed to sleep, for the days and nights rang with the constant cries and swiftly moving feet of well trained and obedient men. She found the rhythmic creaking of the timbered vessel delightful, but hated being confined to her cabin. Later, she learned that she occupied sir James's own cabin; he had moved into the Captain's quarters. She longed to breathe fresh salty air, and, accustomed to exercise, chafed against inactivity. For the umpteenth time that day she took out the clothes that Captain Hastings had managed to procure for her just before they sailed.

'Got a daughter about your age, Miss Crystal. Arabella is her name, and a right pretty little thing she is. So I know what you young girls like to wear,' he told her genially. He had accepted her in that moment on deck when she had challenged Sir James Allenwood; he had

admired her spirit and courage. It was a pity the lass had
to spend all day cooped up alone. He would have liked to
have spent more time with her, but he was Captain of an
important ship and had much to do. It was a shame that
Sir James had taken her in such dislike, for he could have
been some company for her.

'I shall never have time to wear half of these clothes,'
she protested, laughingly.

'You won't say that when you get to England! It's
more likely that you'll be complaining that you've
nothing to wear.'

'But I shall not be going to England, shall I?' She was
downcast. 'I am going to be a servant in Port-of-Spain.'

'Ay, so you are. I keep forgetting.' Captain Hastings
looked at the great mass of thick brown hair, released
from the confines of the Indian braids, which curled
about her face and shoulders. Beneath a high round
brow her delicately arched brows were a perfect foil for
the fiery passion that slumbered, as yet unawakened, in
her eyes. When she spoke seriously upon any topic, she
was intelligent and an excellent companion for a man of
sense. When she chose to laugh, she dimpled delight-
fully and usually won a smile in response, even, Captain
Hastings was surprised to note, from his austere young
master, Sir James Allenwood. All in all, he reflected, he
could not imagine her as servant to any family, no matter
how worthy, in Port-of-Spain. Neither could he see such
an exotic creature in the staid and proper environs of
Westbury-on-Trym, wherein dwelt Miss Vera Allenwood. Still, he thought to himself, he would give his
share of an entire cargo just to see their faces in the
village if Miss Crystal arrived among them! She was a
pretty and very taking young girl, but she was all set to
become a stunningly beautiful woman. 'Now that would
set the cat among the pigeons!' he chuckled.

'What would?' she enquired, turning an interested
gaze upon his smiling face.

'Nothing. Nothing at all.' He flushed, for he could not
tell her what he was thinking. 'Those stones, that's what
I mean. Just lying there on your table. Put them away
somewhere, or you might find that they cause trouble.

'How could they cause trouble?'

'Someone might steal them. That's why.'

'I see. Yes, it is not a nice thought, but it would be unfair of me to put temptation in the way of someone less fortunate than myself.' She put them into the drawer of the table.

Later, a timid knock on her door heralded the cabin-boy, who entered and deposited a tray before her. She liked Ben, and talked to him a great deal. His sandy hair and freckled face amused her, because she had never seen freckles before and wondered at first if the boy had some dreadful rash.

'You a Frenchie, miss?' he asked one day when he had lost his shyness of her.

'No, I do not think so, Ben. Anyway, I do not know what a Frenchie is,' she confessed.

'From France. You talk a bit like a Frenchie. We beat them at Waterloo,' he added proudly.

'The sailors on this ship? They were in a battle?'

'With pirates, yes, but not with the French. The battle with the French was before I was born. Let's see, I'm thirteen now, so it was in,' he screwed up his eyes with the effort that the mental arithmetic required, 'in 1815.'

'I know!' She clapped her hands excitedly. 'I remember that Father Superior told me. There was a great battle at Waterloo, and the English defeated the army of Napoleon Buonaparte.'

'It was just like the way we defeated the pirates. Pirates are bad, miss, real bad. They was fierce and desperate, but we was better.' The boy was stiff with pride, and Crystal smiled.

'What the 'ell you still doin' 'ere?' roared the big unshaven man who had pushed open the cabin door without ceremony.

'Sorry, Mr Stanley!' Ben was scared, and hurried from the cabin.

'It was not Ben's fault, Mr Stanley, I detained him. Please accept my apologies.' She disliked the bullying cook, for she suspected that the deference he displayed to his Captain was very different from the manner he employed to those unfortunate enough to be subservient to him.

'No need for you to be sorry, pretty lady,' he said ingratiatingly, and she felt her skin crawl. 'I'm sure I don't require no apology from a pretty lady what occupies the master's quarters.'

There was something in his expression as it rested on her that made Crystal feel uneasy.

'Must be something special about you to make Sir James give up his cabin. Or,' he regarded her slyly, ''*as* 'e given it up?'

'If you are implying that I occupy the cabin of Sir James without payment, you are vastly mistaken.' She was stung, for she understood him to be suggesting that she was taking something for nothing. Opening the table drawer and beckoning him to her side, she pointed to the precious stones. 'Those are to pay for my passage.'

'Ooh! Now where did a lass like you get stones like that?'

'From my foster-mother, Widela. She was an Indian. I lived with an Indian tribe for eight years,' she said with asperity.

'I wonder what you 'ad to do to earn those pretty stones?' He looked at her with renewed interest. 'Proper little charmer, you musta been.'

'I do not understand you at all. My foster-mother wished to ensure that I reached England. They were her gift to me.'

He dropped an arm about her shoulders, and she stiffened involuntarily. 'Why don't you an' me jump ship in Trinidad? We could 'ave a right good time, and then I could take you to England.'

'If I might make a suggestion, Stanley?' The voice of Sir James acted like the lash of a whip. 'It is that you return to your galley, and leave the future of the young lady in my hands.'

'Yes, sir! Sorry, sir! I got carried away. Meant no offence, I'm sure.' Darting a look of pure venom at Crystal, he departed.

Sir James's level gaze measured her across the small space that divided them. The expression upon his face was difficult to read, and his voice when he spoke was quiet and devoid of expression. 'You are very determined, are you not, to reach England?'

She had been expecting him to upbraid her for showing the stones to the cook, thereby exposing the man to temptation to steal; his question, therefore, surprised her greatly. 'Yes, of course. Father Superior explained my position to me. I can never fit into society in Brazil, for they would not accept me. Your cousin, Miss Allenwood, has an orphanage, and with her help I can enter English society and find a husband. I have quite set my heart on the plan.'

'Did I not make myself clear? Did I not explain to you that I would carry you to Port-of-Spain, in the West Indies, and leave you there with a suitable family?' He had taken a chair and was now sitting astride it, his arms resting along its back.

'I thought to change your mind,' she replied simply.

'Did you, indeed! I wonder how? In the manner you tried to persuade the unfortunate Mr Stanley?'

'That is not fair!' she retorted strongly. 'He implied that I am occupying this cabin without payment, and I wished to show him that I could pay.'

'Do you know why I never carry women aboard any of my ships?'

'N-no.' She was perplexed by his manner.

'Because trouble always follows. Women are a disturbing influence among a crew. They are very determined to have their own selfish way in every matter, and will use any means, no matter how unscrupulous.'

'What very curious women you must know!' She was astonished. 'Is Miss Sophia Jackson such a person?' she blurted out.

'Certainly not! What, pray, do you know of Miss Jackson?'

'Father Superior told me that you were betrothed to Miss Jackson and that she was a very good woman, but that normally you disliked women.'

'Nonsense! Women on board cause too much distraction among the crew, and make discipline difficult to maintain. A disciplined crew is an efficient one; I will brook no indiscipline.' He had spoken with some heat, and now made an effort to control himself. 'You seem to know a great deal about me and my affairs, while I know very little about you. Perhaps you would like to tell me about yourself.'

Crystal was encouraged by the mildness of his tone, since it was vital that she win him to her side. She did not want to be left alone at Port-of-Spain. When Captain Hastings had first suggested conveying her thus far, she had agreed, while privately forming the plan to seek another means of reaching England and perhaps seeking Miss Allenwood on her own. The encounter with the odious Stanley, however, had convinced her that such a scheme was unwise. With his sly eyes and veiled comments, he exuded a menace that she did not feel equal to deal with. She was acutely conscious of her youth and inexperience, and felt very vulnerable. Sir James Allenwood was her only hope of achieving the future planned for her by Father Superior. 'I believe that my parents were killed during an uprising, in Brazil, in 1820.'

'Did you witness your parents' death?'

Something in his tone made it impossible for her to confide in him as she had confided in Brother Michael during their journey. 'No. Later, I was found by some Indians, who took me . . .'

'Where did these Indians find you?' There was a sharpening edge to his tone.

'I am not sure. Somewhere, I think, in the high country.'

'That is, I believe, a very wide area.'

He sounded no more than politely interested, and, reassured, she continued, 'My foster-mother, Widela, had had a vision about me, so they were not surprised.'

'A vision . . . I see. How very interesting.' He bent down to brush a fleck of dust from his knee, clearly rather bored at her answers. 'You spent a long time with the Indians. Did you enjoy your sojourn?'

'Very much! I hated leaving them, for they had become my family. Indeed,' she blushed, and went on shyly, 'I had hoped to stay with them always.'

His face showed some interest. 'Did you marry one of the Indians?'

'No. I had thought that I was to marry Fleetfoot, and I would have been proud to have done so,' she said defiantly, for there was an expression in his blue eyes that she believed to be derision. Clasping and unclasping her hands, she continued, 'I am glad, now, that I did not marry him, for I can see that I did not love him. I did not know what love was, or how important it was.'

Even as she spoke, she realised that this was knowledge that she had only just learned. Since leaving the people on the high plateau, her life had changed as drastically as her thinking. She wondered when this knowledge had come to her, but come it had, and as a result she was quite a different person. A smile curved her full mouth, and her eyes shone softly.

'And then you met Brother Michael,' he said, all the time watching the emotions caused by recollection move across her lovely face.

'Brother Michael? Yes, of course! He was just one of the new friends I made at the mission. But he was my special friend; he was so very kind and patient with me.'

'He brought you here, did he not?' There was no emphasis placed on any of the words, yet an undercurrent of concern lay beneath them.

'And how very glad I was of his protection! The village at which we rested overnight was quite deserted. We thought that the people had been driven away.'

'So you spent the night, alone, with Brother Michael. Where did you sleep?'

Crystal thought she read condemnation of Brother Michael in his tone, and was anxious to reassure him. 'With Brother Michael, of course.'

'At his side, I have no doubt.' His dry tone baffled her.

'He never left me once.' She was defiant again, for she believed him to be criticising her friend.

'My God, I have heard enough!' He leapt up, overturning the chair, his face a mask of fury. 'You have the effrontery to boast of your projected marriage with a savage. I have no doubt that you decided you could do a great deal better for yourself—or perhaps he threw you out? You then have no qualms about seducing that unfortunate young priest from São Paulo, who was clearly besotted by you. What galls me most is that you took in that unworldly kinsman of mine with that ridiculous story!'

Crystal was white with shock and anger, for his reaction was completely unexpected. A day, many winters earlier, came vividly to her mind. Circumstances had forced the tribe to move to a different winter hogan, and they had been driven back, again and again, by a blizzard. They could not return to the old hogan, for it afforded no adequate protection against the ravages of the weather. They had inched their way painfully and often blindly forward, sometimes unsure of what lay ahead, but unable to change course. Such were her feelings now. Sir James's rage astonished her and his accusations wounded her, but she had to persist in her desire to explain clearly.

'I do not understand you,' she said as calmly as she could.

'I do not understand you,' he mimicked cruelly. 'Your story lacks novelty, my dear. After the French Revolution there were many who made their way to England, pretending to be of the nobility. They played upon the sensibilities of the gullible English public in order to secure themselves a position they had not the industry or ability to achieve. You have chosen to depict yourself as a child of fifteen or sixteen. Ha! What a fool you must think I am! Can you offer one shred of evidence to support your preposterous story?'

Crystal went over to the small closet built into the wall of the cabin and removed her bundle of clothes. Untying it, she handed him the contents. 'These are the clothes I was wearing when the Indians found me. My foster-mother kept them.' Her voice shook only slightly, and she averted her face so that he would not see the tears in her eyes.

'Impostor! These could have been purchased anywhere.' He swept the clothes from her hands and threw them on the bed. Taking her chin between long fingers he caressed it lightly, while his cold blue eyes looked into

her face. When he spoke, his voice was soft, almost kind.
'You will never enter English society with my help,
Crystal, for I know you for what you are.'

'What is that?' Her voice was husky, but she could not
look away.

'A harlot, my dear Crystal! A little harlot.'

CHAPTER THREE

'A HARLOT?' Crystal frowned. 'It is not a word I have come across. What does it mean?'

Before the frank puzzlement and clear innocence of her eyes, Sir James found it suddenly difficult to speak with the confident fluency of the past few minutes. Blast the girl! He could not possibly be expected to believe her ridiculous story. No, he would not fall prey to those lovely eyes and apparently honest expression. She was lying. She had to be lying!

'A harlot, Crystal,' he said slowly and deliberately, 'is a girl or woman who sells her body for money.' Even his cynical eyes could not fail to note the mingled shock, dismay and shame in those lovely eyes before they flashed dark green with anger.

'How dare you!' She stepped back from him. 'You choose to insult me! You have reviled and sneered at the so-called savages with whom I lived, but they would never have treated an unmarried girl thus! You are so weak and lacking in virtue that you fail to recognise the quality of your kinsman, the Father Superior. Is he so stupid and ignorant that he would have mistaken my character and disposition and foisted an intriguer on you? He was right; you do hate women! And your hatred makes you blind. It does not suit you to honour your promise, so you would leave me in Port-of-Spain with a family! With your view of me, you would leave me to fend for myself and sell my body in order to live. I would die first! *Die!* It would be better to send me back to the Indians, for they would never so shame and dishonour me.'

'I am sorry, Crystal,' Sir James said stiffly and stood awkwardly. 'I had not meant to distress you.' Her outburst was spontaneous and unfeigned, and he was confused. He could not bear to see the tears which streamed down her face. 'I shall leave you until you are more composed.'

Sir Arthur Allenwood had been a landowner of much importance, and his home, Brentry Hall, had been in his family for generations. A good landlord and just magistrate, he was held in awe by his neighbours. He looked forward to the time when his elder son Philip would inherit his possessions. By the time the boy was nine, he was very much an Allenwood, imperious and fearless of opinion, good or bad. James was very much his mother's son, dark and boisterous, more ready to sport with the local peasantry than to remember that he was an Allenwood of Brentry Hall and must keep them at a proper distance. The memory of his own unfortunate marriage to the daughter of a Peter Luscombe, a Bristol shipowner, always made Sir Arthur wince. It was the one, uncharacteristic, slip in an unblemished life. Carrie Luscombe, although pretty, vivacious and rich, had never understood that she occupied a great position and must act with dignity. Removing her personal allowance, forbidding her the society of vulgar friends and then denying her contact with her sons had all failed to bring the recalcitrant Carrie to heel.

When news was brought that his wife and elder son had been killed when their carriage had overturned, Sir Arthur had been distraught. His niece Vera had acted with the greatest impertinence by suggesting that his wife had been leaving him, taking their elder child with her. It was true that the carriage had been loaded with a vast quantity of baggage, a fact which had probably helped to overturn the unwieldy vehicle. No one, she had told him, would need such an amount of luggage for a sojourn of a couple of days in a town seven miles away. She had said other things that had wounded his pride, things he preferred to forget, about his arrogance and folly. Thereafter, he had never again traversed the few miles that separated his home from hers in Westbury-on-Trym.

But Carrie had left a letter of farewell, and Sir Arthur told the five-year-old James about it whenever he showed a tendency to mope for his errant mama. With brutal frankness and unfailing regularity, it had been dinned into the child that his precious mama had been leaving him, and, not desiring his company, had chosen his elder brother. The more distressed he appeared, the more readily the father repeated the story until James had learned to conceal his feelings. With a scrupulous sense of fairness, Sir Arthur attempted to prepare him for the management of his estates. James applied himself meticulously to the task, but it was not long before he realised that his father would tolerate only one hand on the reins.

When Peter Luscombe died and left his entire fortune and vast shipping interests to his twenty-year-old grandson, shipowners from as far afield as London descended upon the young man, confident that he would sell his interests, and, being a mere lad, would sell at a price advantageous to them. He did not sell, preferring to learn all about the business by going to sea and finding out for himself about sailing, shipping routes, cargoes and trade. By the time he was twenty-one or twenty-two, under the expert and kindly tuition of Captain Hastings, he was a proficient seaman and an able negotiator of all the cargo bought and sold. His cousin Vera thoroughly approved and awaited his return from each voyage with pride and pleasure.

Sir Arthur went from one apoplectic rage to another, talking of harbouring vipers and ingrates. His chief sympathiser was his old friend and fellow-magistrate Lucius Jackson, a landowner in the neighbouring parish of Henbury. Marcus, only son and heir of his father, was a sad disappointment to the worthy magistrate, and the two men commiserated with each other. Marriage, they decided, would settle young James, and who better than to Lucius's daughter Sophia, a good, biddable girl whose only interests, beside attending to her widowed papa's comfort, were her charitable works. The two men were delighted with their scheme, because the young people had always dealt comfortably together.

James concealed whatever he felt upon being informed that Miss Jackson awaited a proposal of marriage from him; his courtesy visits to her home, the home of his friend and his father's oldest acquaintance, had apparently been construed as singling her out for undue notice and attention. Whether James viewed these circumstances and events in the light of courtship was not known, but it was generally felt that the match was a suitable one.

The many voyages that James Allenwood was obliged to make necessitated a delay of the wedding, but there was plenty of time, it was frequently remarked. Unfortunately, Sir Arthur did not live to witness the nuptials or welcome his future daughter-in-law to her new home. If Sophia Jackson was puzzled at the lack of enthusiasm displayed by her betrothed in setting a date for the wedding, then mourning for his father must serve as an adequate excuse. She was too well bred to dwell upon the matter, and it would never have occurred to her to mention it to anyone.

A slight tap on the door made Crystal stiffen. She had been contemplating her woebegone appearance in the mirror, but straightening her spine, she determined that Sir James should not see her distress; from now on, she would present a dignified and impassive appearance.

It was Ben who popped his head through the door. 'Sir James says you're to go up to the quarterdeck to take the air, and I'm to accompany you. Ready?'

It might be an olive-branch, or Sir James might wish for a further opportunity to humiliate her; she could not decide, but she did long for some fresh air. Taking a light shawl and placing it about her shoulders, she followed Ben up the companion-ladder. A light breeze rippled through her hair, blowing it about her face and shoulders while she gulped great draughts of the delicious air. She was conscious of the smallest pang of disappointment that Sir James was not on deck. Had he been waiting her, it would have given her an opportunitty to demand an explanation of his outrageous accusations. Deep down, a feeling persisted that his dislike of her sprang from mistrust and ignorance of the Indians. Loyalty towards her adopted people made her want to defend them against foolish prejudice. That her lack of name or background could be a factor, she dismissed as non-sensical. The English must have some very peculiar ideas, she decided, if such were more important than the character and personality of the individual. Warm balmy air soothed her troubles, and the bright sun dancing over the waves restored her customary cheerful spirits.

'Tell me about England, Ben. Where did you live?'

'In Bristol, the fairest city in the whole wide world!'

Crystal smiled at his ready response and fervour. 'Do your parents not miss you very much?'

'Ain't got no parents, Miss Crystal. They died. Least-ways, me ma did.'

'So, when your mother died, you went to sea?'

'She died when I was a little 'un. I'm one of Miss Allenwood's boys.' Ben spoke with evident pride.

'Miss Allenwood? Tell me all about the lady. I am going to stay with her when I get to England, and I would like to know all about her.'

'You, miss?' Ben's eyes were round with astonishment. 'You a friend of hers?'

'No, I am going to be one of her orphans.'

'You're too old and too fine!' Ben eyed the fine green wool gown that clung to the curves of Crystal's body.

'What is wrong with my gown?' she demanded uncertainly.

'Nothing, miss; that's the problem. Miss Allenwood is real strict and fussy about her children. She likes us all to look,' he made his mouth small and prim, and adopted a high-pitched tone, 'neat and unpretentious.'

'Shall I like her?' Crystal demanded, laughing.

'Course! Everyone likes Miss Allenwood. Just the way they like Sir James.'

'Do you like Sir James?'

'I'd die for him! I was the envy of all the other boys when he chose me. It was the best day of my whole life.'

'Is he not a hard master?' She felt sure that he was, and that Ben was speaking out of loyalty.

'Strictly speaking, Captain Hastings is the master. He gives the orders, and we follows. Sir James don't employ the wrong type!'

Crystal noticed that Ben had paused, and a shadow had fallen upon his frank young face. 'Is something troubling you, Ben? Do tell me,' she coaxed. 'I might be able to help.'

'Ain't nothing you can do, Miss. Truth is, that Stanley is a bad sort. Always moaning and complaining about Sir James. Says he shouldn't be on board at all, and that it's because he don't trust Captain Hastings. But that's not true, miss!' Ben spoke passionately. 'It's because he loves the sea and prefers it to the land. That Stanley is a trouble-maker, you mark my words,' the lad added darkly.

A slight commotion below caused Crystal to glance down and see that her movements were being closely scrutinised by several pairs of eyes. A few half-dressed sailors waved to her and seemed bent upon attracting her attention. She was unsure of herself and, not wishing to appear rude, waved back. They began to call out, smiling and laughing as they did so. She could not understand them, but contented herself with smiling in return. The walk and the sea air had invigorated her and she was in excellent spirits, the fracas with Sir James quite forgotten.

'We'd best get below, miss.' Ben was tugging at her elbow, his face scarlet and his manner uneasy.

'But we have only just stepped out! Surely Sir James did not say that I could only stay for a few minutes?'

'That's it! I clean forgot—that's just what he did say. Only let her out for two minutes. Time to go back.' Again Ben tugged at her elbow.

One of the sailors seemed to be trying to tell her something in particular, and she leaned over the rail, attempting to catch the words.

'Get below at once!' An angry voice behind her made her spin around, almost overbalancing.

She watched Sir James advance towards her, his face set in lines of wrath. 'What is the matter?' she asked him, amazed. He could not pretend to be surprised, since he had given permission for her to be there.

'I will not have you flaunting yourself before my men and wantonly encouraging their advances! You are a guest in my ship, and will behave with courtesy and propriety.'

'What have I done?' She was appalled by his attitude.

'You were asked to take a short promenade in the company of this boy, who can be ill spared from his duties, in order to take some fresh air and exercise.' He was close to her now, and she could see the anger that darkened his eyes and the muscles set in rigid lines round a firm mouth. 'You used it as an excuse to dally with my crew. What were you trying to do? Persuade another gullible wretch to take you to England?'

Ben shifted about uneasily at Crystal's side. 'She didn't understand what they were saying, sir,' he ventured timidly.

Sir James opened his mouth as though about to say something, then changed his mind. 'Get below, Ben. You will be needed in the galley.'

Ben started to scamper away, but was recalled by an imperious summons from Crystal. 'Stay, Ben! Since Sir James seems determined to misunderstand me, we have nothing further to say to each other. You may escort me back to my cabin.' She picked up her skirts and began to follow Ben.

'In future, Crystal, you will take exercise under my personal escort, after dark, since you cannot be trusted.'

Suppressing an urge to cry, she descended the companionway with Ben. 'He is the most infuriating and cruel man!' she exclaimed.

'He's in a right crusty humour today, and no mistake,' Ben sympathised. 'But maybe he's right, and it would be better for you to exercise after dark. Trouble is, miss, you're a sight too pretty, and I dare say the men wouldn't work nearly so hard if you were around all the time.'

That was not the cause of Sir James's anger, but she refrained from disillusioning Ben, who so clearly worshipped him. 'You had better get back to the galley or you will be in trouble, and I should dislike that of all things.'

'Right, miss! I'll bring you some extra-nice grub this evening, if old Stanley lets me.'

Stanley, however, had other matters on his mind, as Crystal discovered very quickly. To her intense astonishment and displeasure, he was in her cabin and seemed to be making a search of the contents of her table drawer.

'What are you doing?' she demanded sharply.

'Taking what's of use to me. Any objections?' Stanley had lifted out the stones and was cradling them in the palm of his hand. There was a gloating expression on his face as he looked from them to Crystal. 'Mind you, I'm not saying that I wouldn't like you thrown in as well! But beggars can't be choosers. So, I'll just settle for these.' He tossed the stones lightly before thrusting them into his pocket.

'That is theft!' gasped Crystal. No Indian ever feared theft from one of his people. The lodge was sacrosanct, and never had to be guarded. 'I shall report you to Captain Hastings and Sir James immediately!' She put her hand on the door-knob.

In a couple of strides, Stanley was at her side and had jerked her away from the door. 'I don't think so, my pretty. And do you know why?'

There was a confidence about the repulsive man, and Crystal could only whisper, 'No.'

'I'll tell you. For starters, Sir James wouldn't believe you. I shall tell him that you and me struck a little bargain. You promised me these,' he patted his pocket, 'in exchange for a good time in Port-of-Spain. Marriage, even. I know all about *you*!' He pushed his face close to hers, his eyes peering into her face, devouring her. 'A nameless little whelp from nowhere wants to go to England to make a fine lady of herself! Pah! Don't fool yourself. Sooner or later, there's only one end for the likes of you.' He laughed derisively at her expression of dismay.

'I haven't the least idea of what you are talking about!'

'Did you think the grand Sir James was going to marry you? He might sport with you, but he'll never marry the likes of you!' Crystal was so obviously astonished by his words that he paused and rubbed a thumb along a stubbled chin.

'Sir James is conveying me to England. I have not the least notion of marriage with him! I cannot think how you came to have such an idea.'

'He's dumping you in Port-of-Spain.' The man's manner was still derisive, but less certain.

'If you will agree to hand back my property, I promise to forget that this incident ever occurred, and none but ourselves shall know of it.' She held out her hand, and expected that the cook would return her stones.

'Very decent of you!' he sneered, 'but I've a fancy to keep these little gems for myself. I'm sick and tired of life in that galley. With these stones, I could buy a snug little tavern in Falmouth and live like a gentleman for the rest of my life.'

Dimly Crystal began to perceive that the gems had more value than she had at first realised. Hitherto, they had been no more than the means to pay for her passage to England and her sojourn with Miss Allenwood.

'I'm keeping these. Understand? If you open your mouth, I'll tell you just what I'll do. I'll follow young Ben, and one day, down a dark alley, where none can see . . .' He threw back his head, eyes glinting evilly, and drew his thumb rapidly across his windpipe in a hideously graphic gesture.

A nightmare vision, familiar now, rose before her horrified eyes of a small dead boy lying in the dust and heat of a summer long since. That fate should never be Ben's. She struck out blindly at her tormentor, screaming and kicking, beating frenziedly against his chest.

'Leave her alone! Bully!' Ben was at her side, his skinny arms flailing wildly.

'Hey! Galley-scum!' Stanley roared in anger and surprise. He lashed at Ben, and his great fist caught the boy on the head, sending him spinning across the cabin, where he fell heavily against the wooden closet.

Stanley paled when he saw that Ben did not move. 'I didn't mean no harm,' he whined. 'It's your fault, doxy!' He looked venomously at Crystal. 'I meant what I said!

You talk, and he', he prodded a finger at Ben, 'gets it. Understand?'

Fear and anger clawed at Crystal's throat, and she was unable to speak. If she reported Stanley to the Captain or Sir James, she risked Ben's life. The insane look in his eyes told her that he was quite capable of carrying out his threat. Dumbly, she nodded.

'What's going on in here, may I ask?' Captain Hastings had entered the cabin and looked at the occupants in turn. 'What is the matter with young Ben?'

'I was looking for him, sir.' Stanley was respectful and quiet. 'When I heard the shouting and screaming from this cabin, naturally I had to look in. Miss, here, was angry with Ben about summat or other, and they were having a set-to. Then he fell over. I swear it was an accident. Miss didn't hit him that hard.'

The Captain looked measuringly at the cook and seemed to be deliberating about something. 'It's the first time I knew that young Ben had a quarrelsome disposition,' he said thoughtfully.

'You never can tell with these youngsters, sir. Especially the ones from the orphanage; the breeding's tricky.' Ostensibly these words had been addressed to the Captain, but Stanley was bending over Ben, examining his injury. He had directed his words and menacing expression at Crystal.

She had never felt so vulnerable and inexperienced. Often the Indians had spoken with fear and hostility of the men of the low plains, and now she understood why.

'He is not dead, at any rate,' said the Captain with relief. 'I've seen injuries like this before, and he might survive; then again, he might not. Like as not, if he does come out of this deep swoon, he will have addled wits!'

'Pray put him on my bed, and I shall care for him myself. I have seen these injuries often, as the braves of the tribe sustained them from time to time, and I have the knowledge to heal him.'

'Don't you think, sir, that it would be better for me to look after him?' Stanley was at his most ingratiating. 'Seeing as the young lady has such a quick temper.'

'I think not. You will have enough to do, for you will

have to make shift without his assistance. Miss Crystal can look after him. We put into Port-of-Spain in a few days, and he can have some proper attention then.'

Stanley hovered about near the door for a few minutes before departing with a grunt.

Together Captain Hastings and Crystal made Ben comfortable, and he promised to send her some water, bandages and ointment.

'I may tell you, miss, that I don't hold with that man's story. Is there anything you want to tell me? You can, you know.' He had seen the hesitation on her face that had replaced the fear he had noticed when he had stepped into the cabin. 'I shall have to tell Sir James about this. He won't like it.' He sighed heavily.

'I am so sorry, Captain Hastings. I feel as though it was all my fault. You did warn me,' she muttered.

'Well, if you won't tell me what happened, you won't. I'll look in later, after this watch.'

For some hours Ben lay without moving, his breathing barely audible and his skin cold and moist. Crystal kept the cabin in semi-darkness, recalling that warriors injured in such a way recovered much more quickly if kept in the dark for as long as possible. While she sat with Ben, she had much to occupy her mind. The hints about her conduct with Sir James she dismissed as irrelevant. What concerned her deeply was the theft of her stones. The opportunity to speak had gone; besides, was it likely that Sir James would believe her? He was convinced she was an impostor, a girl who *would* strike a bargain with a creature like Stanley. The importance of money was only now becoming apparent to her; the English appeared to prize it as much as a name. Although Sir James had waved aside the gems on their first meeting, he seemed almost insulted. With an effort, she tried to recall his exact words: something about not being bought. It was very confusing. Clearly it was not possible to go to England. She could no longer command a passage in this, or any other, ship. Another problem teased her tired brain: what on earth was she to tell Sir James Allenwood when he demanded the stones? If she were to tell the truth, she put Ben's life in danger.

Fervently she hoped that Sir James would maintain his
contemptuous attitude towards them. Sadly she thought
of how her foster-mother, Widela, must have collected
and saved them ever since the moment she had taken
Crystal into her care. For an instant she wondered
whether that was why the Indians had given her the
name of Crystal.

Beneath these evident causes of her present unhappiness she was aware of a deeper pain: Stanley had said
that Sir James would never marry her. That knowledge
ought to have been welcome, for Sir James was autocratic, selfish and without charm or humour, so why
should she feel so depressed?

Ben moaned slightly then, and she busied herself in
bathing his brow and plumping up his pillow to make
him more comfortable. She had decided to sleep on the
floor, on which she had placed some blankets. She knelt
by the boy, stroking his head and making the small
crooning noises that she herself had found so comforting
in childhood.

When the door opened quietly, she glanced over her
shoulder, expecting to see Captain Hastings, but it was
Sir James. For a reason quite unknown to herself, she
began to blush furiously.

'I came to see the invalid, Crystal. Captain Hastings
tells me that you are a capital nurse, and that it is
unlikely that we shall need to fetch a surgeon to attend
Ben.' He sat down on the bed and studied the boy's face
before lifting one eyelid to inspect his eyes. 'Will he
recover?'

'I think so.' Her voice was low, for his nearness
disturbed her greatly. Doubtless, she told herself, she
felt guilty about the fresh trouble she had caused and was
afraid of an angry tirade.

'Sir James, I would like you to know that I am terribly
sorry that this should have happened. I feel responsible,
and it weighs heavily upon me,' she said with quiet
sincerity, but had not dared to look at him, fearing to see
anger or derision.in his face.

He placed a hand lightly over hers, just for a moment.
'I do not blame you in the least.' He spoke so quickly

that she was never quite sure afterwards if he had actually uttered those words.

To her delight, Ben recovered very quickly, although he complained of terrible headaches.

'Only to be expected after the clout you got on the head,' Captain Hastings laughed. 'You'll have to grow thicker skin, if we're to make a sailor of you!'

'I must have had a thick head in the first place, or I wouldn't be here,' Ben ventured cheekily, with a return of his old spirit. 'I'm well enough to move back to my own quarters now, sir. Can I move today?'

'No,' Crystal intervened quickly. She had not had time to warn Ben about the lie she had been obliged to tell the Captain and Sir James. 'I have great experience of these matters, and I believe that Ben should stay here, just for today at least. Perhaps he could return to his own quarters tonight.'

'I see no harm in that. Now, young man, you entertain Miss Crystal, for she has been cooped up with you for three whole days, and you doing nothing but ranting and raving like a thing demented.'

When the Captain had departed, she mixed some medicine for Ben and handed it to him. He was as skinny as ever, but he was no longer so pale and cold.

'Coo! Have I really been here for three days?' He was round-eyed. 'And have you really been with me all the time?'

A blush stole over her cheeks as she recalled the night before. Sir James had insisted that she take some air and exercise and had escorted her on deck. The warmth and dark had been like an intimate cloak, the ship moving swiftly beneath a high, wide star-studded sky. For some while they had walked in silence.

'I have been thinking, Sir James, and I feel that you were right,' she began as pacifically as she could.

'Good heavens!' He laughed; a pleasing sound of genuine amusement. 'I think you must have been confined for too long below decks. I cannot believe that my little firebrand agrees with me about anything!'

There was something so warm and friendly about his

tone that she longed to confide in him, to tell him about the odious Stanley, the loss of her stones, her realisation that she could not survive anywhere without money, but she feared another rejection or unwarranted accusation. 'I am quite happy to be left in Port-of-Spain, if you could find me some suitable employment.'

He had halted beside her and now turned to look at her. In the starlight it was difficult to read his expression, and she began to fear that he might suggest that she had enough money, in the form of the stones, to seek her own employment.

'I think it is a very good idea,' she hurried on. 'Having thought about it, I am sure that I shall not like England at all.'

'Would you care to tell me when you came to this conclusion?'

'No,' she replied.

'I see.' He sounded bored. 'I dare say you are right. If you had decided to journey further with us, it would have put me to a great deal of trouble.'

'If!' she said indignantly. 'What do you mean, if? You have made it clear that you dislike carrying me on board. Those were your sentiments, and I am merely trying to please you.'

'If so, it is for the first time!' He sounded amused. 'It is not you, particularly, whom I dislike; it is women generally. If I were to convey you to England, I am afraid I would need to make provision for a chaperon.'

'That is ridiculous! I do not need a chaperon; I am quite able to take care of myself.'

'Ah! But it was myself I was thinking of.' There was a distinct chuckle in his voice, and she was quite sure that he was laughing at her.

His words had given her an idea. 'Do you think that someone might require *me* as a chaperon? It would be an extremely pleasant occupation.'

'I am very sure they would not, you silly child,' he laughed.

'I am delighted to afford you amusement,' she said with dignity, which seemed to amuse him further. 'If you are going to laugh at me, I am returning to my cabin, for

I am sure you would derive greater amusement from laughing at yourself.' She had been about to storm away, when she recalled that she was very much in his debt and would need his help in the near future. 'Please accept my apologies, Sir James! I must be greatly fatigued. I cannot think how I came to be so rude.'

'I think I prefer your rudeness to this truly dreadful politeness. Can you read?' he asked brusquely.

'Of course I can!'

'Then I must let you have some reading material, for you must be bored with little to do all day than sit with that boy.'

'Thank you,' she stammered, and fled, her feelings in the greatest confusion imaginable.

The books he had sent along for her to read were by someone called Miss Jane Austen; she selected *Emma*, and enthralled by the story, had been unable to put it away.

'Have you, Miss Crystal? Have you really been with me all the time?' Ben demanded again, puzzled by the dreamy expression on her face.

'Yes. Listen, Ben, this is of the utmost importance. That man Stanely took my stones.'

'Your gems? The dirty rotten thief! What did the Captain do?' Ben was indignant, his sandy hair rumpled wildly about his freckled face.

'I have not told him.' Briefly Crystal recounted what had passed between Stanley and herself and the bargain she had made.

'You did that for me, miss?' Tears rose unashamedly in the boy's eyes before he knuckled them away. 'I ain't afraid of Stanley! I'm going to tell the Captain. He'll know what to do, don't you fear. Here, summat's amiss! What o'clock is it?'

'It is early yet, Ben. I cannot think why it is suddenly so dark.'

'Storm,' he responded tersely. 'They comes sudden in this part of the world.' He swung his skinny legs to the floor. 'Got to go, miss! I'll feel a lot better doing my bit than lying here. Canvas and oak, under storm, need men.'

Crystal bit back a smile, for the solemnity with which these words were uttered by the under-sized boy was worthy of a great seaman. Doubtless, when he grew up, this boy, with the heart of a lion, would be just that.

The sky darkened rapidly and the ship passed from rolling to lurching to playing at pitch-and-toss. Crystal understood that the ship and her crew were in the gravest danger and could only wait and listen to the groaning, stressed, timbers under assault from the wind and the enormous waves. Crystal remained alone, unafraid, yet disliking her lack of information. Her inexperience would be a grave handicap, and she feared to hamper the efforts being made to save the ship.

Her thoughts dwelt again and again upon Sir James Allenwood. In their interlude on the deck under the starlight, he had seemed quite a different person. Had she imagined it all? There had been warmth and intimacy and friendship. At the moment it was not sure if they would reach Port-of-Spain, or any other destination. But she knew that she had wanted that part of the journey, by starlight, to continue for ever.

CHAPTER FOUR

PORT-OF-SPAIN was not at all like Rio de Janeiro, and although it did have the same bustling waterfront where shiny-faced black men swarmed about loading and unloading, all industry and endeavour. Crystal was fascinated by the colourful voluminous petticoats of the women and their bright orange bandanas, tied in such a way as to enable them to carry baskets on their heads.

'James! James, my dear boy, this is indeed a pleasure! Welcome to Port-of-Spain.' A short stout man was running up the gangplank, mopping his pink brow with a large white kerchief.

Crystal had been standing on deck watching the scene below and half-listening to the arrangements Sir James was making with Captain Hastings for the repair of the damage. She was amazed to see that pleasure and affection completely altered the austere face of Sir James.

'Charles Stewart, my dear friend,' Sir James exclaimed, going down the gangplank to shake hands with him.

'Was on the watch,' gasped Mr Stewart, very much out of breath and affected by the heat. 'Terrible storm; dreadful business, many ships lost. Glad to see that you survived.'

'Come and drink a glass of rum, and tell me all your news.' Sir James would have ushered his friend away.

'Got a better notion! You come out to Paradise with me. My wife and those two naughty minxes of mine would never forgive me if I did not bring you out to dine at the plantation. Better still, stay with us for a few days. I dare say it will take at least that long to repair your damage.' He looked at the broken masts, and noticed Crystal, for the first time, hovering uncertainly in the background. 'Oh, I did not realise that you had . . . er . . . that is, that . . .' he floundered in embarrassment.

Sir James was in a quandary. It was unfortunate that Charles had seen Crystal, for he had hoped to find a solution to her problem quietly and unobtrusively. The manners and customs by which his world lived would judge this expedition unkindly, and he had the greatest dislike of scandal and impropriety. Charles Stewart was a good-natured, gossipy man who would consider it his social duty to regale everyone with the story that Sir James Allenwood had arrived in Port-of-Spain with a beautiful young girl. Scandal and impropriety quite apart, the very trouble he had most feared had taken place. Women, young and lovely, on board ship, made for unrest and problems. In the ordered world from which Sir James came, young girls led sheltered lives at home, married and settled down to raise families. A quite different type of girl, careless of reputation and easy of virtue, would journey quite happily with a crew, take her reward and then vanish. It had been his intention to find some family who might offer her a home and occupation in Port-of-Spain, for he could not imagine this exotic young creature fitting into life in the humdrum world of his cousin's orphanage. Indeed, if his baser suspicions of her were correct, she would wreak havoc there!

But something about Crystal intrigued him. A strange quality of aloofness would disappear quite suddenly and an impish mischievious girl would be laughing at something she found absurd in English manners and customs. That she was determined to have her own way had, at first, infuriated him. Then, when Ben had been injured, she had nursed him with skill and tenderness, without thought for her own comfort. Doubtless her life with the savages had been one of hardship, but she had given up her bed to the injured boy without thought for her own comfort or any false modesty. During the storm, when she had been forced to remain isolated below decks, she shown courage, and had not once complained or demanded that her needs be met.

He could not be sure if she were all that she claimed to be, or simply an adventuress, but he did not wish to expose her to the censure of the world until he was quite sure. If only Vera were here! She would know exactly what to do. Vera! Of course, the most obvious and by far the simplest solution. He would take her to Vera and let her deal with her. It was inconceivable that he leave her in Port-of-Spain, for what on earth could she do? But Vera could dress her properly, ensure that she received a little polish, and in a couple of years the girl should be able to make a respectable marriage.

'This is Miss Crystal Smith, whom I am escorting to the home of my cousin, Miss Allenwood. I believe you met Vera when you stayed in Bath a couple of years ago.'

'Delighted to make your acquaintance, Miss Smith.' Mr Stewart shook hands with Crystal while simultaneously mopping his brow.

Smith? Crystal was puzzled. Why had Sir James introduced her as Miss Smith? Was this some new and even stranger English custom? How very complicated the English made life. But . . . England! He had said the words which, for her, were invested with magic. She still very much wanted to go to England, but had felt impelled to tell Sir James that she wished to remain on the island because she could not pay for her passage. With the optimism of youth, she hoped that something would occur to solve all her difficulties. In the excitement of the storm, she had almost forgotten about Stanley and his vile threats.

'I am very pleased to meet you, Mr Stewart.' She smiled at him with such unaffected pleasure that he beamed back.

'My girls will be delighted to make your acquaintance, Miss Smith, for they see very few girls of their own age.'

'You go ahead of us, Charles, for I have several matters to arrange here. Miss Smith's chaperon is at this moment unwell—the storm, you understand. We can drive out to the plantation in a couple of hours' time,' Sir James suggested.

'Capital,' declared Mr Stewart, and gleefully hurried home to give his family the very welcome news.

Alone with Sir James in her cabin, Crystal was filled with misgiving, for she could see that Mr Stewart's visit had not given him a great deal of pleasure. 'Do you not wish me to visit the Stewarts?' she asked hesitantly, fearful of the reply.

'No, of course I do not!' he retorted. 'It is most unfortunate. How on earth am I to pass you off?'

Crystal felt deeply wounded. The prospect of the company of girls of her own age was enticing. She longed to know how they dressed, what they discussed, how they spent their leisure hours. Her lively, friendly nature craved companionship.

'I can hardly expect you to remain silent throughout the stay, and yet,' he pushed his hands through his hair and regarded her helplessly, 'I have now accepted Charles's invitation.'

'Are you afraid that I shall talk endlessly of my sojourn with a tribe of savages?' she demanded with some tartness.

What he did fear was that it would become known that she had travelled in his company without a chaperon, but decided not to raise that point again.

'Or are you afraid to expose the Stewart family to the corruption of one such as I?' she asked.

'Not at all,' he responded with asperity, stung by her tone. 'I am sure that you can manage to contain yourself for the very short time we shall be there. I have given orders that the repairs be carried out with all speed. We should be ready to sail by tomorrow evening's tide.'

'I do not think that is the truth; and I dislike those who do not deal in truth,' she said impulsively, and immediately regretted her words, for she recollected that she had lied about Mr Stanley and not told of the theft of her stones.

'Must you constantly argue with everything I say?' Sir James felt goaded. It was ridiculous! He had managed to command the respect and obedience of all with whom he dealt, yet this wretched girl challenged him again and again and brought him perilously close to losing his not very patient temper. 'Find some suitable clothes to wear, and pack what you will need for a stay of one night only. I shall make some arrangements for a carriage to take us to Paradise.' He almost slammed the door as he left.

Crystal dressed carefully in a gown of soft thin apricot cotton. It was extremely plain and showed to advantage her shapely body and long legs; it was made high to the throat and had long tight sleeves. She braided her hair carefully, attempting to take the unruly curls that framed her face. Selecting a pair of slippers, she tried them on, and then wondered if she would be required to walk any distance. Mr Stewart had mentioned a plantation. So she abandoned them and took the soft kid boots from her closet. Pulling them on, she was amazed to find that they were tight. She must have grown since she left the people on the high plateau! The embroidered headband did not look quite right, but she knew that Fleetfoot had admired it and wished for the same sort of admiration again.

'Psst! Hey, Miss Crystal!' Ben entered the cabin, looking mysterious and important. 'Guess what?'

'I could not, Ben. Do tell me?' She had to hide a smile, for he looked bursting with news.

'Old Stanley's gone, and I know where he is. Trying to sell them stones of yours. I'm going to follow him, for Captain says I'll only be in the way here. Shouldn't be a bit surprised if you and me didn't have no problems by this time tomorrow.' He put a finger to his nose, and winked portentously.

'Whatever you do, Ben, please take care of yourself. You recollect his threat?' she said anxiously.

'No fear! I can take of myself better'n that stupid Stanley! He's so drunk already, he'll be unconscious in another hour. He won't even notice the likes of me following him.'

After Ben had departed, she had to decide what she should take with her to the plantation. The dress she was wearing should be quite enough for two days, with some night clothes, some toilet articles and the slippers she had abandoned in favour of her kid boots. As she had no bag, she rolled the articles into a neat bundle and tied it with a piece of string.

The door was pushed open with a slight tap, and Sir

James strode into the cabin and stopped short, his jaw dropping when he saw her.

Crystal was not a vain girl—she thought very little of her looks—but even if she had been, there could be no mistaking the look of undisguised horror on his face.

'Are you quite mad?' he exploded.

'What is wrong?'

'Wrong? You cannot possibly go to the Stewarts looking such an object of ridicule! And that,' he pointed wrathfully to her neatly tied bundle reposing on the floor, 'is not travelling one inch in my company.'

'If my clothes are not proper for the occasion, you will have to instruct me, for I have not the least idea of what I should wear,' she said simply, but he could see the hurt and dismay in her eyes.

Thoroughly nonplussed, he thought with sudden affectionate gratitude of his betrothed, Sophia Jackson. She would never present him with such a problem, being a model of propriety, conversant with his world, at ease in every social situation. Everything about her was calm and restrained, and he felt a longing that she were here at this moment. If she were at his side, he could anticipate the projected visit with pleasure. As it was, heaven only knew what would happen next with the tiresome girl!

'You are surely not expecting me to dress you?' he demanded, expecting a negative reply.

'Yes. At least to choose my clothes, for there is no one else to advise me.'

'You must start by removing those ridiculous boots.'

'Supposing we have to walk? I cannot walk any great distance in those flimsy slippers,' she pointed out reasonably.

'My dear girl, I have not gone to the trouble of hiring a carriage and pair of horses for myself alone! I do not expect you to run all the way behind me to the plantation carrying that ludicrous bundle.'

The humour of the situation struck them both simultaneously, and Sir James tried to suppress a smile but was infected by Crystal's gurgle of laughter.

'Do not argue with everything I say! It is important,

Crystal, if you are to be properly established in England, that you try to present a creditable appearance this evening. The Stewarts are connected to a good many people in Bristol, and I fear that if you do not behave acceptably, you will bring discredit upon us both.' He had spoken more gravely than he intended, and was sorry to see the way her mouth drooped. 'A shawl you must have. Did you not wear a light one, one evening on deck? I shall find a small bag to hold your things. And you must do something with your hair; it is not the fashion to wear braids.'

When he had departed, she looked at her hair in the mirror. He had not said that she looked like an Indian, but that was what he meant. She resented the innuendo, but was not in a position to argue. Unbraiding her hair, she brushed until it shone in a great cloud of curls about her face and shoulders.

'That still will not do!' Sir James had returned and was putting her things into a small leather bag. 'We had better stop and purchase a hat for you.'

'Will you choose it for me?' She dimpled mischievously.

'Certainly not!' he retorted.

So she became the owner of a becoming straw hat that afforded welcome shade, tied over her curls with a broad apricot ribbon. He nodded approval, and gave the horses the command to go.

Sensing that he might have been overly harsh in his criticism of her appearance, he attempted to beguile the short journey to the Stewarts' plantation with descriptions of the island, but eventually her lack of response caused him to relapse into grateful silence. Small talk was of little interest to him, and entertaining sulky young girls, even less.

He did Crystal an injustice, for she was not sulking. She was very much concerned for Ben's safety, and hoped that he would not attempt to do anything foolish and endanger his life. In other circumstances she would have loved to have explored the island with its blue lagoons and lush vegetation.

The horses were bowling up a long avenue, tree-lined

and straight, towards a large square house surrounded by verdant gardens. A wooden veranda ran the length of the house, and a flight of shallow steps led to an imposing front door.

'Paradise,' murmured Sir James. 'Do not forget, I warn you, that your chaperon is unwell and has decided to return to Rio de Janeiro. We are seeking another to replace her. You have spent the past eight years in the mission at São Paulo.'

'You have already explained all this, so I fail to see why you should repeat it!' Crystal was suddenly fearful of meeting these people. Supposing they did not like her? They might react to her in the same way as Sir James.

'I am reminding you because, if you do forget, I shall box your ears when we return to the ship.' His lips were compressed, and she guessed that he meant what he said.

The Stewarts were charming, and greeted Crystal and Sir James with such evident warmth that she lost her fears immediately.

'Miranda is "out",' explained Mrs Stewart to Crystal, 'and Susan will be "out" next year. She is to be presented at Government House. Such a pity that our dear Governor is returning to England.' She sighed, a sound as faded as her appearance.

Casting a look of despair at Sir James, Crystal was annoyed to find that he was being entertained in the liveliest style by the vivacious young Stewart girls. The whole of Mrs Stewart's conversation was quite wasted upon her. Why on earth did she refer to Miranda as being 'out', when she was so very obviously in this room? The light blue eyes of the elder daughter and her fair curls bobbed about her face as she laughed at something that Sir James had said.

The girls were very alike in appearance, both tiny, with exquisitely delicate features, alabaster complexions and fair hair. They were as good-natured as they were pretty, and were delighted to take Crystal to her room to dress for dinner.

'But I am dressed!' she exclaimed when she had

admired the charming room into which she had been shown.

'My dear, we always change for dinner,' Miranda explained with her light tinkling laugh.

'Why?' asked Crystal.

'How very droll you are!' Susan's eyes sparkled. 'I do believe you are making fun of us!'

'Do forgive me,' Crystal murmured. 'I have lived on a mission station for eight years, and I do not have much idea of life in a family house. But,' she confessed naïvely, 'I would dearly love to look as pretty as you.'

'How very sweet you are, you dear thing!' Miranda was warm in her appreciation.

'Why do we not dress her up? Think what fun we could have, Miranda! You could get Milly to do her hair.'

The next couple of hours passed very quickly, leaving Crystal feeling completely bewildered. Dressing for dinner was clearly not a matter of simply changing one gown for another. She was bathed in scented water, and had her hair brushed and twisted by a young black girl until it fell from the crown of her head in deep ordered ringlets about her shoulders.

'She cannot wear a low gown, as she is not yet "out". That means that you have not been allowed to leave the schoolroom and go to grown-up parties,' Susan explained. 'I am so pleased that you are here, Crystal, for I should not have been allowed to join the dinner-party otherwise.' She skipped about the room, quite forgetting that she aspired to her sister's level of sophistication.

After much argument and dispute the girls decided that Crystal was to wear a pale cream gown with an additional flounce pinned to the bottom of the full skirts, for she was much taller than the Stewart sisters.

'How very grown-up you appear!' Susan was envious, as her gaze swept over Crystal. 'I can hardly credit that we are both sixteen.'

'I do not suppose that there is much time for childhood on a mission station,' Miranda declared wisely.

Crystal continued to be entranced with everything about the Stewart girls and their delectable house. Her bedroom was decorated in pale pinks and blues, the washbasin and jug were painted with flowers, and fine muslin curtains were draped about the bed.

'To keep out the nasty creepy things that fly about at night, tormenting one,' the girls explained.

'I do not fear them at all, for I am used to sleeping out of doors,' Crystal said without thinking.

'Sleep out of doors?' squeaked Susan. 'Whatever can you mean?'

'You droll thing! I do believe that you are teasing us again.' Miranda smiled placidly. It was quite beyond her comprehension that anyone slept anywhere but in a comfortable bed.

'I meant that we frequently left the shutters open at the mission, as it is very humid in Brazil,' she explained hastily. Deception was alien to her nature, but she was fearful that Sir James might indeed box her ears if she committed any more solecisms.

It was fun to dress up and take a great deal of time brushing and arranging one's hair, but it seemed to occupy the greater part of the girls' conversation and activities. Crystal was not sure that such a way of life, purposeless and frivolous, would recommend itself to her energetic soul. She had misgivings about life in England and wavered once more, thinking that perhaps she might ask Sir James to find her some employment in Port-of-Spain after all.

After much preening before the mirror, twitching of curls and pirouetting of flounces, the girls decided that they were ready to go down to dinner. As they advanced down the broad curved staircase, Crystal was conscious of a desire to look well in the eyes of one person and felt an unaccustomed shyness steal over her. She found she could not look at Sir James, who was with his hosts.

'Well, Sir James, what do you think of Crystal? Is she not quite lovely?' Miranda had tripped gaily across to him, quite conscious that she herself presented the most pleasing picture, a confection in cerulean blue.

'She is well enough.' He spoke dispassionately, although his eyes rested on her for a long moment. She felt a stab of disappointment.

Thereafter Sir James devoted himself to entertaining Miranda and Susan, and Crystal was forced to acknowledge that he succeeded admirably. The dinner-party was a great success, for the conversation sparkled about the candlelit, flower-decorated table. She had no idea that one meal required a veritable battery of heavy silver knives, forks and spoons, but as one succulent dish followed another, she gave herself up to the enjoyment of eating until the ladies withdrew to leave the gentlemen to the enjoyment of private conversation.

'For, my loves, talk of slaves and reforms and pirates cannot be of the slightest interest to us,' Mrs Stewart informed them.

'I should think not!' Susan fluttered her small white hands, and shuddered so much that her curls quivered about her head.

'What are pirates?' Crystal asked in her accented English.

'My dear! Do you not know anything? How very remote that mission of yours must have been!' Miranda was far too well bred to question Crystal, for she was their guest. But, really, a babe-in-arms must know that the most vicious and unprincipled pirates had plagued the Caribbean for two hundred years.

'The pirate problem has been almost settled, so there is not the slightest need for us to dwell upon the subject.' Mrs Stewart rang for some tea. 'Come, my loves, let us have a little music.' She settled languidly on a deep sofa and looked expectantly at Miranda and Susan.

'Do you play in instrument, Crystal?' asked Susan, as her sister began to play upon the pianoforte in an alcove near the window.

'I played the pianoforte, once, many years ago,' she responded slowly, remembering.

'Many years ago? Why, you are still a young lady, so it cannot have been so very long ago. Do play something for us, for to have a newcomer among us is such a novelty.'

Miranda stopped her idle strumming on the keys and joined her sister's entreaties. In the face of such cajoling, it would have been boorish to refuse. Crystal knew that, but did not feel that she could explain her reluctance.

'I was a very little girl when I learned this piece, so I may warn you that you must not expect excellence.' She did not look at the music on the stand, but played from memory the piece she had been practising for her mother on that day, so long ago. At first her playing was hesitant in the extreme, and she was obliged to repeat herself a few times before she felt confident enough to play it through. She did not know, but it was a piece arranged for the pianoforte from a suite by Handel, charming and elusive, and the notes fell around the cool airy room as though they belonged there.

A polite ripple of applause greeted her and she turned, flushed with success, to find that Sir James had entered the room with Mr Stewart, and was regarding her with the oddest expression in his eyes.

No one pretended that her playing had been more than passable, and she was not requested to play again, but for Crystal, the occasion had been momentous. She was transported back in time, to another room. A fair woman had been embroidering, and had said, in English, 'Pray continue that piece, Maria', so, responding to that voice, she had played. It was the first time that she had recalled the past without pain. She turned a glowing face on Sir James, longing to share her discovery with him.

Then Miranda played prettily, but Susan had real skill and entertained the company creditably.

'Am I not the luckiest man alive, James? I have the most charming and talented family. It must commend married life to you.' Mr Stewart beamed with affability as he surveyed his womenfolk.

'How is dear Miss Jackson?' enquired Mrs Stewart. Upon hearing that she was well, she continued in her tired voice, 'I am so hoping that she will be able to find our Miss Watchett some useful occupation for a couple of months. She is Susan's governess, but really we do not need her services any more, and she is very anxious to return to England as soon as possible. Some young man, I believe.'

'A curate,' giggled Susan, 'for whom she entertains a hopeless and unrequited passion.'

'Hardly hopeless and unrequited, since they are to be married shortly. I do wish you would not speak in such a silly fashion, Susan! It makes me wonder if you are quite ready to dispense with Miss Watchett.'

'Oh, Mama, you promised that she could leave as soon as some arrangements could be made for her,' wailed Susan.

'I believe that I may be of some assistance,' Sir James interpolated. 'Crystal's chaperon is unwell and wishes to return to Brazil, so we need a replacement immediately. Do you think Miss Watchett would be willing to travel tomorrow?'

'Oh, yes!' Susan jumped up, clapping her hands excitedly.

Seeing that his wife's feelings could not be determined, Mr Stewart hastily assured his guests that the governess would be ready to sail on the evening tide.

It was with genuine regret that Crystal parted from her new friends, but her period of vacillation was over: she was resolved on going to England, as she had now several reasons for wishing to stay with Miss Allenwood. She resolved to tell Sir James the truth about the stones and Stanley, and risk his wrath. If they could not be recovered, she must beg him to take her none the less, if only to honour his promise to the Father Superior.

Sitting beside him in the carriage that bore them back to the ship, she tried to find words to tell him of her thoughts. He looked deeply preoccupied, his handsome face marred by a frown. She racked her brains to think of what she could have said or done to have vexed him —perhaps she should not have allowed the Stewart girls to dress her up, but the temptation to look pretty had been irresistible. She had played the piano clumsily —she realised that when she heard the performances of Miranda and Susan—but surely that could not have angered him! Despite his abstraction, she had spoken to him twice but he had not appeared to hear, as he handled the reins with great skill and ease. The horses, rested after a night in the Paradise stables, were fidgety and restive, so she decided to wait until they were back on board the *Bristol Flyer* to make her confession. In the meantime, she gave herself up to the pleasure of sitting beside him and watching, not the cane-fields or the lush vegetation, but a sight infinitely more pleasing to her eyes.

CHAPTER FIVE

'LIAR! YOU must have made some arrangement with that man to sell your stones. You caused his death in a drunken brawl, and risked Ben's life when he retrieved most of them for you.' Sir James flung the gems down on the table in the cabin.

'I have already told you that he threatened Ben's life,' Crystal reminded him in a horrified whisper.

'I have only your word for that!' he told her curtly. 'I should have obeyed my first instinct in Rio and refused to take you. I have been stupidly misguided; you obviously thought that Stanley was going to cheat you, and sent Ben after him.' He pushed a hand wearily through his hair and sighed heavily. 'Women cannot be trusted!'

'That is not fair!' she burst out. 'I told you the truth about myself but you chose not to believe me; you called me horrible names, and accused of such evil things that you made me afraid of you.' He looked as though as she had struck him. 'You cannot know what it feels like to be continually doubted and reviled! I wanted you to think well of me, but you persisted in misconstruing my every action. How could I know how to behave in your society? You deal in prevarication and dishonour as easily as breathing. I have been used to the very opposite. How I pity your Miss Jackson; she will have the most wretched life with you.'

He eyed her with disapproval. 'Please do not mention Miss Jackson again. She has never caused, and will never cause, me a moment's anxiety.'

'She would, if you called her a harlot!' she retorted.

'Miss Jackson would never give me the slightest reason to so accuse her. Her manner is at all times, I am thankful to say, above reproach.'

'I wish I had never left the Indians, I was happy there!'

An emotion, long repressed, began to stir within him.

He wanted to believe her, and the sadness in her eyes moved him. The mention of Miss Jackson had been distasteful in the present circumstances, and he was surprised to acknowledge that it aroused no particular feeling. That was the sort of marriage he wanted; he was tolerably certain that his father had married a pretty face and had suffered disillusionment and pain as a consequence. Certainly he could never contemplate marriage with a girl such as this one, for he would never have a moment's peace! His conscience began to prick him. If she was speaking the truth, he had done her a grave injustice. The charge that he had made her afraid of him hurt him very much, for he had had experiences that led to the concealment of events and emotions.

'Can we agree,' he began, more mildly, 'that the incident is closed? Stanley is dead, and already replaced. No great harm has come to Ben, and you have recovered most of your gems. By the by, you had better give them into my keeping. Miss Watchett is due to arrive at any moment, and we sail within the hour.'

'But you do not believe me?' she persisted.

'I should like to,' he responded stiffly.

'Alone?' Miss Watchett turned pink with embarrassment and averted her gaze from Crystal's astonished face. 'My dear Miss Smith, it is not usual for a young girl, or indeed for an unmarried lady of any age, to be in the company of men without protection.' Miss Watchett had been scandalised to find that the woman she was supposedly replacing had already left.

'Why should I need protection from Sir James Allenwood and Captain Hastings?' Crystal was thoroughly confused.

Her perplexity seemed to allay Miss Watchett's unexpressed fears. 'Well, Miss Smith, I shall be very pleased to give you instruction for the next few months.' She did not say that she had been very handsomely recompensed by Sir James to do so, and that this pecuniary advantage brought her wedding to her impoverished curate much nearer. 'Indeed, it will be a diversion, for these long voyages can be most tedious for women.' She arranged some books and papers upon the table. 'I think we could begin this morning with some reading.' She picked up the volume of Miss Austen and regarded it with approval. 'You can read aloud to me, so that I can judge how far you have already progressed. You must work very, very hard.'

Never had an admonishment been less necessary, but several times she laughed aloud, for it struck her as irresistibly funny that English women should consider a walk in the shrubbery as exercise! If they genuinely liked a man whom they wished to marry, they must publicly convey the opposite impression.

One cold clear evening, when Miss Watchett did not feel up to their stroll on deck, Crystal went alone and encountered Sir James.

'I trust you have enjoyed this stage of the voyage, Crystal? We should be in Bristol in a few days.' He spoke quietly, and stared out to the darkened horizon.

'Very much, thank you. Miss Watchett has been kind enough to give me lessons every day. I am sure she would much rather have been reading or sewing. And I liked the novel, *Emma*.'

'That is good.' He was not looking at her, and she felt that he was not much interested in anything she had to say. 'It is very well written.'

'I could not understand why the Reverend John Elton would not marry Miss Harriet Smith.'

They were walking side by side, but occasionally when his arm brushed against her, he moved away instantly.

'I am sure you must recall that he gave his own explanation of that.' It sounded to her like a snub.

'It did not make sense to me, Sir James,' she persisted. 'The heroine, Emma Woodhouse, befriends the beautiful Harriet Smith from the little boarding-school in the village, and then wishes to promote her friend's happiness and well-being by arranging a marriage between her and the young vicar, John Elton. It seemed perfectly suitable, so why should he be annoyed at the prospect? That is what I cannot understand.'

'She was of obscure birth and had no dowry, Crystal.'

'Is that so important?' She turned away and stood by

the rail, knotting and re-knotting the fringe of her shawl.

He did not miss the anxious inflexion in her voice, or pretend to misunderstand her. For a few moments it seemed as though he would not reply. 'I am afraid it is.'

'Does that mean that I shall never marry?' There was the smallest catch in her voice.

He raised a hand as though he would touch her averted shoulder, but allowed it to drop. 'Of course you will marry. You are a very lovely girl, and you should have no difficulty in finding a husband.'

'But not of your station?' Her voice was faint.

He replied, with absolute finality, 'But not of my station.'

Crystal's eyes sparkled with pleasure as she surveyed the round mahogany table in the cabin shared by Captain Hastings and Sir James. It gleamed with silver cutlery and glowed under the light of many candles, and reminded her of the delicious dinner she had shared with the Stewarts. On the morrow they would berth at Bristol, and to celebrate the end of a long and successful voyage, the ladies had been invited to dine with the two men.

'I am sure I do not recall when I last looked forward to an invitation with such pleasure,' Miss Watchett trilled as she fastened a cream ribbon through her mousy locks. 'It just goes to show, does it not, that being confined in a ship makes one appreciative of the simplest pleasures?'

'I look well tonight, Miss Watchett. I think that life on board ship . . .'

'Heavens above! screeched that scandalised lady. 'Never say so, Crystal!' She had long abandoned the formal 'Miss Smith'. 'You should never say such a thing; it is the height of impropriety! One should say, in fact, the opposite. 'I do not think this ribbon, or coat, or gown becomes me", then await a response from the person to whom you are speaking.' She seemed to be seriously agitated.

'And if one receives a compliment?' Crystal was becoming more and more impatient with the petty narrow code of English social life.

'Turn aside,' Miss Watchett turned a plump shoulder, 'and murmur that the speaker is mistaken or misguided. But never admit that the compliment has pleased you. It would be highly improper, as it would be for you to compliment a man.'

The men then entered the cabin. Captain Hastings looked scrubbed and genial and shook hands with his guests as though they had come a great distance to his table. He beamed with pleasure and radiated good humour. Sir James towered over him, and looked distinguished in a well-fitting coat that complemented pleasingly his dark hair and blue eyes. Captain Hastings noticed that Sir James's eyes lingered on Crystal and he, too, admired the girl afresh. She had grown in the six months she had been with them and had bloomed like a flower in summer. Although her skin had lost its honeyed tone and was now almost translucent, the curve of her cheek was delicately pink, like a wild rose. Her hair was thicker, and still sprang from a round brow in great massed curls. But none of these features was noticed before her magnificent tawny emerald eyes, for the amber lights were particularly vivid tonight in the shimmer from the many candles. Sir James had better find the girl a husband and forget all about orphanages and occupations, he considered, for she would wreak havoc wherever she went. He had to remind himself that he was a happily married man with a daughter of the chit's age, for he wanted to bow and kiss her hand like a silly young man of twenty! Silly old fool! he said severely to himself. Aloud, he invited the company, 'Well, come and take a glass of sherry, and we shall drink a toast to our two fair guests who are in particularly fine looks tonight.'

Accepting a glass of sherry, Crystal looked straight at Captain Hastings, and told him, 'That is a very stupid thing to say.' She knew at once that this was the wrong thing, for the others gasped and looked shocked. 'I am sorry. I had thought that was the English way to receive so charming a compliment,' she stammered, and blushed in the greatest confusion.

'Pray tell me, Crystal—for I am sure you will know the

proper thing to say—' Sir James's grave voice was belied by the slight twitch at the corners of his mouth and the gleam of amusement in his eye, 'what have you to say of *me* tonight?'

Looking briefly at his commanding appearance, she said as civilly as she could, 'I think that you look truly terrible.'

The men roared with amusement, and even Miss Watchett could not help laughing, which made her seem younger and much more attractive. It was impossible not to be in a good humour after such a beginning, and the four of them enjoyed a light-hearted evening.

It was cold in Bristol, buy Crystal barely noticed, for she was awestruck by the number of tall houses, shops and buildings that sprang up from the very quays where numerous ships were docked. Upon the many hills that swept up from the River Avon there seemed to be yet more houses, churches and high buildings, banked one upon the other until the skyline was an uneven myriad of steeples, towers, roofs and slates of every colour. Vendors thronged the quays, but how very different from Port-of-Spain! England in March was cold and blustery, with chilly little winds that sneaked round unguarded feet and legs. The people who milled about selling hot pies, muffins and items of haberdashery were sharp of face and small of person, their clothes drab and none too clean. She had mastered English, and under Miss Watchett's guidance spoke almost flawlessly, but the accent of these mean, pinched-looking, people absolutely baffled her.

Now that they had actually arrived, she experienced a reluctance to attend to her baggage and make arrangements to leave the ship for ever. Sir James had been a very important part of her life for the past six months, her friend and her foe. Whenever she felt downcast, she had only to recall those brief moments beneath the starlight when they had shared something important. Was it friendship? Striding about the quays with his coat unbuttoned and his cravat loosened, the wind lifting his black hair, he presented an attractive and commanding

appearance. Men of all ages deferred to him and scur-
ried to do his bidding. Clearly, then, he was a man of
some importance in this place.

A tall fair-haired young man was swinging along with
an easy grace. His face was creased into a good-natured
grin, and the hand he extended to Sir James was long and
shapely. The two men chatted for a few minutes before
mounting the ramp to the ship. For some reason Crystal
felt shy of this personable stranger, and whisked herself
from view. He reminded her a little of Fleetfoot with his
animal-like quality, which even at a distance disturbed
her a little.

'My sister will be sorry to learn of your early arrival,
for I know that she had looked forward to meeting you
herself. But she will not be returning from our aunt's
house in Gloucester for at least another week.' The
fair-haired man's voice was as pleasing as his appearance, and there was a hint of laughter behind every
syllable. He sounded full of mischief, very different from
Sir James; Crystal was curious, and wanted to meet him
as a refreshing change, for she had begun to form
the impression that the correct code of behaviour in
England entirely precluded the possibility of smiling or
laughing.

'And how is Sophia?' Sir James asked courteously. 'I
trust that she is in good health?'

How cold he sounded, how uncaring! Crystal thought
that the Sophia to whom he referred must be his
betrothed, although she might have been his housekeeper's cat for all the warmth in his voice. This tall,
merry-faced stranger must be his prospective brother-
in-law.

'Capital! Blooming as usual, and very busy about her
various charities, tireless girl. Wish I had half her energy
and application!' His ready laugh rang out over the deck.
'As a matter of fact, I am here to redeem myself for my
idle ways. Your cousin Vera has commanded me to fetch
whatever little urchin you have for her from this voyage.
It seems that she received a letter from Vernon Marshall, that missionary fellow related to you, promising to
send her some brat from Brazil—an English brat. So

here I am in Bristol to see my friends, visit the theatre and do some good works.'

'Crystal!' Miss Watchett called her from behind. 'Should you not be attending to your luggage? I am sure that we shall be able to disembark in a few minutes.'

The men turned quickly at the sound of Miss Watchett's voice, and the tall man spotted Crystal. His merry grin disappeared, to be replaced by an expression of bold approval. His eyes travelled from the top of her curly head, over her bosom to her shapely waist, and down to the soft leather slippers that peeped from beneath the hem of her plain blue gown. His lips formed in a soundless whistle, and he glanced at Sir James, his expression changing from surprise to laughter. 'You sly dog! I always thought you were too much of a Calvinist —that you would be the last man in England for a little adventure of this sort!' He dug his future brother-in-law in the ribs playfully. 'Not the woman-hating man of iron we all took you for, then?'

'You quite mistake the matter, Marcus.' Sir James looked at his most forbidding, his eyes darkened to pewter grey, and his jaw was set rigidly. 'This is the young person I have been transporting to my cousin's orphanage. Please meet Miss Crystal Smith. Crystal, this is my future brother-in-law, Mr Marcus Jackson.'

Responding to the engaging smile and obvious admiration, she tripped forward with unaffected pleasure, her cheeks suffused with becoming colour and her great eyes shining. 'I am so pleased to meet you, Mr Marcus Jackson.' There was the merest trace of an accent in her husky voice.

'May I say that the pleasure, beautiful young lady, is all mine. The thought of transporting you to Miss Allenwood's home fills me with rapture.' This speech ended, he caught her hand and pressed his lips to the back of it.

Over his head, Crystal shot Sir James a startled glance before her amazement turned to amusement. 'I wonder, Sir James, if I should treat Mr Jackson to some real English politeness? How was it again I should receive the very great compliment?'

The meaning of the remark was lost upon Marcus, but

the saucy look accompanied by the most enchantingly
dimpled smile was not. What surprised him most of all
was the answering smile of deep amusement in Sir
James's eyes. The staid, sober Sir James Allenwood
smiling at some orphanage wench! And smiling in such a
way as he had never smiled at any woman before! Sophia
had better take her elegant little nose out of her good
works and put it into her wedding preparations before it
was too late!

'As you are so keen on good works, you may certainly
convey a lady to her destination,' said Sir James.

'With pleasure, dear boy. With the greatest of pleasure,' Marcus answered with absurd promptitude, his
eyes never leaving Crystal's face. She blushed in confusion before looking away, for she had once seen such a
look in the eyes of Fleetfoot, but Mr Jackson had an
effect on her that Fleetfoot had never produced.

'I am so very pleased that you are desirous of engaging
upon an act of chivalry, my dear Marcus, for there is,
besides, a lady who must be escorted forthwith to her
relatives. It will put you to no great inconvenience, for
she has a married sister living up in Clifton.' If Sir James
could be accused of malice—and truly it could not be
said of him that he was malicious; overbearing perhaps,
certainly arrogant; but rarely succumbing to malice
—there was a hint of such amusement in his face now.
'Come up here, Miss Watchett, and meet Mr Jackson.'

Marcus Jackson's face was a study of conflicting
emotions as Miss Watchett's plump form made its
breathless way on deck. He was far too well bred and
good natured to allow his dismay to show, and he bowed
gallantly over her hand. 'I shall be charmed and honoured, Miss Watchett, to be allowed the privilege of
taking you to your relatives in Clifton. I could only wish
the journey were twice as far, for the pleasure your
company must surely give me.'

Even the rigidly correct and pious Miss Watchett, her
nuptials now very close, thanks to the handsome gift
bestowed upon her by Sir James Allenwood, was not
impervious to this overflowing charm and twinkling eye.
'So very honoured, Mr Jackson,' she fluttered, blushing

like a young girl, and said, turning to Sir James, 'Could you ask one of your men to bring up my trunks?'

'Surely there is no hurry?' said Marcus. 'We could all dine first. There is a very good inn just over the bridge in King Street, where we could have a very good dinner and still be in Clifton before dark.'

'But we would not reach Westbury-on-Trym before dark if we delayed,' cut in Sir James smoothly. 'I must convey Miss Smith there without delay.'

'Then you do not propose remaining in Bristol tonight?' The question was lightly asked, but Crystal sensed a hidden meaning beneath the innocuous words.

The two men measured each other for the space of a few seconds. Marcus Jackson's face held only bland enquiry and the veriest hint of mockery in his laughing dark eyes. 'Certainly not, Marcus,' Sir James returned stonily, the deep furrow, that Crystal had not seen for some while, returning to his brow. Some hostility lay between the two men: its cause unfathomable, its effect obvious.

'Say your goodbyes, Crystal, then go below and make sure that your possessions are in order. We may depart, I hope, in twenty minutes.'

'Do you not stay to ensure the unloading of your ship?' Marcus enquired.

'That is Captain Hastings' province, and he is quite capable of that task. I shall naturally return tomorrow, and perhaps you would like to dine with the Captain and myself at my house in Queen Square?'

'I shall be honoured,' returned Marcus civilly. 'I shall be taking a greater interest in the affairs of the neighbourhood, Miss Smith, and promised to call upon you to see how you are.' He bowed over her hand, and she felt his breath fleetingly as he kissed her hand very lightly. The quick intake of breath at the physical contact was alien to her, and not unwelcome.

'We are sorry to lose you so quickly, Marcus, but you must be anxious to be on your way.' Taking his prospective brother-in-law firmly by the arm, Sir James led him away from Crystal. He shook hands courteously with Miss Watchett and escorted her to the quay.

*   *   *

The open carriage had climbed a very steep hill. Bristol seemed to be built upon hills, and they were now traversing a pleasant tract of grassy land. Sheep were dotted about, and cows were being herded by men and boys in white smocks. The air was fresh and clean and like no other that Crystal had ever breathed; it was pleasant and smelt of damp grass, without the icy, biting, quality of the high plains. She had never seen such greenery and marvelled at the many shades of the grass, trees and plants. When she looked at her companion, she was aware that his face wore a shuttered look. Although she knew that he was not a happy person and lacked the exuberant quality of Marcus Jackson, he had never seemed so serious and preoccupied as at this moment. Briefly she was reminded of the weeks when Brother Michael had withdrawn from her to some remote corner of his mind. She had become accustomed to Sir James's moods, and normally would not have been unduly troubled. Their time of parting must come very soon, and her heart was heavy. There was so much she longed to say to him, but Sir James was not a confiding person, and being such did not invite confidences.

'What is this place called?' she asked, to break the silence that had grown like a wall between them.

'Durdham Down,' he replied. 'We should arrive at our destination very soon, for it is only about two and a half miles further.'

Crystal shivered, for she viewed her new life, a life without Sir James, with a certain amount of apprehension that she had done her best to conceal. She determined to accept her fate and make the best of her new life.

'I am sorry, Crystal,' he said, with such kindness that she stared at him. 'I had not taken your wishes into consideration when I chose an open carriage. I could not bear to be confined or driven by anyone, but you must be very cold.'

So unexpected was this concern for her comfort that Crystal was speechless.

Sir James halted the horse, and pulling on the wooden brake, looped the reins over the hitching-knob. He

produced a thick fleecy rug from the box under the seat
and arranged it about her knees. His head was close to
hers, and she could feel the warmth of his body as it
moved nearer. The light pressure of his hands as he
tucked the rug round her caused ripples of confusion, for
he stirred some warm fiery emotion in her that made her
breathless. When he pulled the hood of her thick cloak
over her head and face, his fingers lightly brushed her
cheeks, and her heart quickened.

'Crystal, I should like you to know something.' He
was very serious, his blue eyes darkening to grey, and
they looked deeply at each other for a fraction of a
second.

'What is it?' she whispered.

'I do not know if my original suspicions were correct,
but I hope they were not. I have come to admire your
spirit, courage and fortitude in the few months that we
have spent together. With all my heart, I wish you well in
your future.'

Praise from Sir James was very rare, she guessed, and,
much moved, she caught his hand and kissed it fervently,
for it seemed to be an English custom. She felt it clasp
her own for a moment before being drawn abruptly
away.

'Really, Crystal!' He was half amused, half angry.
'You must learn to conduct yourself!' Then, more softly,
for he had seen the stricken look in her eyes, 'English
women do not kiss men's hands.'

'But Marcus kissed my hand,' she pointed out, miser-
ably aware that some spell had been broken.

'Mr Jackson,' he said heavily, 'is a law unto himself.
Do not model your behaviour upon that of Mr Jackson.
And never address a gentleman, or refer to him, by his
first name.'

'But you called him "Marcus", and you call me
"Crystal", and . . .'

'For heaven's sake! Do not be forever arguing with
me.'

'I fear I shall never adapt to your way of life,' she said
dejectedly.

'You will never be required to adapt to my way of life,

but you will find that life in England can be very good. I shall arrange for the sale of your stones. When they are cut and polished, they should be worth enough to ensure that you have a respectable dowry. My cousin should then have little difficulty in finding you a husband.'

He did not look at Crystal throughout this speech, which chilled her more than any icy wind.

'Do you think that Mr Jackson might like to marry me?' she enquired. The thought of his breezy manner and merry face cheered the bleakness that had descended upon her.

'Certainly not!' he responded, with such abruptness that she was startled. 'A most unwise choice!' Compressing his lips, he gave his horse the order to trot, and looked thoroughly forbidding.

'But he seemed to like me very much.' She was puzzled by the sudden change in his manner.

'Mr Jackson seems to like all women with whom he comes into contact! It is reckoned to be one of his many charms.' Sir James's voice and manner were crushing in the extreme.

The brief accord that had sprung up between them had quite disappeared, and the remainder of the journey was passed in silence.

CHAPTER SIX

DENEWOOD HOUSE was situated at the end of a tree-lined avenue, stoutly built in an earlier generation, and its small turrets and many windows lent a peculiar old-world charm to the plain grey edifice. Although it was almost in the centre of the village of Westbury-on-Trym, it was so quiet as they approached the front door that they might still have been in the middle of Durdham Down. The many trees round the house gave it an enclosed, entirely private, atmosphere that was extremely pleasant, for Crystal was unused to the proximity of the many houses and people that crowded the village. Although the village was surrounded by many farms, Sir James had explained that the River Trym carried shipping right into its heart.

There was neatness and order everywhere, and a smell of the wax that had emanated from the furniture in the Stewarts' house in Port-of-Spain. The room in which Crystal awaited Miss Allenwood was furnished in a plain but elegant style, with a great quantity of delicate china figurines and a profusion of flowers arranged in bowls. On the marble shelf above a bright fire was a gold-coloured clock beneath a glass dome. She had never seen anything so fascinating, and reaching up, touched it lightly. It chimed, a high tinkling sound, and fearing that her touch had caused the sound, she jumped back in alarm. It was thus that Miss Allenwood made her acquaintance.

'I am truly sorry, Miss Allenwood! I fear that I have damaged your clock, for I touched it, and it made a sound.'

'Well, Miss Smith, honesty is a quality I like very much, but do not fear that you have caused any damage. That clock chimes upon the hour, and that is what has just occurred,' she explained kindly.

Vera Allenwood was a sturdy spinster of about forty

with a weathered complexion, as it was her habit to spend as much time out of doors as possible. An excellent judge of character, she had chosen to treat with reserve the cautionary advice of her cousin James. She liked her newest charge immediately, for beneath the imperfectly concealed anxiety of her newest charge she saw poise and a natural dignity. While a man might see only the beauty of her face, Miss Allenwood saw the courage and strength of purpose, and warmed to Crystal.

'Sir James tells me that you have had a most interesting life, Crystal.' She sat upon the large sofa and patted the place beside her. 'Come and sit down and tell me about it yourself.'

'I fear that Sir James does not believe me,' Crystal said hesitantly.

'I have had some correspondence with my kinsman, Vernon Marshall, and Sir James had told me something of your background. All in all, they speak very well of you, but I prefer to form my own judgments.'

The greater part of Miss Allenwood's success with her young charges lay in her ability to convey to them that they had her undivided attention and her absolute belief in them as people. It was inconceivable that they should lie or be guilty of any failure to obey her rules. Crystal fell under her spell, and found herself relating, without any reserve, her whole history. She spoke with restraint of Sir James and, in doing so, unwittingly revealed her feelings to Miss Allenwood. Wisely, that lady forbore to press her upon the subject, which appeared to cause her embarrassment.

'Sir James has always been a difficult boy. At least,' she amended, 'since his mother and brother died.'

'Brother? I did not know that he had had a brother.'

'Philip was a few years older than James, and if he had lived, he would now be Sir Philip. But we can none of us turn back the clock and must learn to accept our fate.' It was one of Miss Allenwood's favourite dictums, and one which Crystal was to hear many times in the following year.

They were crossing the yard at the back of the house

towards a number of low stone buildings. 'These are the workshops, where the boys learn woodwork.' Miss Allenwood pointed to a building at the extreme end of the enclosed yard. 'Abel Poundford instructs them. He is a bit crotchety now, but a good teacher, and my boys do very well when they go out into the world.' She spoke with affection and pride. Pushing open the door of a building close to them, they went into a long well-lit room. Down the centre was a long table, and at it sat girls from anything between twelve and sixteen, all intent upon various pieces of needlework and dress-making. At the head of the table was an open-faced young woman, clearly superintending the progress of the work of each girl.

'Good afternoon, Miss Allenwood,' they chorused, pausing in their work, and looking at their benefactress with contented faces.

'I would like you to meet Crystal Smith. Miss Smith has agreed to come and live here and help me with the running of the house,' Miss Allenwood said with brisk decision.

An excited murmur ran round the table, and Crystal herself became the object of curious scrutiny. But none was as surprised as she! Assist Miss Allenwood? The thought had not occurred to her, for she would have counted herself fortunate to be numbered among the girls who were learning to sew.

'It is not at all as I expected, Miss Allenwood.' They were now drinking tea from delicate china cups in Miss Allenwood's sitting-room. 'Miss Watchett led me to understand . . .'

'My dear, do not be forever telling me what Miss Watchett says and thinks, for I am finding it most tedious. It is true that most orphanages are not run as mine is,' she conceded, 'mainly because those in charge do not have my wealth. After the war with Napoleon was over, the real battle then began, here in England. Many men did not return, and those who did were unfit for work; hundreds of children were orphaned or aban-doned. Oh, I could have provided for many more.' She rose, and pulled a bell beside the fireplace. 'I decided, however, that I would treat the children as though they were my own. They are given as much education as they are capable of absorbing, and the boys learn a trade, and then either start in a job or receive a sum of money to set up in a business. To the girls I give the same sort of training, for it is better to be occupied than idle; but they also have a sum of money for their dowry on marriage . . .'

'But Miss Watchett told me that the barriers against such girls . . .' Crystal faltered into silence before the glacial light in Miss Allenwood's eye.

'That woman has talked a great deal of nonsense! Of course there are barriers, but they are manufactured by men and can be broken down by men and women with a little resolution of character. Ah, Elsie!' A neatly-dressed girl of about fifteen had entered the room. 'Take away this tea-tray, and prepare the small room next to mine for Miss Smith.'

Crystal was deeply gratified by the trust shown in her by a woman she admired and respected so much. The efficient running of Denewood House required considerable organisation, and it was clear that Miss Allenwood commanded her small world with the same unquestioned authority as Sir James commanded his fleet of ships.

'I am deeply conscious of the honour you bestow on me, in asking me to assist you,' began Crystal shyly.

'A job you will be quite capable of doing very well,' Miss Allenwood said briskly. 'Sir James has told me that when he has sold your stones, he thinks they will fetch a considerable sum of money. You are not an orphan needing my charity, Crystal; you are an orphan needing my help to launch yourself upon the world. We shall see how you develop over the next few months. And I must confess that it would make a very pleasant diversion to have the company of a young lady.'

Crystal's room in Denewood House was tastefully furnished. She especially liked the walnut writing-desk with the small drawers and pigeonholes, and the quantity of writing-materials. Composing a letter to the

Father Superior would be her first task in the morning, she vowed. It was some time, however, before she was able to sleep that night, for she had much to occupy her mind. Much of what Sir James had had to say she attributed unfairly to the unfortunate Miss Watchett. It seemed that his rejection of her sprang from some personal motive and not, if his cousin were to be believed, from considerations of the conduct becoming to each class. Very much depressed, she eventually fell asleep.

There was no opportunity the next morning to write any letters, for Ben had come to pay a visit, and he later sought out Crystal.

'You've taken the old girl's fancy.' Ben winked conspiratorially at her. 'You're in for a right old time of it! I heard her telling Sir James that she is going to make sure that you practice the piano and learn some languages and dancing and such.' He looked sympathetically at her, as one who is obliged to bear sad tidings. 'Seems she has her heart set on taking you to parties and dances.' He wrinkled up his nose. 'Only thing I can't make out is why she should think you have the money to pay the piper. Those stones of your'n weren't worth nothing. That's what got old Stanley into trouble.'

'What are you saying, Ben?' she asked faintly.

'Terrible brawl, there was,' he told her enthusiastically. 'I would've been a goner if Sir James hadn't come up at the very minute he did. Smashed his way through half a dozen of them, and rescued me. Too late for old Stanley, though. But he arranged for a really lovely burial—better than the old codger deserved! Anyways, musn't stop gabbing all day, got to see the others and have a little chin-wag. See you when we're next in Bristol!' He scampered off and left a bemused Crystal to reflect upon what he had told her.

Hurrying to her room to brush her hair and tidy her appearance in order to look her best before confronting Sir James, she tried to decide what to say to him.

'Gone?' Crystal tried without success to conceal her disappointment. 'Did he not wish to see me?' she blurted out.

'I expect he will return tomorrow, for he promised to have tea with us. He expressed a particular desire that you would be present, as he has something particular that he wishes to relate to you.' Miss Allenwood watched Crystal's transparent face with compassion.

They spent what remained of the morning looking through the accounts, and Crystal learned that the orphanage was, as she had suspected, run on lines of the greatest competence. The home farm produced enough for their wants, and the surplus was sold in the village or occasionally was given to relieve the poverty of the most needy families. The clothes worn by the children were all made in the sewing-rooms, and the products of the wood-workers and lace-makers were sold at handsome profits.

It was usual for Miss Allenwood to take her noonday repast with the children, and Crystal saw that they regarded her without a trace of self-consciousness and much affection. She responded to the conversation of each one with an appearance of absorption, which flattered and encourage many small confidences.

'I usually rest now,' Miss Allenwood explained when the meal was over. 'Perhaps you would like to go to the sewing-room and make the acquaintance of Mary Goddard?'

Glad to fall in with the suggestion, she went to find Miss Goddard, who was alone. 'I hope I may sit with you for a while?' asked Crystal. 'Perhaps there is something I could do?'

'You are most welcome to talk to me.' Miss Goddard gave one of her rare and charming smiles. 'As for doing something, that is up to you. Perhaps you would like to make a dress for the wedding?' Crystal looked puzzled. 'Unless, of course, you are planning to have one made by the village dressmaker. But I can assure you that we are quite skilled here in Denewood House.'

Crystal's perplexity continued. 'I do not doubt that, Miss Goddard, but I do not know of which wedding you speak.'

'The wedding of Sir James to Miss Jackson. It takes place in a few months. Surely you knew of it?'

'Yes. Yes, of course. I had forgotten it for the moment.' Her spirits sank unaccountably. She knew that Sir James was betrothed, but somehow the event seemed remote and unreal.

'Miss Jackson is the most beautiful and gracious lady. She has promised me some employment after her marriage, and that will be wonderful for me. Sir James owns houses here in Bristol and in London, and it is Miss Jackson's wish that, after the marriage, Sir James gives up the sea and makes his permanent home in London.' She selected a length of pale thread and, frowning with concentration, began to thread her needle. 'I should think it will make a most welcome change, for her life in Hembury is not easy. Her father is a most exacting man.' She broke off as she contemplated her idol. 'She bears everything with such fortitude.'

'Quite a paragon, in fact,' replied Crystal with unwonted tartness.

'Indeed she is! Although there are many who say that she is too old for him. I expect you know that there is a slight difference in their ages, as she is twenty-eight or so. But she is so sweet and kind that he must count himself the most fortunate of men. They are a most popular couple, and Miss Jackson has been gracious enough to allow the orphans to attend the wedding, provided they remain at the back of the church and do not make a sound.' Her frank open face looked at Crystal with such expectation that her sentiments were shared, that her companion kept her reflections to herself.

'I should very much like to make myself a dress, if you would help me,' said Crystal, anxious to change the subject.

'By all means. We can start with making a pattern.'

The next couple of hours were spent in deciding upon materials, styles and the method of making the chosen gown. Mary Goddard was an expert needlewoman, and Crystal could quite see why Miss Jackson should want to employ her.

*   *   *

Miss Allenwood usually dined alone in a small room beside her sitting-room. 'From now on, you will dine with me, Crystal. It will be refreshing to have someone to discuss the affairs of Denewood House with; someone who cares about it, as I care.'

This little speech touched Crystal deeply, and she became aware that Miss Allenwood's life must be somewhat lonely. During dinner she told her about the incident on board the *Bristol Flyer* when she had almost caused Captain Hastings and Sir James offence. Much amused, Miss Allenwood demanded to know more of her impressions of polite behaviour.

'I can see that we are going to deal very comfortably together. I need someone to cheer me up, and you are the very person I would most desire, for you have some very unusual views on life.'

Elsie, blushing and giggling, admitted Mr Jackson to her mistress's and Crystal's presence on the following afternoon.

'You seem to take a great interest in my work all of a sudden, Marcus,' Miss Allenwood said. 'Do you mean to mend your ways?' She noted with interest that his eyes had approved Crystal's appearance and that she had flushed rosily.

'That's it! Hit the nail right on the head, Miss Allenwood.' He looked at her with such an outrageous twinkle in his eye that he drew a reluctant laugh from her. 'When Sophia returns, you will be able to tell her that I have been all that is saintly.'

'And why, pray, should I tell her anything so untruthful?'

'Because I mean to reform, and I have come to offer my services as a riding instructor.' He looked at Crystal, and smiled engagingly. 'There must be someone here who would like to learn to ride a horse.'

Riding was not a sport in which Miss Allenwood was experienced, but she could appreciate that Crystal might be interested. 'What an excellent idea, Marcus. Unfortunately, Miss Smith has no habit, and until one has been made for her, she will not be able to avail herself of your kind offer. If, however, you care to call in a week or two, I am certain she will be delighted to accept some instruction. Now, if you would ring the bell, you may stay and have some tea with us.'

For the next few minutes Marcus entertained both ladies with his witty and entertaining conversation, and when Sir James was admitted later, he found an atmosphere of the greatest good humour prevailing. Crystal was in her best looks, simply attired in a gown of deep blue wool, her hair neatly bound at the nape of her neck, her cheeks suffused with a warm glow and her eyes sparkling.

'Marcus?' Sir James's eyebrows rose. 'What an unexpected pleasure,' he declared frostily. 'Do we owe your visit to anything in particular?'

'I do not believe that I need explain the presence of any of my guests to you, James. Sit down, and don't be so testy.' Miss Allenwood appeared to be amused at something. 'Marcus had very kindly offered to teach Crystal to ride a horse, and naturally I have accepted for her. I do believe the dear boy,' she tapped his knee playfully, 'has decided to reform his silly ways.'

Sir James looked unconvinced, but sat down and addressed some commonplace remarks to his cousin.

After tea, the greater part of the conversation having been borne by Miss Allenwood and Mr Jackson, she said to him, 'You must come and view the stables, Marcus, and advise me where I can best stable a horse for Miss Smith.' So Crystal and Sir James were left alone.

'I would not advise you to encourage his advances, Crystal.' Sir James had meant to discuss other matters, but it irked him to see Marcus sitting so comfortably in his cousin's sitting-room. Crystal's reaction to his nonsense had irritated Sir James, for he felt that, beneath the surface charm of manner, Marcus Jackson was without heart or principle. His chief claim to notice were his attractive appearance and engaging manners; he frequently overspent his very generous allowance, and had not the slightest interest in the management of his father's estates. He was frequently the cause of his father's bad temper, but was quite content to allow his sister to soothe the old man and coax him into repaying his latest debts.

'I was not encouraging his advances. I was enjoying his company. You are most unjust, Sir James,' she replied, deeply disappointed, for she had looked forward to this meeting. 'Why should it be of any concern to you? I understand that you have some particular reason for wishing to see me.' She looked at him directly, all trace of the friendly sentiments she had shown to Mr Jackson quite gone.

'I have sold your stones, and they have fetched a very good price. The sum raised has been invested in my own shipping lines. You will receive a quarterly dividend, which should be quite sufficient for your needs and will enable you to marry well,' he told her formally.

Crystal was unbearably hurt by his manner, for she guessed that there would be very few meetings between them in the future. She appreciated that he had shown her unusual kindness and forbearance in providing her with a chaperon, and could not begin to know how she felt, but why must he be so cold and formal? For so many months he had been a constant presence in her life; now that he was absent, she felt curiously bereft.

'Yesterday Ben told me that the stones were worthless, and that that was why Mr Stanley was killed. Is that true?' she asked, wishing to know the exact circumstances.

'No. That is . . . Stanley was certainly killed in a drunken brawl.' Sir James appeared to be very much vexed. 'Your stones were of great value, and the sum has been invested for you. Do you doubt me?'

'No, of course I do not. But Ben said . . .'

'For heaven's sake! You are the most exasperating girl I have ever met! Ben says, Ben says . . . ! You are prepared to take the word of a boy of fourteen against the word of a rational man of four-and-twenty! Next, you will no doubt be looking to Mr Jackson as your close friend and intimate adviser.'

Her chin shot up, and she flashed fire in defence of her new friend. 'At least he does not constantly upbraid me!'

she retorted. 'I like Mr Jackson very much indeed, and he likes me.'

'He will never marry you, so do not waste your time in that direction.' He regretted the words the very moment he had spoken, and could not think what had possessed him to utter such sentiments.

Tears welled into her lovely eyes and spilled down her cheeks.

'Crystal! Please forgive me.' He was at her side in an instant, and gathering her into his arms, attempted to erase her distress. The fragrance from her skin and hair filled his nostrils, and her softly yielding body quivered with suppressed sobs. Unwittingly he began to caress her, and bent to murmur in her ear, 'Please do not cry! I did not mean to hurt your feelings.' His voice was barely above a hoarse whisper, for he experienced an over-whelming desire to kiss her. Shyly she turned a face glowing with love up to him; her lips were parted and her eyes were luminous. His clasp tightened about her, and his lips hovered above her mouth. Then without ceremony he pushed her away, muttering hoarsely something about forgetting himself. He pushed his hand through his hair in a now familiar gesture, and walked to the fireplace, where he stared into its depths as though seeing flames for the first time.

The next minute, Miss Allenwood returned to her sitting-room with every appearance of one well pleased. 'So, James, Crystal, have you settled all your business quite satisfactorily? Marcus assures me that my stables are quite adequate to hold your horse, Crystal. James, do you think you might look about for a nice quiet horse for a lady to ride?' Thus she continued, apparently oblivious of the tension that crackled across the room and the trance-like attitudes of those she addressed.

'I fear not, Vera,' Sir James said, as though striving to master some strong emotion. 'My wedding plans must be immediately executed, and I shall have little leisure to attend to Crystal's affairs.'

With only the briefest of formalities he took his leave, and Miss Allenwood smiled as one satisfied with the progress of a favoured project.

CHAPTER SEVEN

'IT IS HARD to imagine that you have been here for one whole year; I cannot think how I managed before you came to Denewood House. Perhaps I am getting old, but everything seems such an effort, and it is such a relief to hand over the management of the house to you, my dear.'

Crystal looked with concern at Miss Allenwood, of whom she had become very fond; it was true, she did look tired and strained. 'I am sure, dear Miss Allenwood, that it is the unusual heat that is affecting you. You must allow me to do more for you, as it distresses me to see you so fatigued.'

Vera Allenwood sighed contentedly at the thought that she had devoted her life to her work and received much respect and affection in return. Crystal had been a joy and a revelation to her, and she had come to love her dearly and rely on her completely.

There had been great excitement the Christmas before, when Sir James was to come for a visit. Crystal had dressed herself becomingly, only regretting that she had never been able to tame her unruly curls. He had not, however, been able to come, but had sent a great basket of presents. The gift for Crystal bore her name, and when she opened the tiny package she gasped with astonished pleasure, for it contained a beautifully wrought gold chain from which was suspended a cross. It was an adult version of the child's cross and chain she still had in her possession.

The gift had given her much upon which she longed to reflect, but there was little leisure in that busy time for privacy. Although they had shared a moment of intimacy in Miss Allenwood's sitting-room, she thought often she must have imagined the episode, for the sensation of physical awakening had been instantly crushed. Had Sir James not selected a name for her that denoted the sphere of life to which he believed she rightly belonged? The Miss Harriet Smith of the novel was, like herself, of obscure birth and penniless. Despite his protestations about the value of her stones, she believed that Ben had been speaking the truth. She formed the conclusion that Miss Allenwood had provided the money, for she had declared early on that she had taken a liking to Crystal and wished to make provision for her. Initially, believing herself to be very much in Miss Allenwood's debt, she had worked hard, never grudging any exertion. Now she was sincerely attached to her, and her efforts were made for the sake of that attachment.

'It is infamous, is it not, that Mr Lucius Jackson should have left his affairs in such disgraceful order?' Crystal said to her benefactress.

'It is very easily explained. Marcus is a young ne'er-do-well, and Sophia is better able to manage the affairs of the estate.'

'But to stipulate that Miss Jackson's marriage could not take place until her brother had married! Surely that is infamous?'

'Are you really so grieved on Miss Jackson's behalf?' enquired Miss Allenwood with affectionate mockery. Crystal had the grace to blush, but did not respond. 'Possibly dearest Sophia would do better to give her brother more responsibility. It might encourage in him a more adult attitude.'

'It is strange that I have never met Miss Jackson. I have heard so much about her that I feel I know her quite well.' Crystal longed to know about her, but had always been reticent about asking Miss Allenwood for information. She had formed the impression that she did not altogether approve of her cousin's choice of bride.

'Miss Jackson had a great deal of respect for her late father and for Sir James's father, and as they chose to disapprove of me and my chosen life, she maintained that disapproval.' Miss Allenwood indicated that she found such behaviour hurtful.

'How much easier life would have been for you if only they had given you some support!' Crystal said warmly.

'I am not repining.' Miss Allenwood chuckled with amusement. 'The truth is that I am glad they all stayed away, for they bored me to death with their silly notions and stifling small talk. I would much rather have you here, for you entertain me.'

'Indeed, I love you dearly and love being here.' Crystal rose gracefully and crossed to the sofa upon which Miss Allenwood reclined. Dropping a kiss upon her brow, she smiled at her with affection. 'You have been like a mother to me, and I shall never want to leave.'

'Enough of that cajoling nonsense!' Miss Allenwood smiled with a return of affection. 'You will be late for your ride with Marcus if you delay much longer. Go and change into that smart new habit.'

'Are you sure you do not mind my going?' Crystal looked again with concern at the tired face of Miss Allenwood.

'No, you need the exercise. You do too much, and I should like an hour alone.' Crystal's words had given her an idea, and she wished for time to execute certain plans. 'You may call upon Mrs Hastings and pay my respects. I believe she may have news of Sir James, for his ship is due to berth at any time. You may also ask that little baggage, Arabella, to have tea with us tomorrow afternoon. I should like to see her again, especially now that you two girls have become such friends.'

Promising to make the call, Crystal hurried away to change her clothes. She liked Arabella Hastings, with whom she often walked in the nearby woods and promenaded occasionally in the village, but she could never feel any degree of close friendship with her. They were the same age, seventeen, but Crystal felt much older and more experienced, and guiltily she was aware that, sometimes, Arabella irritated her. Lately a slight tension had developed in their friendship, for Arabella, in love with Marcus Jackson, resented the easy terms upon which her friend stood with him. She expressed surprise that Miss Allenwood allowed Crystal to ride about the countryside unattended with him, and was sure that her mama would be too careful of *her* reputation to permit such an occurrence! Was Mr Jackson particular in his attentions? No? How very extraordinary, for she was quite sure that a dozen people had remarked upon the way that Mr Jackson's eyes never seemed to leave Crystal's face. How very stupid people were, for everyone knew that, according to the terms of his father's will, his sister had to approve his choice of bride before the estate would be handed over to him. Arabella had become delicately hesitant before declaring that she thought it was to be regretted that Miss Jackson should have such antiquated notions about respectability.

Crystal was always amused at her friend's hints and conversation. It was true that she was quite fond of Marcus Jackson, but he had not the power to engage her deeper affections, and he knew it. She did not feel like confiding these sentiments to Arabella.

The riding-habit, of excellent cut and made in olive green cloth, fitted like a glove, and showed Crystal's figure to perfection. Pinning her hair up, she arranged her riding-hat becomingly and pulled on a pair of leather gloves.

'There you are, Crystal.' She had gone into Miss Allenwood's sitting-room to make sure that she had everything she needed, and found that lady sitting at her writing-desk. 'You may take this letter to my man of business.' She shook the sand from the letter, and addressed it. 'If he is not there, just leave it with his clerk.'

'Certainly, Miss Allenwood. Is there anything else? I do not wish to plague you, but I feel that you would be better for some rest today. I can read to you this afternoon, or play the pianoforte, whichever would please you best.'

'You may sit and gossip with me, for you are sure to see a few people when you are out riding. I am not much inclined for anything else, now that you have taken the burden of running Denewood House from my shoulders.'

Watching the tall graceful figure ride slowly down the drive beside the attentive Marcus, she sighed. 'Yes,' she murmured. 'She is like a daughter to me.'

*   *   *

'Do we have to call on Mrs Hastings?' Marcus was pulling a wry face. 'We have spent half the morning running Miss Allenwood's errands. Could we not ride to Brentry, where there is a lovely gallop near the Monkers' farm?'

'Mr Jackson, I declare you are the most disobliging creature!' Crystal laughed. 'We have delivered a note to Miss Allenwood's solicitor. It has taken us a mere five minutes; the call on Mrs Hastings should take not more than ten, for we cannot, with civility, shout our message from horseback and gallop away.'

'Arabella's simperings annoy me. I would much rather be with you.'

Marcus had used his coaxing tone to no avail, for ten minutes later they were being graciously received by Mrs Hastings in her morning-room at Northover Lodge. 'Well, Crystal, how does Miss Allenwood go on?'

'She feels the excessive heat, I fear, and is somewhat tired and wanting in spirits,' replied Crystal, accepting a glass of lemonade from her kindly hostess.

'I do hope that we do not suffer any of these dreadful summer fevers. I recollect that there was a dreadful outbreak of typhoid a few years ago.' She turned her stately person to smile at the entrance of her pretty daughter Arabella. 'Bella, my love, come and greet our friends.'

'I declare I am vexed to death with you, Crystal!' Arabella spoke to her friend, but pouted at Marcus. 'You have neglected me disgracefully this past week.' She tossed her curls and turned a shoulder pettishly away from Marcus. 'I have not been allowed out of doors since mama became convinced that the countryside is over-run with rioters.' She sighed deeply, and turned limpid eyes on him. 'It would be so very different if I were you, Crystal, and had a gentleman to escort me!'

Mrs Hastings was a sensible, practical woman who saw that Marcus and Crystal, while they made a handsome couple, were not in the least in love, and she could not object to their weekly rides in full view of all their acquaintance about the countryside. It was known, of course, that Marcus Jackson must marry soon if he were to secure his considerable inheritance, but that his sister should be prevented from marriage until that time was a very shabby arrangement. Typical, Mrs Hastings had remarked, of the tyrannical Lucius Jackson. She viewed her daughter's infatuation for Marcus with tolerant amusement; from a worldly point of view, Arabella would be doing very well for herself to catch such a handsome prize. But there were rumours, if one could believe rumours, that Marcus was as active in his amorous life as he was inactive in every other sphere. She could not wish for such an alliance for her only child until the young man had shown himself willing to assume his responsibilities and follow some rational pursuits.

'I do not recall, Bella, ever saying that the countryside was over-run with rioters. I believe that the very poor are presently disgruntled because they wish the government to allow the importation of foreign, cheaper, corn.'

Marcus moved restlessly. He had little taste for serious conversation, and exchanged a sympathetic grimace with Arabella.

'Miss Allenwood invites you take tea with her tomorrow afternoon. I hope that you will be able to come, Mrs Hastings.'

'I am sorry, Crystal, but that will not be possible. We expect Captain Hastings to be here by tomorrow. Bella will then have all the escort she craves, for she has become inordinately fond of walking all of a sudden,' Mrs Hastings apologised.

Tomorrow! So soon! If Captain Hastings was returning, Sir James would be with him. They had been on some long-projected trip to view the new steamships, and the date set for their return had been uncertain. Crystal's heart began a slow hammering, and her throat felt constricted. Hitherto he had always called to see his cousin on occasions when she herself had been absent. Miss Allenwood had told her of the postponement of the wedding, which was understandable at first because Miss Jackson was obliged to observe a period of mourning. Miss Allenwood had been irritated by the terms of Lucius Jackson's will, but had observed to Crystal that any court would set aside such an unreasonable condition upon application. No such application had been made, and the only conclusion that the interested could draw was that one or other of the parties was not over-anxious for the nuptials to take place immediately.

It was with difficulty that Crystal paid attention to the remainder of the conversation, and was relieved when they eventually could pay their respects and leave.

'Wait, Mr Jackson!' Crystal called. 'I want to ride properly.' It was the custom for a woman to use a side-saddle, and although she had worked hard on her accomplishments to please Miss Allenwood, her body and spirit rebelled against this ridiculous mode of riding. Today she felt an upsurge of joyous spirits, and wished to express her feelings.

'You *are* riding properly. You ride superbly!' Marcus shouted exuberantly. He revelled in the admiration their appearance excited whenever they rode together. To his intense astonishment, she had dismounted and was taking the saddle from her horse.

'Here!' she commanded a watching urchin. 'I shall give you a shilling if you mind this saddle for me.'

The lad sprang forward, promising to mind the saddle with his very life, if need be. Crystal leapt up, and throwing her leg over the horse's back and taking the rein, cantered up beside Marcus. His mouth hung open ludicrously, then he threw back his head, and giving a shout of laughter, urged his own horse forward. Together they raced over Durdham Down to the place known as the Sea Wall. They were breathless and dishevelled, but she glowed with a radiance Marcus had never seen before. She had lost her riding-hat, and her neatly pinned hair, loosened from its bindings, spilled about her shoulders.

'You are a magnificent girl, Crystal. There are not many girls who would do as you have done!' He devoured her with his gaze, noting the sparkle of her eyes, her parted lips curved with merriment. He almost fell in love with her at that moment.

'Was it so very wrong?' She laughed with pleasure, for she had loved the freedom of the wind and the gallop.

'No,' he prevaricated slightly. 'Only a few very conventional people would regard it as slightly improper. Do not look concerned, for only you and I shall know, and we can find your hat on the way back.' He bent forward to pat his horse's neck. 'We had better rest the horses before returning, as they are hot and tired. Let us tether them here, and take your favourite walk along the Sea Wall.'

Strictly speaking, the name Sea Wall was not accurate, for the term applied to a high promontory at the edge of Durdham Down that looked down into the Avon Gorge. It was a view much beloved by walkers, sightseers and painters, and Crystal had come to love this place. Whenever she looked down and saw a great ship, she wondered if it belonged to Sir James Allenwood; she often thought about where he might be when he was not at his Brentry estates.

Although Crystal and Marcus would not permit the animals to fill themselves with grass, they walked them to a trough for water. When they led them back up to the edge of the Downs, a number of fashionably dressed men and women regarded her with some disdain, and, grinning at each other, they mounted up and began to return at an easy canter. There was a long stretch of empty smooth green before them, and a rising surge of excitement in Crystal.

Marcus turned and glanced at her, catching something of her feelings, and laughed in easy comradeship, so that she felt happy and relaxed.

He called across, 'Let us have a race to where you left your saddle, and you owe me a forfeit if I win!'

'I agree,' she called back, and digging in her knees and crouching low, she rode recklessly across the Downs, gaining on him all the time. It was a glorious feeling, and for a time they rode neck and neck in perfect harmony with each other, their horses and the earth about them, lulled by the rhythmic drumming of hooves. She had a wild exultant feeling in throwing off all the constraints of society outside the walls of Denewood House. Ahead of them, she espied a carriage that seemed to be stationary by the tree where she had left her saddle, so she reined in her horse and slowed down, but Marcus, racing ahead, did not see it, for it had moved away.

'I win!' he shouted triumphantly as he turned his horse where the urchin sat with the saddle. 'I claim a kiss. I have won a forfeit from you! Come down!' He had leaped from his horse and thrown the reins to the ragged child. 'Come down, my adorable Crystal, and kiss me, for I have won you fairly and squarely!'

She dismounted, meaning to saddle her horse and ride at a more sober pace back to Denewood House, but she could not help laughing at his flushed face and eager smile. She was sure he was not serious in his intent.

'If you dare to make such a spectacle of yourself, I shall box your ears!' Sir James Allenwood stepped forward, his expression forbidding, his voice icy.

Crystal flushed scarlet, all her pleasure in the ride gone, her feeling of reckless exultation subsiding to shame before the scorn and condemnation in his eyes. Never had she seen Sir James look more angry. His frown was deep, his jaw set in a firm uncompromising line, and his mouth had thinned. She dared not meet his eyes, but she could guess that they had darkened to that shade of stormy pewter she had once learned to dread—a long time ago.

He surveyed her from head to foot. She had fulfilled all that early promise of voluptuous beauty, radiating grace and vitality. Her flush became more painfully vivid beneath his glare. 'So! This is how you comport yourself about the countryside, while my poor cousin doubtless imagines you to be taking some unexceptionable exercise! You are little better than a gypsy. Not even the most hoydenish girl in the county would behave as you are behaving now! How could you, Marcus, allow her to make such a complete fool of herself? If she has not the sense or the breeding to guide her behaviour, you should have advised her.'

'Do not blame my poor brother. He has clearly been led astray by that person.' The speaker had a high, clear, exquisitely modulated voice.

She was sitting in the carriage, very upright, and Crystal had never seen anyone so perfectly proportioned or so very lovely. There was a resemblance to the Stewart girls, but only a resemblance; for Sophia Jackson was tiny, with a small, short nose and a little curved mouth. The hand that held the lace parasol was encased in a white glove, and she stared straight ahead of her and not at the group who stood a little distance from the carriage. Crystal felt large and clumsy beside this fair model of feminine perfection. Hatless, her hair blowing about her face, cheeks flushed, she wished she were a thousand miles away!

'Sophia, my love, this is Miss . . .'

'I do not wish to be introduced to that person.' Miss Jackson cut her betrothed short, her cheeks reddening, as she spoke to her coachman. 'Kindly drive me home. Marcus must follow behind, for,' she spoke ominously, 'I wish to speak with him on the subject of being led astray by persons of the lower orders. That person can make her own way back to the orphanage.'

'Escort your sister back to Henbury, Marcus, and I shall take your horse. I have a few things to say to Miss Smith that she will not care to have anyone overhear.' Sir James spoke curtly, and Marcus nodded.

'James!' An outraged Miss Jackson looked at him in surprised disapproval, and Crystal saw that her eyes were a most beautiful shade of violet that perfectly matched the ribbon of her white muslin dress. 'You surely do not propose to leave me alone?'

'Hardly alone, my love. In the care of your brother.'

'After the way he has behaved, I am surprised that you trust him to care for me!' The petulance did not diminish the flute-like tones of her voice.

'But he was not responsible for his actions, as you so rightly pointed out. And,' he reminded her, 'you wish to speak with him. As I wish to speak with Miss Smith.'

Trying desperately and unsuccessfully to restore some order to her hair, Crystal gave up the attempt and decided to adopt a note of cheerful unconcern. She had longed to see Sir James, and bitterly regretted that their first meeting after such a lapse of time should be under such inauspicious circumstances. He, she decided, was making a great deal of noise over nothing in particular. Had she behaved so very badly? Her conscience told her that she had certainly not behaved well. She gave the staring child a shilling, and picked up her saddle. Before she could lay it over the horse, it was taken from her and thrown to the ground.

'What are you doing?' she demanded breathlessly, for Sir James stood so close to her that he almost touched her.

'More to the point, Crystal, what are *you* about?' He sounded so stern that her resolve almost crumbled and she longed to weep.

She longed to call out after the departing carriage for Marcus to return and explain matters. She stifled a feeling of disloyalty to her friend, for she thought that he could have very well explained to his sister and Sir James that it was a crazy wager, and had never happened before. That Marcus was financially dependent upon his sister until he chose to marry a bride of whom Miss Jackson approved, she knew, but that need not have weighed with him. For if anyone was in disgrace, it was surely not Marcus.

She began uncertainly, 'I am really not sure just what it is you wish me to explain.' He was so close that she could feel his breath on her cheek and smell the tangy salt air that clung to his clothes and his person. As she had not done a year ago, she could appreciate the lean masculine strength of the man. She flushed and lowered her eyes, afraid that they might betray her.

'Do not lie to me, Crystal! I left you, with some reluctance, in my cousin's charge. I would have been glad to have had my fears and suspicions of you allayed. Vera loves and trusts you, she is always warm in your praise, and this is how you repay her! Making love with Marcus Jackson! Openly and without shame! How could you so dishonour and betray her? The whole countryside must have seen you riding bareback, and not only that, but engaging in a race with a young man! He announced to the whole world that you are his, and demands a kiss!' He was becoming more furiously angry with each word he spoke. 'Are you?' He was white with anger.

'Am I what?' Crystal was hurt and puzzled, and it did not occur to her that he was disproportionately angry over an episode witnessed only by themselves.'

'*Are* you his?' he demanded harshly.

'No,' she whispered, blushing with shame. She could not feign ignorance of his meaning. The charge that she had in some way brought shame and dishonour upon Miss Allenwood wounded her more than anything else. Tears began to trickle down her cheeks.

'Do not put on that display, for it does not deceive me! Recollect that I witnessed such a display once before, and I was not deceived then! It is obvious that you are trying to entrap Marcus Jackson, but even he cannot be such a fool as to be taken in by you!'

Raising her hand, she struck him on the mouth. 'You are arrogant, cruel and pompous!' She was now as thoroughly angry as he. 'You never have any amusement yourself, and you do not want anyone else to enjoy life. The Father Superior was right: you do dislike women.' She spoke meaning to hurt him as he had hurt her, and succeeded better than she knew. 'You think that any woman who is not a pale little doll is a slut! I cannot see the harm in riding astride. I did it for several years. Or do you choose to forget that?'

'I do not choose to forget what you are so willing to remind me of!' His voice shook with fury. 'I recollect that you told me you wished to marry some savage, you brazenly confessed to sleeping with a man of religion, you created a furore on the *Bristol Flyer* that caused the death of a very good seaman. Now I find you attempting to seduce the brother of my future wife!'

'And how do you know that I am not lying to you again?' Her voice was husky with emotion. 'How do you know that I have not already seduced him? Think how fortuitous it would be for you and Miss Jackson if I were to marry Mr Jackson. You would then be free to marry, and there would be no further excuse for delay.'

His face whitened beneath its deep tan and his lips tightened ominously, so that Crystal was afraid that she had pushed him too far.

'Your schemes could well rebound, Crystal! You may have forgotten, in your ambitious calculations, that Miss Jackson's consent is necessary for her brother's marriage. And I should counsel her to forbid her brother to marry so far beneath his station.'

This enraged her quite as much as it was intended to. Again she raised her hand to strike him, but he forestalled her.

'Oh, no you don't, my little firebrand! Once is quite enough. In civilised society we have other ways of settling our disputes.' He caught her hand in a vice-like grip and forced it behind her back, his body pressed close to hers.

'And how do you know that she will not be obliged to consent? I might already be with child!'

If she had struck him again, he could not have looked more stunned. She tried to twist away from him, appalled by the words she had blurted out in a moment of extreme anger.

'Do not struggle. I have no wish to touch you.' He pushed her away, as though disgusted.

They did not exchange another word on the way back to Denewood House. She longed to tell him that she had told a foolish lie, but the contempt with which he had treated her had made her so angry that she was beyond reason. She vowed to herself that she would never again allow him to intrude upon her every thought, or fill her dreams. From this moment on, she would never think of him again.

CHAPTER EIGHT

'ADOPT HER?' thundered Sir James. 'Have you gone mad, Vera? Adopt that slut—some nameless hussy from the gutter? I will not allow it!'

'My dear James, calm yourself, I beg you.' Miss Allenwood spoke wearily. She deeply regretted her cousin's reaction to her scheme, and was puzzled by the vehemence of his objection. 'Indeed, you do her an injustice, for she is the sweetest and kindest girl alive. I love her dearly.'

'She has the knack of winding people round her little finger,' he said bitterly.

'You are unkind, James. You grow more like your father every day.' She raised herself from the sofa where she had been resting. 'I wish you would stop this dreadful pacing about, for it makes my head ache.'

He was shaken by her altered looks and the lack of her usual robust demeanour. There was talk of summer fever, and several of his poorer cottagers had been stricken. He would have to deal with that problem later in the day.

Noting his grim and cold expression, Miss Allenwood felt a pang of regret for the loss of the lovable little boy who had disappeared on that day, many years ago, when the wilful and passionate Carrie Luscombe had decided that she could take no more of her husband's bullying ways. Much as she had sympathised with Carrie, she could never quite forgive her for leaving James behind. The outgoing little boy had shut himself away behind a wall of chill civility and impassive indifference, having assumed too much money and authority at too early an age. Vera had wished him well, but had been saddened to see that his new duties, which he assumed with such ease, had encouraged the worst aspects of his autocratic temper.

'I had thought that you were fond of Crystal. At one

time, I had hoped to promote a match between you. Silly of me, wasn't it?'

'Promote a match between me and that—that trollop?' He looked thunderstruck. 'Doubtless you had forgotten that I am betrothed to Sophia,' he said with depressing formality.

'I had not forgotten that the match was forced upon you by those deplorable old men,' she retorted acidly.

'You quite mistake, Vera. Sophia is everything that is amiable. It is true that I had not thought of marriage at the time, but I am most sincerely attached to her; she is the wife I would have chosen.'

'And how is dearest Sophia?' She hoped to banish the stormy look from his eyes.

'Well, I thank you. She sends her regards.'

'You must be looking forward to your wedding,' she persisted.

'Very much.'

'James, I know you cannot approve of my intention to adopt Crystal, but it is, nevertheless, my wish. I fear that she might be quite alone, soon. The allowance you make her is more than adequate for her needs here, although she never touches a penny of it. I cannot think why.'

'It is not an allowance. I sold her stones at a good profit, and invested the money in my own company. She is merely paid dividends.' Sir James did not look at her while speaking, and she nodded as though satisfied with his answer.

'I want you to promise me something.' Her voice was solemn. 'If anything happens to me, I want you to take care of Crystal, and ensure that she marries well.'

'She won't marry that scoundrel, Marcus!' he snapped.

'Marry Marcus? Of course she will not. Whatever put that idea into your head?' She looked amused. 'They are the greatest of friends, but she has not the slightest idea of marriage with Marcus Jackson, I can assure you of that.'

He was much too fond of her to disabuse her mind, and kept his opinions to himself. 'Where is the paragon now? As she is so fond of you, I quite thought to see her here, attending to your wants. She was cavorting about on the Downs yesterday with Marcus, but today she is absent.' He could not resist criticising Crystal.

'I sent her to rest in the garden. She works too hard, and has been cooped up here too much.' Miss Allenwood closed her eyes and sank back on the pillow he had placed behind her head.

'I promise you that I shall care for Crystal.' He leaned forward and dropped a light kiss on her brow. 'Please do not worry about her any more.'

Striding across the smooth lawn in the hot bright sunshine, Sir James was feeling savage. The minx had cajoled his cousin, he was sure, into this adoption proposal. Without pausing to analyse his feelings, he contented himself with feeding his anger towards the girl who constantly occupied his thoughts, aroused his passionate anger and quite destroyed his peace of mind.

Crystal was asleep beneath the shade of an oak in an attitude of complete abandonment. Her apricot dress was spread about her, crumpled, and her impossible hair was loose. He experienced an almost overpowering urge to take a handful and feel its silkiness. Although she personified innocence and purity in sleep, he knew better!

His shadow covered her, and she slowly opened her eyes. Stretching voluptuously, she smiled sleepily up. He found her every movement sensuous and provocative, and it angered him, for he considered it part of her design. 'Oh, it is you!' she said sharply, and jumped to her feet, now wide awake and hostile. 'Your cousin is in her sitting-room, if you wish to see her.' She walked ahead of him, head high and hips swinging.

'I want to talk to you.' His stride matched hers.

She had had a trying morning, for a mood of irritability had seemed to prevail at Denewood House, as unwelcome as it was singular.

'You may say all you have to say out here, for once indoors, I have much to occupy me.' Crystal stopped on the narrow stone terrace that ran along the back of the house, and sat upon a stone seat. She sternly quelled her tumultuous heart, but could not help thinking how plain and dull and undistinguished all other men seemed beside this tall broad-shouldered man with his tanned face and thick black hair. Summoning her courage, she broached the subject she supposed to be uppermost in his mind. 'Doubtless by now you will have spoken to Mr Jackson and discovered that we had no more than a silly wager. It had never happened before, and it was entirely my idea to remove the saddle and ride bareback. I had no idea that it was so improper, and he assured me that it was not.' She watched him, trying to gauge his expression, for it was shadowed on the terrace and the light played tricks. 'I must also beg your pardon for having spoken so stupidly of my relationship with Mr Jackson. You provoked me, and I spoke in anger. I was deeply mortified when I thought about it afterwards.'

He wavered, tempted to believe her. Marcus had said nothing about the episode, and the general feeling in Henbury House, the Jacksons' home, was that the incident had never happened.

'Sir James, if you do have something to say, will you come to the point?' Crystal was becoming impatient at his silent stare. 'Miss Allenwood is far from well, and I do not like to leave her for long.'

'You do not object to making yourself an object of Marcus Jackson's sport, or lolling about in the garden!' He spoke with heat, having stopped his pacing to stand a few feet away. A bee droned near by, and the still hot summer air was heavy with the scent of flowers. He looked levelly at her, and she returned his gaze with as much composure as she could. 'Did you persuade my cousin to suggest adopting you?' he said gruffly, for her look disturbed him.

Her eyes widened in startled wonder. Whatever she had been expecting him to say, it was not that. Adopt? Did he mean that Miss Allenwood wished to adopt her as a daughter? How good and kind she was! And how unnecessary her action, for Crystal was devoted to her already and needed no proof of her affection. 'No, I had no such idea!'

'Liar!' he flung at her. 'You bamboozled a trusting woman; I can quite imagine it. You have made yourself indispensable to her. How clever you are, Crystal; you are to be congratulated! The allowance I make you is not sufficient, and you are greedy for more. Miss Jackson might spoil your plans to ensnare her brother, so you ensure that you will have a comfortable life by becoming the adopted daughter of that foolishly doting woman. I told you once, a long time ago, that I was not sure if my suspicions of you were true or false, but that I admired you, despite that. What a fool I was!' He spoke with such bitter self-derision that she was wounded. Taking a step closer, he towered over her. 'You will never inherit this house, or my cousin's fortune. I shall make it my personal business to block your schemes!'

'I really must protest, Sir James,' Crystal said in distress. 'I never thought of such a thing!'

'Did you not? Can you deny that you have already made yourself almost a daughter of the house? You read to my cousin each evening, play the pianoforte and talk to her?' There was so much contempt in his voice that she became angry. 'Riding a horse, as though you were a lady! And dressing in that way! I tell you that it does not befit your station.'

'How dare you, you odious, self-righteous man! You accuse me of scheming and plotting because I have given Miss Allenwood help and affection. What have you or any of her relatives ever done for her? Nothing!' Her scorn quite matched his own, and he was startled. 'Oh yes, every so often you would send a parcel, much as you would send a parcel to some elderly servant. You would descend from on high to pay a visit, and everyone must be conscious of the honour you pay. You would choose some boy to treat as a slave in one of your ships. Very fine! Very noble! But you got a good employee every time, did you not? Did you ever stop to consider how much work your cousin took upon her shoulders or whether you could lighten her load?' Drawing breath, she saw that the lines of his face were tight with anger. 'All the times you graciously stopped at the house and barely had time to drink a cup of tea with her, did it ever occur to you that she might like the company of her equals to talk to . . . maybe to dine with? You cannot be unaware that people of your rank, *her* rank, snubbed her most cruelly for undertaking this venture. She is never invited anywhere by anyone except by Mrs Hastings. Of course she has come to depend upon me, for I am the only friend and companion she has.' She was magnificent in her fury, an avenging goddess, with the sun glinting on her skin and throwing lights on her hair. There was grace and a wild beauty in her every movement.

Sir James appreciated none of this, for he was stung by the truth of her words, and liked her not at all for pointing out the things he should have seen for himself. He had depended upon Vera's unspoken sympathy many times during the wretched years when his father had lamented the loss of his elder son and constantly reviled his late wife. Although he had not seen her often, his father's stubbornness had ensured that she had been like an oasis to an unloved child. He had defended his cousin against his father's opposition, but had done little in a practical way to assist her. He winced when he thought of how lonely she must have been in this great house; loneliness was something he understood very well. She could hardly regard her charges as her equals —not, that is, until Crystal came. Damn her! He scorned her contempt. He experienced an unaccustomed desire to wound the little baggage as she had wounded him. 'Don't think to act the lady on account of those worthless bits of glass that that savage entrusted to Vernon Marshall! You are here because I chose to bring you. You have money because I gave it to you. You shall not profit from this situation, because, as I have given, so I shall take away.' He was too angry to consider his words and too provoked to feel contrition. 'I shall talk to you when you are calmer and in a more reasonable frame of mind.' Turning abruptly on his heel, he strode away.

The small sitting-room in Henbury House, which had long been considered Miss Sophia's special province, was cool and gracious. It was carpeted in thick pale grey, and the walls were lined with very pale grey-striped paper. Velvet curtains hung at the windows, and a few sofas and chairs dotted about the room were covered in white satin. It formed a most desirable background to Sophia's fair beauty. Her fragile loveliness was deceptive, for she had needed a will of iron to deal with a father who changed his mind frequently and was a careless and often unreasonable landlord, and with a brother she adored, but knew in her heart of hearts to be a spendthrift weakling.

Sophia had a sense of her own importance and what was due to an old and established family. She above all others perfectly understood her father's will. Marcus would be quite likely to run through his inheritance very quickly, so he needed the right sort of wife to ensure that this did not happen. Sophia could choose the right sort of wife for her brother—certainly not that ill-bred creature with whom he had been riding on the Downs. Heaven forbid! The name of Jackson would be dragged through the mud in no time at all. Arabella Hastings was a sweet and biddable creature who would never disobey her sister-in-law, but unfortunately her worthy father was not of the Jacksons' rank. In the meantime, Sophia had no real objection to delaying her own marriage, although it would add to her consequence to be Lady Allenwood. She enjoyed being the complete mistress of Henbury because it suited her to command everything to her complete satisfaction, and she knew much more about estate management than her feckless brother. She anticipated with some pleasure the search for a bride for her brother: a well-born girl with a good dowry and a placid disposition would be admirable. For too long Sophia had lived under the yoke of a bad-tempered father whose will almost matched her own, and was determined that while she would be Lady Allenwood, she would remain mistress of Henbury. Marcus's bride must be a girl who would accept her sister-in-law's advice and management. There had been several young girls who lived in the vicinity of her aunt's house in Gloucester. She would pay another visit to that city and select a suitable one. Marcus would have no option but to agree, unless he forfeited his allowance; it would be quite simple.

'It is good to be here, Sophia!' James relaxed into a chair opposite her and watched with satisfaction as she executed some delicate lacework. Frequently he felt stifled and confined in this room, which was essentially feminine and very much suited his betrothed, but today he was glad of its restful repose. At least she never stormed at him or disturbed him. She was all that he would desire in a wife, peaceful and undemanding.

'That wretched girl!' he expostulated.

'My dear James, please moderate your language,' she remonstrated quietly. 'Pray tell me in what way she has upset you now.'

'My cousin wishes to adopt her and make her heiress.'

'How very shocking,' Sophia remarked placidly. She turned her work, and held its spidery fineness up for admiration. 'Is that not a delicate piece?' she asked.

'Yes, lovely,' he almost snapped. Leaping to his feet, he began to pace the room. 'She had the impertinence to upbraid me . . .'

'Your cousin?' Sophia's brows arched in surprise.

'No! That wretched girl!'

'Do stop marching about, James! I cannot see that it matters. Persons of that order are frequently given to coarse and ungovernable emotions, but it is not for people of our condition to notice them. They cannot affect us. Now if *I* were to upbraid you, it would be quite different.'

'You would never upbraid me! It is a pleasure to be with you, Sophia, for you are always so restful. Not like that she-cat!' he said vehemently.

She was feminine enough to resent, just slightly, the effect the wanton Miss Smith was having upon her sober unemotional betrothed. Although he was four years her junior, she loved him for his quiet restraint, and because he was the opposite of her blustering father and had all the qualities her loved but weak brother lacked.

'I cannot see what all the fuss is about, James.' She folded away her work. 'As I understand your cousin's affairs, you are one of her trustees, are you not?'

'You seem to understand a great deal about business!' He was nettled.

'You, above all people, must know that I have had to.' There was the faintest reproach in her voice. 'It is quite easy: you simply refuse to agree to such a wild scheme. In fact, I would regard it as evidence that your poor misguided cousin is no longer fit to manage her affairs. Surely it would be a kindness to prevent such an occurrence?'

Her calm and entirely reasonable attitude and suggestion had the effect of darkening Sir James's humour and making him more disgruntled than ever. Sophia forbore to comment further, and deciding that they were all finding the extreme heat trying, rang for some cool lemonade.

'Are you sure you wish me to continue reading, Miss Allenwood? The news in this paper is all rather depressing, for it talks of nothing but the demands for the reform of Parliament, and opposition from those who fear revolution. Perhaps it is making your headache worse?'

'No, no, dear child. I don't really care for the news any longer, but it is so pleasant to have you read to me. It is a luxury I have learned to enjoy. You have been such a comfort.'

Putting aside the newspaper, Crystal watched her friend with the deepest anxiety, for she looked tired and drawn. She wondered whether she should mention the conversation she had had with Sir James; certainly she would not tell her that they had quarrelled. 'Dearest Miss Allenwood, Sir James has told me that you wish to adopt me. There is not the slightest need, for I am fully sensible of all you have done for me. I love being here, and I love you dearly, so there is no need to make any change.'

'There is every need to make a change, Crystal. You have been like a daughter to me, and I wish the world to recognise you as such.' There was a dreamy look in her eyes. 'With money and position, you could marry as you choose, and you are the sort of girl who would be happy in marriage. You might even marry someone who would allow you continue the work I have started here.'

'You will be well quite soon,' Crystal said quickly, fear sharpening her voice.

'Of course I shall be well quite soon. I have always enjoyed excellent health. I am feeling the heat, that is all, and I must confess that I am enjoying being cosseted; it is a new experience for me. Probably that is why I am allowing myself to be such an invalid.'

'Perhaps you should go to bed. I shall send for the doctor to attend you.' Crystal spoke with decision, for it occurred to her that Miss Allenwood was really ill.

'Yes, I shall go to my room presently. But I am determined to adopt you, and I have sent for my man of business to arrange everything. James will have to agree, of course.'

'He will never do that!' Crystal said without thinking.

'Has he discussed the matter with you?' Miss Allenwood's eyes rounded with surprise.

'Yes. He told me that he would never agree.'

'We shall see about that!' Miss Allenwood's face showed two angry spots of colour. 'James is becoming as autocratic and unreasonable as his father, and that woman will not improve his temper.'

Crystal had no difficulty in identifying the person to whom Miss Allenwood referred, but she could not imagine anyone, let alone the tiny Miss Jackson, influencing Sir James. 'He said my stones were worthless. I had suspected as much from something Ben Hardy told me,' Crystal said quietly. 'So, you see, you do not need to do any more for me.' She did not mention his revelation that he provided an income for her. The knowledge that he had paid for the privileged position she had enjoyed at Denewood House made her feel uncomfortable. That he should have displayed his mistrust and dislike while doing so, confused her. It was a long time since an understanding had flowered briefly between them.

'I should not worry overmuch, Crystal, despite what my cousin may have told you. He has given me his word that he will take care of you, and I have never known him to break his word.'

*   *   *

The doctor was with Miss Allenwood, and Crystal had almost finished her evening duties. She felt wearier than ever, for the children had been unusually difficult and she had had to coax them to eat their supper and go to bed. She longed for a moment to herself when she might review the events of the day.

'Miss Crystal! Miss Crystal!' Hannah Baker and Sally Jarman burst into the sitting-room. 'You know that woman we went to help—Mrs Monker?' Crystal recalled that Mrs Monker, a farmer's wife, had requested some help, for she had been most unwell. It was the place to which Marcus was fond of riding, and Mrs Monker always gave them a mug of cider and some bread and cheese. Miss Allenwood was especially kind to Mrs Monker, for she felt that her husband Jake was thoughtless and demanding. Marcus enjoyed a harmless flirtation with the daughter of the house, young Lottie.

'What is it, girls?' Crystal was unable to stand their bubbling excitement.

'She's dead! Dead!' Hannah was filled with childish dread and excitement as the bearer of such fearful news.

For an instant, Crystal heard again the toll of the bell at the mission at São Paulo, and she felt chilled in spite of the heat of the evening.

'It was typhoid,' Sally whispered. Both girls were fearful, and looked to Crystal for guidance.

'Send Abel Poundford and Mary Goddard to me, then get some supper and go to bed.' She spoke with brisk authority, but her heart thudded with dread.

Crystal had become resigned to the ominous appearance of the rose-coloured rash that appeared upon child after child, and sat patiently at the bedside of many a small victim in the night hours when the terrible stomach-pains were at their worst. She had ordered that all the water for the house be boiled; she recollected that the Indians had boiled drinking-water when they could not find a pure spring. The bedding and clothes of the dead were burned immediately. When Abel Poundford gave up his tenacious hold on life, she grieved deeply, but when Mary Goddard quietly gave up her dreams of the future and died, Crystal began to find her burden intolerable. Summer fevers were not uncommon and usually passed as quickly as they had come, but this outbreak was vicious and unprecedented in the placid villages round the great port of Bristol.

Sophia Jackson was tireless in her efforts to help those devasted by death and sickness, and her betrothed, Sir James, worked beside her to quarantine the afflicted households. He had also helped to establish many relief schemes in the city, and had donated a great deal of money to Miss Jackson's charities to help the typhoid victims.

Crystal envied her, for she had someone to help her during this dreadful time. Miss Allenwood, already unwell, had succumbed to the fever, and it must only be a matter of time until her indomitable strength gave out. No harvest would be gathered this year from the home farm, but that was of small consequence because the few children left were already very ill.

'My poor girl! You are completely worn out!' The concern in Sir James's voice was very real as he took Crystal's slim hand in his own. 'You must rest, for there is nothing more you can do.'

The almost tender look in the blue eyes that regarded her with such compassion made her want to cast pride to the four winds and lean her weary head against his broad chest and weep out her misery and fear. But she could not forget that he had made terrible accusations against her, and his dislike and mistrust had persisted from their first meeting.

'You must go to your cousin, Sir James. She is very sick, and would like to have a member of her family with her at this time.'

He was shocked by her seeming lack of emotion. Vera had spoken of this girl as her intended adopted daughter, but she displayed no grief, no fear—nothing beyond weariness. He could not but admire her, for she had run the orphanage, tended the sick and buried the dead with stoic calm, but her composure irked him: it was unwomanly. It was a still hot day and the air was stifling, and yet, weary as she was among sickness and death, she showed a vitality and a strength of purpose that lay like a reservoir beneath her calm surface. She baffled him, and was rarely from his thoughts. There was some quality about her which was entirely alien to the precisely ordered world in which he moved both on land and at sea. He could not be in the presence of this strange girl for more than a few minutes without wishing to control her elusive quality that defied his understanding. He had been astounded at his cousin's suggestion that a match might have been made between himself and Crystal. Although he loved and respected Sophia, he was fully aware that this other girl was becoming a dangerous obsession. Assuredly he did not love her—his feelings at times bordered on hatred—and her physical proximity sent almost unbearable ripples of disturbance through him. His visits to Denewood House had been timed, whenever possible, to avoid her, for he had experienced more than once an overwhelming desire to kiss her. The disclosure she had made about her relationship with Marcus had revolted him, and for an instant he had wished to kill the unfortunate young man. She had then denied that such an intimate relationship existed, but she could not have lived as she had done and remained innocent, no matter how much he might wish to believe otherwise. There was no innocence about Crystal Smith! He had given her a name, an income, a place in his own society; while he might wish that he had never met her, he had, as yet, no wish to let her go. His own emotions and responses confused him. Thank heavens that his cool, well-bred Sophia never drew such a response from him! With her, he could be rational, tranquil and content. They would deal as amicably after marriage as they dealt now.

Crystal sat impassively by the bedside of the dying woman. She could not allow her sense of loss and bereavement to show on her face, for she would not distress her friend in her last moments. Going calmly about the duties of the sick-room, she longed to ease the look of bewildered hurt on Sir James's face.

'You will take care of Crystal, James?' The voice was so low that it was almost inaudible. 'She would not allow the lawyer in to see me, and now I fear that it is too late.'

'Yes, Vera. I give you my word to care for Crystal.'

He glanced at Crystal—an unguarded and involuntary look—and she guessed that he had not given the matter much thought. Passionately she hoped that he would allow her to continue running Denewood House, for the remaining children, and others, would need the love and care of the orphanage. This house was more dear to her than any other place, and she had been busy, happy and fulfilled here. He must understand that. 'I am sure that Sir James will do the right thing,' she murmured, taking the dry hand in a light clasp. 'Goodbye, dear Miss Allenwood. Thank you for everything you have given me.'

A slight pressure was exerted on Crystal's hand and Miss Allenwood smiled up at her, murmuring something too faint to be heard. Crystal left the room quickly, sure that her friend would prefer to spend her remaining moments with one to whom she was related. Also she was very much afraid that her composure would break down. She would weep later, in the privacy of her own room.

Already Miss Allenwood's sitting-room felt lonely and desolate, and Crystal moved restlessly about, picking up an ornament, discarding a flower from the rose-bowl, for it had been several days since she had had leisure to change the flowers. She touched the chiming clock on the mantelshelf, before going to the window to gaze out at the flowerbeds in the vain hope that she might, by looking at something beautiful, ease the grief she felt inside. When she observed a stocky man with a quick aggressive gait crossing the lawn, an involuntary shudder ran through her; it was Jake Monker. She had met him only briefly, and had disliked him. There was no one to answer the inevitable summons on the door, and with the greatest reluctance she went to meet the unwelcome visitor.

As she opened the door, he paused in the act of raising a clenched fist to bang upon it. He was short and powerfully built, with a broad nose and dark, close-set eyes. He was clad in the gaiters and smock of a farmer, and although he presented a clean appearance, there was an air of corruption beneath the veneer of rural honesty. She shuddered again, and the man, who had been regarding her with sensual appreciation in those small eyes, snatched the hat from his head and wiped a large hairy hand across his thick lips.

'Why, I do believe I 'ave the pleasure of seeing Miss Crystal Smith!' There was a forced geniality in that heavily burred West Country voice. 'I 'eard that Sir James, my landlord, was 'ere, and wishful of a word, urgent-like, I took the liberty of presenting myself. But, as I'm 'ere, I reckon I can kill two birds with one stone.' He jabbed a stubby finger at Crystal. 'You'll be outta work soon, and I need a nice girl like you about the place to see to my poor motherless children.'

'But surely, Mr Monker . . .'

'Jake, my lovely girl. You call me Jake. That's what you're to call me from now on.'

'Mr Monker,' she said firmly, trying to avoid the greedy look in his eyes, 'your daughter Lottie must be fourteen or fifteen, almost as old as myself, and surely Caleb is at least sixteen! They do not need mothering.'

'My poor little Lottie ain't a woman.' As he took a step forward and touched her breast lightly, Crystal recoiled. 'Not like you are! Oh, don't turn away from Jake Monker!' He had turned back his upper lip in a semblance of a smile, and there was menace behind the expression in his eyes. 'I always gets what I want. I'm that kind of man.'

She closed the door in his face, her heart pounding with apprehension, for she had not forgotten that Miss Allenwood had said he was not kind to his late wife. Sir James had mentioned that he was the best of the tenant farmers throughout Henbury, Brentry and Westbury-on-Trym: if there was trouble with any of the farmers who were dissatisfied with the Corn Laws, or who grumbled against the landed gentry or spoke of reforms, Monker was the man called in to mediate and talk the kind of sense that held the community together in stability and order.

A door closed quietly somewhere in the distance, and slow footsteps approached. Crystal hurried back into Miss Allenwood's sitting-room to await Sir James, guessing that the coming interview would be painful. She attempted to dispel the anxiety that Jake Monker had engendered in her, and schooled her features into passive acceptance of the news she dreaded to hear.

He entered the room, and there was such a look of deep unhappiness about him that she went immediately and folded him into the warmth of her embrace, while he sighed against her, 'She is gone.' He spoke simply, but she could sense the emotion behind his words.

A shadow fell on their passionless embrace, and turning her head, Crystal caught sight of Jake Monker at the window. 'I had forgotten,' she said quickly, her voice husky with unshed tears. 'Jake Monker has come to see you on some urgent matter, and you should go out and speak with him.'

He placed his hands on her shoulders and looked into her anxious eyes. 'I promised my cousin that I would make suitable provision for you, and I shall make satisfactory arrangements for your future as soon as I can.'

'You should go.' She felt her apprehension lift, and looking into his clear blue eyes, an absolute trust in him filled her. He might be arrogant and have previously shown his dislike of her, he might think that she had schemed to become Miss Allenwood's heir, but he had given his word, and she did not doubt for an instant that he would keep it. The disquieting fears caused by Jake Monker subsided.

'And that's about it, really, Sir James.' The manner adopted by Jake Monker with other men, particularly his superiors, was vastly different from that of a few minutes ago with Crystal. ''Tis you must go and negotiate; that was the word I got.' He spoke briskly and decisively, and Sir James listened with attention. 'They are holding Captain Hastings to ransom in some foreign part, and Mr Stewart says you got to go in person and talk terms and 'and over cash. They won't deal with no agents; seems they seen you a couple of times.'

'I have often been to Port-of-Spain, although I have never been down the coast that is a hideout for the pirates.' They were walking down the drive to the road. 'It could not have happened at a worse time. Typhoid everywhere, my cousin dead, and there are certain matters I cannot impose upon my agent or Miss Jackson.'

'Truly sorry to 'ear about Miss Allenwood. A very fine lady, and one that'll be sorely missed.' Monker turned to look squarely at his employer. 'If there be anything I could do, Sir James, you only got to ask. I 'opes you know that.'

'You are a good man, Monker. Thank you.' Sir James considered his extreme good fortune in these troubled times: he was blessed with good dependants, an able agent, and a reliable woman in his betrothed, Sophia Jackson.

Monker nodded back at the orphanage. 'That'll 'ave to be closed down, shouldn't wonder. Wouldn't be fair to put little 'uns into a place where they all died of the disease. Per'aps you might like to put Miss Crystal into some good family until you comes back? Somewhere where she'll be cared for like a daughter of the family.'

'A capital notion!' Sir James briefly clasped the shoulder of Monker. 'The very thing! I wonder I did not think of it myself.' He decided to ask Mrs Hastings to take Crystal into her home until such time as he returned, and then he could arrange for her future at his leisure. Arabella Hastings was about the same age as Crystal; they got on well together and would be company for each other.

'This is very dreadful news, my poor James! Only tell me what I can do to ease your burden.' Sophia was all concern as she bade her betrothed to enter her sitting-room, and rang for some tea. 'Will you dine with me before you go?'

'I shall not have time. I must arrange for my cousin's funeral, then catch the evening tide. If we sail in a light, fast craft, we can be in Port-of-Spain very quickly. Unfortunately, Mrs Hastings insists upon accompanying me.'

'How very improper!' Genuine shock registered on Sophia's lovely countenance.

'It is not the propriety that concerns me. I believe her to be much concerned for the well-being of her husband.

'Even so, her place is not to be gadding about on the high seas! She should leave that to you, and await him here.' Something like disgust pulled down the corners of her exquisite mouth.

For an instant he saw another mouth—wider, with full sensuous lips—and quickly banished the image. 'Tell me, Sophia, if I and not Captain Hastings were held hostage for ransom by pirates, would you await me here? These are desperate and dangerous men who have been known to drive the hardest bargains and treat their victims with vicious cruelty. Would you rest easily, here, if I had been captured by such men?'

'Surely there is law and order in Trinidad? You are always telling me how wonderfully pleasant and civilised Port-of-Spain is.' She was almost pettish in her response.

'Those pirates are a law unto themselves! Most people are terrified of them.'

'James, you are exaggerating, I am sure of that. The sooner you give up the sea the better. Indeed,' Sophia's tone was almost playful, 'I am convinced that this little escapade with Captain Hastings will convince you to give up all thoughts of the sea from now on.' His expression hardened, and she saw she had misjudged her handling of him. 'I cannot conceive what you think *I* should be able to do. I should be quite heartbroken, of course, but I should be quite out of place in a ship!' she said piteously.

His conscience smote him. 'Of course you would, my darling!' He caught her against his chest and held one fragile hand. What a brute he was to think that his fragile Sophia could endure the rigours of such a journey! His mouth sought hers, but she averted her face in pleased confusion.

'James! We need not make this an occasion for unseemly conduct!' She pushed him away, gently but firmly. 'I am confident that you will all be among us again before long.'

'Oh, Lord!' He spoke ruefully, for in his sudden rush
of tender emotion towards his betrothed he had almost
forgotten Crystal. 'I had hoped to lodge Crystal Smith
with Mrs Hastings and Arabella until I returned.'

'That is now out of the question?' Sophia said sharply.

'Of course it is! Where will Arabella reside?'

'In Bath, with some relatives of Mrs Hastings.'

'I wonder if they could be prevailed upon to take
Crystal for a time? My cousin intended to make Crystal
her adopted daughter and heiress, and I must deal with
that upon my return.'

The arrival of the tea-tray helped Sophia to cover her
dismay. This would never do! 'You may go,' she said to
the maid. 'I shall pour.' Partially filling a china cup with
pale gold tea, she gazed thoughtfully at a group of
Dresden figurines. 'It would not be a good idea to send
the young person to Bath. Marcus is still there.'

'Still skulking, you mean!'

'Marcus is visiting some friends,' she said with some
asperity, for she disliked anyone criticising her brother.
'I thought it would be a good idea if he remained there
until the epidemic had run its course. But I very much
fear that the young person would do all in her power to
attach him if they were thrown continually together. It
would not be desirable.'

He was stung by her tone. In other circumstances he
might have shared her sentiments, but he disliked hearing Crystal referred to as 'the young person'. 'I think it
would be a good idea,' he said obstinately. 'It would
bring our marriage much nearer. She is to inherit a good
deal of money, she has certain graces, and she will no
doubt wish to take her place in society. Besides—' he
forestalled further argument '—I gave Vera my word,
and I intend to keep it.'

Sophia Jackson had dealt for long enough with the
vagaries of an obstinate temperament to know how to
deal with this mood. She said in deepest astonishment,
'My dearest James, I never for a moment intended you
to do otherwise. But only consider the disservice you
would be doing the girl. Your cousin, I collect, never
actually made a will, and unless you handle this matter

with the utmost discretion, you would subject both
yourself and me to the most unwelcome speculation
about your interest in the girl. I gather that Miss Allenwood spoke to no one but yourself of this worthy plan?'

'No,' he admitted.

'And further consider,' she continued persuasively,
'that if you were to announce to the world that she is to
be handsomely provided for, she would be the object of
every fortune-hunter in the county.'

He saw the force of her argument, and the obstinate
look wavered, then left his face. 'Then what *can* I do
with the wretched girl? I gave my promise.' He pushed a
hand distractedly through his hair.

'Why, leave her in my care until such time as you
return. You can arrange matters then. There cannot be
any great urgency.'

'You are too good!' He was much moved by her offer,
for he knew that she disliked Crystal and was acting in
such a way only for his sake. 'As soon as the observances
due to my cousin are completed, and you have agreed to
a marriage for Marcus, we must be married. I shall not
be put off any longer.' He spoke with warmth, and
looked at her with such admiration and affection that she
was moved to extend her hand to him in farewell, and
allow him to hold that hand for longer than the occasion
merited.

It seemed to Crystal as though the funeral bell had tolled
without ceasing for many weeks. The funeral service for
Miss Allenwood was very short, and she was barely
conscious of Sir James leading her back to Denewood
House. It was so empty that she could not bear to walk
through rooms that had resounded to the happy chatter
and laughter of children. As though guessing her
thoughts, Sir James led her out into the little garden at
the furthest corner of the south lawn, much beloved of
Miss Allenwood. It was enclosed with hedges, and they
sheltered the profusion of bright flowers. The evening
light bathed the garden in a bronze glow, and the air was
sweet with the scent of the blooms.

'I suppose I should offer you something to eat . . . It is

customary, I know, but I am alone here now . . .' She could not go on, for her voice was suspended by tears. Stumbling, she put out a hand blindly, as though to ward off the inevitable loneliness. Her heart was full of grief at the death of her friend and the passing of a way of life she had come to love.

'Crystal, do not be afraid to grieve. I know a little of such feelings.' He caught her to him and gently began to caress her.

'I am so lost!' She wept against his coat. 'I have lost my only friend. And now you must go, too!' Until his disclosure that he was leaving immediately, she had felt only anger and hostility towards him; now she felt desolation, for he was her link with the past, and she had always envisaged a future in which he was somewhere in her background. 'Take me with you,' she whispered, almost to herself. Raising a tear-drenched face to him, she implored again, 'Please take me with you. I know that the mission you undertake is fraught with peril. If anything happens to you, I wish to be at your side. If you do not return, I cannot live without you.'

Her admission astounded both of them. Crystal was deeply conscious of his closeness and longed to yield to him. A world without Sir James would be unbearably void. She recalled several small incidents when he had shown kindness and forbearance with her youth and ignorance. He did not question for a moment the need to go to the help of Captain Hastings, although she recalled from her conversations with the Stewarts that such a mission would be dangerous in the extreme. Love! So this was love! How strange it was; she must have loved him, without realising it, for some time!

Her scent filled his nostrils and her body quivered slightly beneath his touch. His eyes, which had begun to smoulder, devoured her face as though seeing it for the first time. Then she touched his cheek, and he stepped back as though a spell had been broken. 'I cannot take you, Crystal.' His voice was hoarse, and he sounded quite unlike his usual decisive self. Abruptly releasing her, he left the garden quickly as though blinded by some unsuspected vision.

CHAPTER NINE

JAKE MONKER said with heavy sincerity, ''Tis sad old times for us all, but we must pull together, and we shall succeed, with the help of the Lord.'

'So I can rely upon you to attend to those matters on the Brentry farms, Monker?' Sophia was much impressed with this stalwart man. 'You may deal directly with the agent upon all future occasions, for I am sure that you will exercise sound judgment,' she said graciously, even sympathetically.

Jake Monker watched her face out of the corner of his small crafty eye, and drew a stubby finger along the heavy line of his jaw. 'Sir James was concerned that the girl from the orphanage, Crystal Smith, would be all right. I didn't like to interrupt them because 'e was too busy comforting 'er, 'er 'aving just lost Miss Allenwood. Mighty concerned for 'er, 'e was.' Seeing the way Miss Jackson's face tightened at the mention of the girl's name, he hid a satisfied smile and allowed the import of his words to sink in before continuing, 'I 'ad been going to offer the girl a good Christian 'ome—my own—for I know 'ow young girls can come to grief if left to their own devices, and the traps there are in this bad wicked world. It would serve me well, for I would 'ave someone to instruct my poor motherless girl, Lottie, in the management of the 'ouse.'

Sophia's heart leaped with gratitude. This was the very solution to a vexing problem! Sir James himself had suggested that Crystal be lodged with a family. If her very strict conscience nudged her a trifle—for she well knew that, no matter how worthy Monker was, it was not quite the home Sir James had in mind—she consoled herself with the thought that it was the only feasible alternative, and it was merely a temporary and quite unexceptionable arrangement. She most assuredly did not want that beautiful and disturbing girl under her own roof, for she had witnessed Marcus's eagerness when he was to accompany her on the weekly riding expeditions. Her handsome and impressionable brother would return from Bath very soon, and would be head over heels in love with Crystal if she stayed under the same roof. However well dowered, the girl was of unknown and probably questionable origins, and she appeared to exercise a most undesirable effect on men—and quite deliberately contrived. It was really most fortuitous that Monker was prepared to take the girl into his home. He must be quite five-and-forty, and a sensible man of the land and community, and surely above the wiles of Crystal Smith. 'This is most kind of you, Monker. You shall, of course, be recompensed for your trouble . . .'

'I wouldn't 'ear of it, Miss Jackson! No more than me duty, and the girl shall earn 'er keep. No need to trouble yourself further. I'll go and collect 'er today.'

Well satisfied with the disposal of an irritating problem and the saving of the expense of Crystal's upkeep, Miss Jackson was in a charitable humour. 'No, I shall bring her to you myself, at six-thirty.'

Denewood House was cold and lifeless. The dormitories that had resounded to the clatter of running feet and childish voices were silent; the rows of little iron beds like sentinels on lonely endless duty. The dining-room and workshops through which Crystal walked for the last time were shadowed with a thousand happier recollections. And Sir James . . . They had shared a special experience in the garden, and the emotions and memory of that encounter sustained and nourished her now. Although he had taken abrupt leave of her, she believed that he returned her feelings, and had not spoken because he was not free. She no longer felt bereft, and already longed for his return. Somehow, she was convinced, everything would be resolved for the best when he returned to England. Loving him as she did, she would will his safe return. Her love would be his safe passage and talisman against all danger.

The sound of the carriage on the gravelled drive announced Sophia Jackson's arrival, and Crystal hurried down to greet her. When she had received word earlier that day that Miss Jackson was to collect her, she had been astonished, and then delighted, for it could mean only that she was to stay with that lady until Sir James returned. Her lips curved with tender appreciation of this proof that he lost his doubts of her. Those vile doubts he had expressed so unequivocally a lifetime ago must have been quite vanquished. Her hurt and anger, she now recognised, had sprung from the quite natural desire for his good opinion. She did not give a rap for the petty restrictions of the English class system, but the code of Sir James's world made his betrothal to Miss Jackson as binding as a marriage. Crystal was sure that, somehow, her own longing for him must eventually be transformed into reality. She was unsure how this was to be achieved, but for the present, her love and hope must sustain her.

'Could your man bring down my trunks?' she raised a shining face to the small lady who sat upright in the back of the open carriage.

A tiny frown marred the flawless beauty of that fair face, and colouring faintly, she raised her gloved hand in assent, as her coachman had already climbed down to carry out the order he anticipated. Miss Jackson was in a slight quandary, for it occurred to her that Crystal might think that she was to stay at the Jacksons' own home. She was attired as though she were on a social visit, and really that cream muslin dress became her almost indecently well, revealing as it did the rounded curves of her figure. The thick mass of hair caught up at the crown of her head fell in lustrous curls about her neck and shoulders and was unconsciously fashionable, and the sparkle in those clear green eyes bespoke an assurance that irked Miss Jackson. Yet she experienced some hesitation about telling Crystal where they were going, and bade her climb up into the carriage.

'We must proceed to our destination without delay, for you are expected, and will be a most welcome visitor.'

Crystal felt a pang of remorse as she looked at the delicate profile beside her. She longed to confess to Miss

Jackson her feelings for Sir James, but how could she? Instead, she said eagerly, 'You are so good, Miss Jackson! You cannot imagine how happy I am to be coming to stay with you.'

The attractive inflection in the girl's husky speech and the belief that she, an orphanage girl, was to be elevated to the status of a guest in the rigidly correct Jackson household irritated Sophia and caused the last of her scruples to flee without regret. 'I fear that you are in some error,' she explained as the coach moved away. 'It would, of course, be delightful to have you to stay with me, for my maid is taking some holiday to be with her sister during her forthcoming confinement. Fortunately,' she prevaricated very slightly, 'Sir James Allenwood made provision for you before departing, and you are to be placed with a good and worthy family until his return.'

The warmth of the afternoon breeze turned to a chill, and Crystal felt a dreadful apprehension gnaw at her stomach. The small upright figure had uttered this speech with composure, turning her violet gaze guilelessly upon her. As the carriage began the descent into the village of Brentry and to fork on to a farm track, the happy bubble of self-confidence and happiness that she had felt since Sir James's departure began to evaporate, and she felt sick with some nameless fear.

'Miss Jackson—' she clutched at the hand of the woman beside her '—are you taking me to Jake Monker?' She knew that the question was unnecessary, for she had ridden this way often enough with Marcus.

Sophia's slender eyebrows arched in surprise. 'So you know him?'

'Mr Jackson and I used to ride this way. Mrs Monker was always kind to us, and we used to rest our horses at her farmhouse. I—I have met Mr Monker,' she faltered unhappily, aware that she could not confide her fears. 'I will do anything or go anywhere, but do not make me go to Jake Monker!'

Sophia was seriously perturbed, because the girl was looking and talking quite wildly. How very fortunate that she was not coming to stay at their own home, as

such emotional outbursts would be most embarrassing.
'As you know the family, you will doubtless feel quite at
home there.' Crystal continued to look terrified. Really!
How irrational the girl was! Clearly the recent experiences at the orphanage had unhinged her, and a period
of quiet and hard work in the home of a sensible yeoman
should cure her of such foolishness. Or had she really
thought to step into the world of the Jacksons and the
Allenwoods? 'You are not being sensible, and Sir James
would be very annoyed to know how little you value his
judgment.' She had hoped that her calmly worded re-
proof would have the effect of dispelling that distraught
expression and hectic flush. Because she was unimagin-
ative, she was quite unable to account for Crystal's
outburst, and supposed that the worthy but misguided
Miss Allenwood must have filled her with unsuitable
notions, and was glad that she had not courted that
lady's society.

A neat, well-constructed farmhouse lay ahead, and
the surrounding yards were immaculate and free of
rubbish. A large vegetable garden could be seen to one
side of the house and trim brick dairies lay at the
back.

Grey clouded the mellow evening sun, and a great
weight crushed her happy confidence as Crystal again
heard his words: 'I shall make satisfactory arrangements
for your future.' She was betrayed! How foolish she had
been! She had but imagined Sir James's response to her
own ardent feelings—she knew that now. He had never
revised his ill opinion of her. What silly notions had she
entertained? Some foolishness about spending her life
beside the man she loved? He had promised that he
would thwart her supposed plans to enter English
society, but she had never had any such plans!

The unusual circumstances of her early years that had
given rise to suspicions of her now came to her rescue.
She had learned that to show one's feelings to the enemy
was to give the advantage; so no one should ever know
that her courage almost failed her as she looked at the
assembled Monker family, and saw beneath the smiles
their greed and stupidity. Jake had nudged Caleb, a

gangling boy with vacant eyes and loose lips, into performing a bow. The youth placed a bony hand across his
stomach and bent stiffly forward so that his lank mousy
hair flopped over his face. Under other circumstances,
Crystal would have found the episode amusing. Lottie,
conscious of scrutiny, allowed her lids to drop over her
protuberant eyes and pouted before lifting one plump
shoulder in a dismissive gesture. Jake missed this
action, for he had stepped forward to the carriage.
After performing his greeting to Miss Jackson, and
accepting her refusal of refreshment, he turned to
Crystal.

When he laid a thick hand on her knee, she willed
herself not to cry out, for her skin crawled under the
unwelcome contact with the man she already feared and
hated. 'Welcome, Miss Crystal! Welcome to your new
'ome.'

The interior of the farmhouse showed evidence of
much neglect. The front door led straight into a large
kitchen dominated by a great wooden table and flanked
by a modern-looking range. A flight of stairs leading up
was situated at the far end, opposite the door. On the
wall close to the door was a massive stone sink with a
water-pumping handle above it. It was modern, indeed!
Crystal's look of surprise gratified Monker. He had
carried her trunks to the bottom of the stairs and
dumped them there.

'I'll get our Caleb to carry them up just as soon as 'e
gets back. I sent the two kids out to the village for the
evening, just so's you and I could get to know each other
and be real friendly-like.'

Crystal felt nauseated. This man's wife was but lately
dead; she had kept his house and borne his children, yet
with her barely cold in the grave, his hot lustful eyes
were undressing the girl who stood before him.

That Sir James could have so betrayed her caused her
the very deepest grief. He had relegated her to the care
of this man, and if this was what he considered proper
provision for her, it spoke volumes. Crystal was a
passionate, spirited girl, who was loving and could
inspire love in others, but at that moment the alien seed

of revenge nearly found soil in which to root. Banishing the thought, she determined to accommodate Jake Monker while seeking a means of escape. The restricted life she had led at Denewood House had left little leisure for meeting people or making friends. Mrs Hastings and Arabella might have been allies, but they were not here. Suddenly she thought of Marcus, who might be rather weak and given over to the pursuit of pleasure, but surely he would not refuse to help her out of this predicament?

'I'll show you to your room. It's a right pretty little room, next to mine.' Monker leered at her, and pushed her up the stairs ahead of him.

Several sturdy oak doors opened from the long low landing, and he opened one and admitted her into a square, sparsely furnished room with a clean although desolate appearance. A spotted pier-glass enhanced one corner, and he pointed to it proudly. 'Belonged to my Hannah, did that; real proud of it she were! Take a look, and see if the sight of you wipes that sour look off your face.' Monker stuck his thumbs into the broad leather belt with its heavy buckle, and puffed out his chest. Drawing in his stubbled chin, he watched her movements. 'Move real pretty, you do, Crystal,' he said softly, with a throaty chuckle. 'I do like that dress! I can nearly see through it, and nearly ain't good enough for Jake Monker! Take it off!'

'Take my dress off?' she gasped, and whirled about to face him. 'Are you mad?' Instinctively her hands had risen to her breasts, and fell again as quickly.

'That's right, me little dear.' She could smell the tobacco-soured breath and almost feel the rough stubbled chin against her cheek, for she was slightly taller than him. 'You 'elp my kiddies by day, and at night you and me can sport together. That'll be your reward. Now take off that dress! I wants to get a good look at you.' He fumbled at the flimsy material at her throat and shoulders, his breath coming in uneven rasps, while the buckle of his belt dug into her soft flesh.

'Get away from me!' she commanded, and pushed

him with all her might. 'If you touch me again, I shall tell Sir James Allenwood upon his return.'

'Don't act so 'igh and mighty! Aren't I good enough?' he demanded, although he did retreat from the blazing anger in those eyes turned on him with such unexpected vehemence. 'Well?' He advanced towards her. 'Aren't I as good as Sir James Allenwood? I saw the two of you that day, shameless hussy! Well, what you gave 'im you give me, and you won't find me ungenerous.'

'I gave Sir James nothing,' she managed to say. Only my heart, once, she whispered to herself, when I was very naïve and stupid.

'I got eyes in me 'ead, and I'm not thick. If 'e was going to treat you right, you wouldn't be 'ere right now, would you, Miss Hoity-Toity? So stop looking down your nose and be a good girl and act sensible.'

Monker had started to unbuckle his belt, and she felt sick with shame and fury, for his words had lashed her. She backed away, and tried to leave the room, but he impeded her with unexpected swiftness in that thick muscular body. 'I said take that dress off, my pretty, or I'll rip it off you!' A clumsy hand began to knead her breast, and she could feel the calluses through the thin material.

'If you really believe that Sir James and I are lovers,' she said, desperately playing for time, 'how do you think he will react if he knows that you are keeping me here against my will and are prepared to rape me?'

The directness of her speech stilled his fumbling hands, and made him look at her with something approaching fear in his small cunning eyes. 'Against your will?' He gawped at her, his mouth hanging open. 'I ain't keeping you 'ere. Go where you like!'

The realisation that she had nowhere to go struck Crystal afresh. At one point she had believed that she had some money of her own, and even if there were funds placed to her credit in a bank, she had no idea how to set about retrieving it. In any case, it was not her money. She had nothing! She was forced to accept that until Sir James returned and made some decision about her future, she would have to remain in this house.

Nothing would induce her to betray the utter sense of desolation which crept over her, or the fear that Monker could induce in her.

Fear flickered again in those shifty little eyes. 'As for rape—you're mad, girl, mad!'

Crystal knew that she had won the advantage. 'Yes, rape! Until Sir James returns I must stay here, for, as you pointed out, I do not have anywhere else to go. But I am not here for your sport!' Her terror had made her voice strong, and her imperious stature made him quail before her. 'If you lay a finger on me, I shall go straight to Miss Jackson and tell her what you are about. Then I shall go to the Reverend Mr Alcott and ask him to give me sanctuary.'

'She-cat!' muttered Monker, buckling his belt. 'But you needn't think no orphanage slut's 'aving this decent room! Little place by the scullery, just off the kitchen, is good enough for the likes o' you.'

Crystal breathed a sigh of relief and ran out and down to the kitchen.

'There.' He indicated a small cupboard, like a cell, with a narrow iron bed. There was no window and it was dark and stuffy, but it was safe, and well away from Monker. 'I tell you, my fine lady,' he hissed in her ear, 'you'll regret turning down Jake Monker afore you're much older. Now you ain't the fine visitor 'ere no more, waiting to be served by my poor wife. So get out of that finery and into something more fitted for work, then get this place cleaned up.'

It was dark by the time Lottie and Caleb returned, and they flung themselves into the now beeswaxed kitchen, gaping about them in surprise.

'So this is the poor little orphan!' Lottie circled her, a plump hand on her rounded hip, head to one side. 'Bit of a come-down in the world, ain't it, Crystal?' The girl was pretty in her pert way, but her bodice was cut too low over her full breasts for Crystal's taste, and something of her thoughts must have showed in her expression. 'Don't look at me like that!' Lottie noted Crystal's fine skin and thick hair, now confined beneath a white cap, and the plain gown of dark green covered with a white apron. There was a quality about the tall shapely girl that she herself lacked. 'You never had much time for me when you used to come here with Mr Marcus. Well, you'll have to cut your clothes now to fit your cloth!' She sniggered unpleasantly, and Crystal flushed at the reminder of former, happier times. 'I reckon she's too much of the fine lady for us, Pa!'

'Is she to be our new Ma?' Caleb's dull eyes looked with hostility at Crystal, then questioningly at his father.

'That she ain't!' He looked broodingly at Crystal, and a light shone in his furtive little eyes. 'She's our skivvy. She's 'ere to do all the 'eavy work so you can learn to be a fine lady, Lottie. You mind 'ow she speaks, and copy 'er. You were right about Mr Marcus Jackson; 'e was real struck by you. I reckon you could do worse for yourself than get 'im for 'usband.'

Monker had ordered Crystal to prepare a meal for the family and she had baked a steak and kidney pie in thick juicy gravy, encased in a steaming crust. They fell upon it with snatching hands and slobbering mouths, and the very sight of this, accompanied by their noises while eating, made her glad to escape to her little cell.

'Skivvies don't eat with family,' Monker instructed her, in order to demean her in front of his children. 'Get!' he snarled, jabbing a finger in the direction of her cell-like room. 'And when family is about, stay out of sight and mind your manners.'

When the family left the kitchen, for it was now their custom to sit in the large, over-furnished parlour each evening, Crystal returned there to wash the dishes and scour the pots. No task was too onerous, but if she failed, Monker would cuff her across the head with a deliberate punch. Caleb often tried to bully her, but one look from those stony eyes caused him to retreat quickly, although in his father's presence he would snigger at her discomfiture and heap insults upon her.

Only Lottie, with her impertinent voice and pretty face, seemed to be kind to her. Gradually the girl's speech and manner improved, and she became less abrupt and would ask Crystal all manner of questions about her life at Denewood House. She always brought the conversation round to Marcus Jackson, and avidly drank in every detail that she could wrench. That he had indulged a flirtatious nature she could not doubt; that Lottie should have taken seriously his careless good-humoured dalliance appalled her. But any warnings she tried to give fell on angry ears. Lottie merely assumed that she was jealous, and Crystal was wise enough not to persevere.

'You're turning out real nice, Lottie,' Monker commented upon his daughter's improved speech and manner. 'Shouldn't be surprised if you didn't marry Sir James 'imself!' He laughed at his witticism, but there was a serious intent about the jest and he watched Crystal with a new consideration in his ambitious eye. 'I wonder that Mr Jackson don't stop by any more. 'E used to be glad of 'is bread and cheese and drop of cider, as I remember, when 'e was out riding. Next time 'e comes, I want 'im made real welcome, you understand?'

Crystal did understand. 'That would not be fair, Mr Monker.' They had reached a tacit understanding, by which she went about her duties unhampered by his lustful approaches and he was kept at bay by her icy disdain and the threat of exposure to Miss Jackson.

'What wouldn't be fair?' he demanded belligerently. Every so often his lust made him vent frustrated anger on her.

'To give Lottie ideas above her station,' she responded calmly, for she was beginning to be fond of the girl. 'With some training and guidance, she could make a good match with a farmer, but she would never be accepted by the likes of Sir James Allenwood. And well you must know that Mr Jackson may not marry without the consent of his sister. If you keep telling her that she could look so high, she will become dissatisfied with a man of her own station.'

''Ow dare you?' he spluttered, but his shrewd mind told him that she spoke the truth. 'Orphanage slut! My Lottie's good enough for anyone—better'n a slut like you any day of the week! You could teach 'er 'ow to walk and talk an' 'old a cup. I got money, plenty of money, to dress 'er up real nice. Any man would be proud to take my little Lottie.'

'You are making a very big mistake.' She resumed her mending of a smock, hoping that her silence would drive him from the kitchen.

'I heard all that!' Lottie descended the stairs, her face a mask of spite. 'So I'm not good enough for gentry? Let me tell you this much, Pa, she's afraid I'll take her fine friend away from her. The talk in the village is that Mr Marcus is sweet on her, but not sweet enough to have her for a wife.'

'What's this?' Monker struck the table with a heavy fist, causing the mugs and plates to jump. 'You after young Jackson?'

'Certainly not!' Crystal replied as coolly as she could, for this conversation was distasteful. She looked into the faces that watched her: Jake Monker, heavy-jowled and suspicious, Lottie's protruding eyes spiteful and angry. 'It is hardly a question of whether you are good enough for Mr Jackson; his sister would never consent to a match with you. She is conscious of her social position, I believe. As to myself, Mr Jackson and I were no more than friends. Can you have forgotten that Sir James Allenwood is betrothed to Miss Jackson? You cannot imagine that he would break his engagement in order to marry another.'

'That's where you're wrong, me girl!' Monker said with malicious triumph. 'That's what 'e may 'ave fobbed you off with, but the truth is that 'is pa made that match for 'im. I been around a sight longer than you, so don't think to come in 'ere telling Jakie Monker what's what! I was tenant to 'is father, Sir Arthur, an' a rare old codger 'e could be, at times! When 'is eldest son was born, about the same time as Miss Jackson, 'im and Mr Lucius Jackson 'atched up this little scheme to get the two children wed. But Philip died when that mother of 'is, no better'n that she should 'ave been, ran off and their coach overturned. So what more natural than the two old gentlemen should decide to marry off the daughter of one to the son of the other! Keeps the land together. And if Sir James's 'eart's in that marriage, I'll eat my own boots!' He roared with laughter, and stuck his feet up on the table. 'I reckon any man, even a sensible one, will take to a pretty face.' He looked at her slyly. ''E didn't seem averse to you, now did 'e?'

'What are you talking about, Pa?' Lottie said, avid with curiosity.

'Only that Miss, 'ere, and Sir James, knows a sight more about each other than she lets on. And I don't reckon that Sir James is quite so devoted to Miss Jackson as 'e lets on.'

'Ooh! You don't say, Pa!' Lottie's eyes were round with astonishment, and she looked at Crystal with something akin to respect.

'Only 'e wouldn't 'ave someone like 'er to wife. She don't even know 'er own name. I knows your name ain't Smith!' He spat triumphantly, revelling in her discomfiture. 'I 'eard young Ben 'Ardy talking about you. She lived with savage Indians, so God knows what she got up to!'

'Dirty slut!' breathed Lottie ecstatically. 'And she keeps telling *me* how to behave. The cheek of her!'

'Who's your ma and pa, then?' Lottie demanded unkindly, as the girls crossed the yard with buckets of warm frothing milk to the dairy. Since the exchange in the kitchen, Lottie had resumed her former hostility.

'I do not know,' confessed Crystal, incurably honest.

'Well, at least I know who my ma and pa are. I've got a name, which is more than you've got. The name you have is what Sir James gave you; and he's not likely to change it to another!' She tittered unkindly. 'So you needn't act so high and mighty with me.'

Setting the pails on the scrubbed table of the dairy and opening the shutters to allow some light, Crystal sighed heavily and regarded her seriously. 'Lottie, do you really wish to marry Sir James?'

'Well, no, not really, not since you ask me outright. It's only pa's fancy.' She dropped her taunting manner and looked thoughtful. 'But I do like Mr Jackson; he's so gay and full of fun. And he's got a way of smiling at a girl.'

Crystal knew this to be true, for no one could be as charming and attractive when he chose. The girl must be lonely, for her father's absurd pretensions had caused him to deny her friendship with other girls of her age and status. Caleb was stupid, and when not working, spent his time at the local public house drinking cider with other village louts. He was fond of Lottie in an amiable way, but could be no company for her. It was his dearest wish that his father be allowed to buy the farm from Sir James, and much of his conversation was upon that topic. If ever Monker became too cruel or aggressive, or struck her, Crystal would remind him of her threat to go to Miss Jackson and denounce him. It was her only weapon. But Lottie was different.

'You know, Lottie,' she began carefully, for she had seen the wanton sideways look that the girl had cast on one of her father's young workers as he crossed the yard, and had noted the imperceptible jerk of his head as he signalled to her to follow him to some assignation. 'It's not wise to dispense your favours among your father's farm-hands.'

'And what's it to you?' demanded Lottie shrilly, alarmed but defiant.

'Why, nothing!' Crystal feigned astonishment. 'But do you think that Marcus Jackson would want soiled goods in a wife?'

'I haven't done anything,' mumbled Lottie. But she kept darting anxious looks at the window, and had begun to fidget as though wishing to be gone.

A cold biting wind seemed to enter the kitchen from every direction, and even the heat from the range did little to disperse the icy draughts. Crystal was weary, for there was much to be done. In the deepest recesses of her mind she admitted her anxiety at lack of news concerning Sir James, but it was not reasonable, she argued to herself, to expect news so quickly.

Suddenly the door opened, and the fair curly head of Marcus Jackson appeared. The merry twinkle in his eyes lifted her spirits immediately. 'Mr Jackson!' She ran to him with a glad cry, extending both hands. 'How very glad I am to see you. Pray, come and sit down and tell me all the news. How is Arabella? Is there any news of Captain Hastings and Sir James?' She was eager and breathless.

'Steady on! Steady on!' he laughed at her gently. 'Arabella—the most adorable girl in the world!—sends you her fondest love and begs the pleasure of a visit from you, for she is bored to death in Bath with only her aunt's society. Now that I am not there to dance attendance on her, she recollects all her old friends.' His twinkling eyes had softened.

'Good heavens! Do you mean that you and Arabella are to be married?' she said, pleased and astonished.

'In love, yes. But married—not yet,' he admitted ruefully. 'My sister has refused her consent. She has commanded me to return and learn all about the management of the estates. And I, all willingness to comply, for I should wish to be my own master when I marry, am here to receive instruction.' There was now a seriousness about Marcus that he had lacked before. Obviously, thought Crystal, Arabella Hastings had exercised a praiseworthy influence on this volatile and pleasure-seeking young man.

'I cannot conceive why your sister should refuse her consent to your marriage with Arabella. Surely it is everything that is suitable?'

Marcus accepted the bread and cheese that Crystal had placed before him and murmured his thanks for the tankard of cider that she put by his elbow. 'She thinks I might do better for myself. In fact, she has met some girl in Gloucester, cousin of an earl, and is going mad for me to meet her.' He spread a slice of bread lavishly with creamy butter. 'The way she carries on about the wretched girl! Apparently her only virtue is that noble connection. It's my believe that my precious sister fancies the earl herself, and proposes this match for me only so that she can gain entrée to his circle. Very devious is my sister! And a proper devil, once she's got the bit between her teeth.' He took a long draught of cider. 'I've got to convince her to let me marry Arabella. If she continues to refuse her consent, I shall apply to the court to overset that stupid will of my father's. Only, of course, I would much rather not subject my future wife to that sort of scandal.' He was unusually serious, and there were grim lines about his mouth.

Crystal was much impressed with the change in him, and wondered that Miss Jackson could not see that his love for Arabella had brought out such good qualities in him. 'You must love Arabella very much,' she said.

'I adore her!' He settled comfortably down in the wooden chair near the range and savoured the warmth of the kitchen.

'Is there any news of Captain Hastings?' she asked shyly. She longed to hear him mention Sir James's name, and could barely contain her curiosity.

'What a selfish devil I am!' He clapped a hand to his head. Pulling a small packet from his pocket, he handed it to her. 'A Christmas present from James, for you. I am so full of myself that I had quite forgotten. Say you will forgive me?' He smiled winningly. 'Now I promise that I shall not budge from this chair until you open it, for I have wagered with Sophie, who was mightily put out that James should have sent you a present, that it is a book.'

The happy interlude was cut short by the entrance of Monker. Crystal hoped that he would not touch the small parcel on the table, and was relieved when he shook the snow from his coat and stamped his feet before greeting the visitor with affability without appearing to notice it.

'This is a most welcome surprise! But you should not be sitting out here in the kitchen with Crystal, Mr Jackson! You shall come into the parlour with me, and sit at the fire. Is it lit?' He shot the question at Crystal, and was satisfied when she nodded. 'Go and fetch a bottle of brandy. Mr Jackson and I must 'ave a little toddy to welcome in Christmas, the season of cheer. You must give me all the news of Captain 'Astings and Sir James. Do they return soon?' He ushered his guest into the parlour before Crystal could hear the reply. A moment later, he put his head round the door. 'Go and

find Lottie,' he hissed, 'and get 'er togged up, present-
able. Tell 'er Mr Marcus is 'ere!'

With some consternation, Crystal realised that she
had not seen Lottie all morning. Certainly she was not in
the house, so putting on a thick cloack, she went outside
and began to search. Her mind was much occupied. Sir
James's sending her a present indicated that he had not
yet returned; that he was alive and well must be certain,
for Marcus would surely have told her of any accident.
She wondered what Mrs Hastings was doing, and how
she would react to the news that Arabella and Marcus
wished to marry. The snow, falling thickly, covered over
any footprints, but she guessed that Lottie might be in
one of the barns. The murmur of voices from the big
hayshed rose at her approach; the farm-hands were
eating pasties there and enjoying a respite from work.
Jake Monker was a hard taskmaster.

'Has anyone seen Lottie?' Crystal asked. There were
some stifled titters, and the youngest boy coloured and
looked away. 'If you know where Lottie is, you had
better tell me, for her father wants her and will be very
angry if she does not come into the house at once.' She
had spoken more sharply than she intended, for she
guessed that Lottie must be with one of the boys, and
was ashamed of the girl's wanton behaviour.

'She's in the dairy!' the youngest boy blurted out.

There was a flurry of movement in the furthest corner
of the dairy as Crystal pushed open the door. 'Lottie!'
she called. 'Come out, your father is looking for you. He
wishes you to . . .'

'Get out! I know you're only here to spy on me!' Lottie
stepped forward to retrieve her bodice, which was on the
floor. Her half-naked state seemed to bother her not at
all. 'You always want to spoil my fun! I don't believe pa
wants me at all.'

'Yes, he does. Mr Jackson has come to pay a visit, and
he wishes you to meet him. When you are presentably
dressed,' she added with emphasis, for Lottie was making no effort to dress or restore order to her tousled hair.
These words, however, exercised a magical effect on the
recalcitrant girl. In less than a minute she was dressed,

and pulling the hood of her cloak over her curls. 'If you tell pa about this,' she jerked her head in the direction of a sheepish, tousle-headed boy who was dragging rather ragged clothes over his clumsy body, 'I'll tell him that I came in here to put a stop to *your* carry-on.'

'You wouldn't dare to tell such a lie!' Crystal said, furious.

'Wouldn't I just! And pa'll believe me a sight quicker than he'll listen to you. So don't try to make trouble, I'm warning you!' She flounced from the dairy and ran across the yard to the house.

Monker was waiting for them in the kitchen. 'What you been up to in the dairy at this time of day?' he demanded.

'Cleaning up after Crystal, Pa. She never leaves the place the way I know you like it,' Lottie responded promptly.

'That's my girl!' Monker patted her fondly on the shoulder. 'Now you go up and put on your prettiest dress, for Mr Jackson is stopping to eat 'is dinner with us. The snow is too bad for 'im to risk taking 'is 'orse out. You fix us a real nice dinner, Crystal, same as what the grand folk 'ave. And we'll eat in the best parlour, like gentry.'

Monker was occupied with getting his son suitably attired, and Crystal slipped into the parlour to find Marcus. He was esconced in a chair by the fire, sipping brandy, and bore every appearance of a man contented with his lot.

'I need to speak to you, Mr Jackson, before you go,' she said hurriedly, casting anxious glances over her shoulder. Jake Monker would be very annoyed if he caught her talking to him. Lottie would assume that Crystal was flirting with him, and probably stage a scene.

'I only agreed to stay in the hope that I might have five minutes' conversation with you, for I am beginning to guess how matters stand here.'

The approach of Lottie put a stop to any further exchange. She was sumptuously clad in bright blue satin,

low cut and profusely embellished with great quantities
of bunched lace. Fortunately she possessed no jewellery, but she compensated for this deficiency by generous use of a violet perfume. Conscious that her appearance had stunned Mr Jackson, she tossed her head, lifted
her plump shoulders coquettishly and pranced into the
room. By exercising the strongest self-control, Marcus
did not look at Crystal, but turned his eyes, brimming
with glee, upon Lottie.

He was bowing deeply over her hand when Monker
pushed Caleb through the doorway. 'There you are!
That's 'ow gentry behaves. Take plenty of notice of Mr
Jackson, for I'm sure if you was to pattern yourself on
'im, you'd be a gent in no time.' Monker poured brandy
into their glasses, and looked about him with satisfaction. 'We always togs out in our Sunday best to eat our
dinner. We're a cut above the others round 'ere,' he told
a bemused Marcus.

'And you, Crystal, do you tog out in your Sunday best
for dinner?' Marcus managed to say, with only the
faintest tremor in his voice.

'She's the skivvy. She don't eat with the family,' Caleb
informed him.

Roaring loudly with laughter to cover his annoyance,
Monker playfully cuffed his son on the back of the head.
'What jokes these young 'uns do come out with! Is the
dinner ready yet, girl?'

'Yes, Mr Monker. If you would like to go into the
dining-room, I shall bring it in.'

Crystal presented them with a large tureen of the stew
she had made that morning, and Marcus's polished
manners allowed him to convey the impression that he
found nothing strange in this noonday repast. Even
when Caleb gave up the attempt to manage a small juicy
dumpling with a knife and fork and resorted to the more
familiar manual method, he evinced nothing but pleasure in his company. Lottie, who always enjoyed her
food, was finding it difficult to simper while doing justice
to the savoury excellence of the stew.

'And when did you say that Sir James returns?'
Monker enquired.

Crystal almost dropped the dish of potatoes, so anxious was she to hear the reply. She was longing to know, even though she had vowed to put him from her mind; he was the only person who could rescue her.

'Fairly soon, I believe. That is what brought me here today. I am commanded by my sister to beg that you will allow Miss Smith to go over to the Hastings' house and make sure that all is in order for their return.'

'Don't they 'ave no servants of their own? Monker demanded, a shade of aggression in his voice.

'Certainly they do. But, assuming that the family would be from home for Christmas, the servants were despatched to their own families. If you are not able to oblige, I can ask my sister to make other arrangements.'

He spoke lightly, but Monker was quick to detect the faint threat behind the words. He did not wish Miss Jackson to think that he was ill-treating Crystal; she might dislike the girl, but he was tolerably certain that she would not condone the treatment she had received.

'Oblige? Of course! I would oblige your good sister in anything. Crystal and Lottie can go together.' He beamed with approval at his daughter. 'There's no one so handy about the house as my Lottie.'

'I would not dream of troubling Lottie,' Marcus said smoothly, his mouth quirking humorously at her. 'Indeed I should not like to see so fine a young lady demeaned by heavy work.'

In spite of herself, Crystal felt some compassion for Lottie. She was the victim of her father's foolish ambition and Marcus's lively sense of humour.

'A fine young lady she is, to be sure. And she'll make an even finer wife, one of these days.' Monker winked at Marcus.

Marcus looked much struck by this thought, and Crystal began to feel uneasily that he was hatching some mischievous plot. Much as she liked him, she could not forget that he was essentially weak, and a man who might use people if it suited him. Later, she was sure that this was so, for when he was taking his leave of them, he begged most charmingly to be allowed to pay them another visit very soon. This request, to which Monker was delighted to accede, was accompanied by a wickedly attractive smile bestowed on a blushing Lottie.

'Perhaps Caleb could walk over with my horse when the snow stops. I must make the attempt to go home now, or my sister will be anxious about me.'

When Marcus had departed on foot, Jake Monker rubbed his hands with glee, believing that his stratagem had been successful. 'You'll be Mrs Marcus Jackson by next year, you mark my words! Come 1831, you'll be a lady. That'll make them all sit up! I'll take 'is 'orse over to 'Enbury myself, for I'm wishful of a few words with Miss Jackson.' He looked at Crystal moodily. 'What was that parcel what was on the table?'

'Parcel?' Her heart jumped into her throat. She had hidden it under her mattress, for she was certain that Monker would take it from her. There had not been time to open it. 'I cannot think what you mean . . . unless you mean the little package that belonged to Mr Jackson. I believe he said he had purchased a book.' She was relieved to see that Monker accepted her words without further comment.

Later, in her small room, she opened the parcel and found it to be a volume bound in red leather and lettered in gold, *Northanger Abbey*, by Jane Austen. With fingers that trembled slightly, she opened it and saw that the first page was inscribed in a large bold hand: 'To Miss Crystal Smith, on the occasion of Christmas, 1830, from her friend James Allenwood.' Clasping the book, she lifted it to her cheek. He had remembered her! He had sent her a book. How she would treasure this gift!

CHAPTER TEN

IT HAD stopped snowing and the land was covered in a glistening mantle, every sound muted, the air expectant and hushed. While Crystal and Marcus walked to North-over Lodge, the home of Captain and Mrs Hastings, he eulogised all the way about Arabella: she was a divine creature; he had never been in love before; marriage would exactly suit him, for it was time he settled down. Did Crystal not agree that Arabella was the prettiest name she had ever heard? Had not Arabella the most pleasing disposition? Dutiful and amused, Crystal said all that was proper. To be walking out of doors with so cheerful a companion suited her happy mood. She told Marcus a little of her life with the Monkers, and he was appalled.

'I believe I can help you, Crystal, for I very much want to. I have a plan. It came to me earlier, during that preposterous luncheon.' He laughed at the recollection of the repast.

'It is not kind of you to encourage Lottie, Mr Jackson, because she truly believes that your intentions are serious. I am afraid that her father has encouraged her to believe that you might marry her.'

'That is exactly what I want her to think! It will give me the excuse to visit you. It galled me to see you waiting on them. Listen! My sister will not consent to my marriage with Arabella, but if she believed that I were interested in another, one who was not my equal, she would be only too pleased to agree to my marriage to my dearest girl. Then, as soon as we are married, I should employ you as my wife's companion!' His eyes sparkled. 'Is that not a splendid idea?'

'But would your sister truly believe that there was the slightest danger of your marrying Lottie?'

'Lottie? Good Lord, no! If my sister does not know that Lottie Monker is known as a wanton baggage, then

she must be the only person who ignorant of that fact,'
he said with contempt. 'I mean that you and *I* should
pretend to be in love. We could ride about the countryside together, be seen to hold hands, to kiss, even.
Sophia would get to hear about it, and would be
alarmed.' He began to laugh. 'I remember that after that
little game of ours on the Downs—you recall the day we
had the race?—she was furious with me, and feared that
I might fall in love with you. Then she told me that
nothing would induce her to consent to a marrriage with
you.'

Crystal felt as though Marcus had slapped her. The
bright colour caused by a walk in the cold fresh air had
deepened to a blush of mortification. Could Marcus be
so blinded by love that he did not know how callous his
words were? Did he believe that she had no feelings. She
could not doubt that his opinion of her was one shared by
the rest of the world, but was this how Sir James viewed
her? The cold wind of reason chased away her profound
depression. Of course that was how Sir James viewed
her—he had told her so, often enough. She believed,
despite the social difference between them, that he had
cared about her, and that thought had made her happy,
but he had placed her at the mercy of Jake Monker. It
would be easy to pretend to be in love with Mr Jackson,
so handsome and charming. If Jake Monker wished to
think he was courting Lottie, so much the better. If Sir
James thought that she loved Marcus, and was annoyed,
better still, because she would be suitably revenged. The
prospect of congenial employment as companion to
Arabella was sufficiently enticing to make her agree to
the wildest plan.

'I think that that is a good idea, Mr Jackson. I am sure
that your sister would be so upset by the thought of your
marriage to me that she would be pleased to agree to
your marriage with almost anyone in the world,' she said
carefully, attempting to keep the irony from her voice.

'Splendid! You are the best girl in the world, next to
Arabella!' Laughing, he swung her round and kissed her
on the cheek.

They spent the remainder of the walk hatching absurd

plots, staging assignations and laughing a good deal. It was so long since Crystal had laughed or enjoyed any light-hearted conversation that she felt her spirits restored.

'What does Miss Jackson desire me to do?' she asked Marcus when they entered Northover Lodge. The house seemed in excellent order.

'Strictly speaking, nothing,' he admitted ruefully. 'She does not exactly know that you are here. It is all part of my little plan.' It was very difficult to resist Marcus when he chose to exert charm. 'She asked me to see one or two of the servants who might be staying in the neighbourhood, and ask them to prepare the house in case the Hastings family returned for Christmas.'

'Do you mean that they might not return?' Her spirits plummeted unaccountably.

'We hope they will return as soon as possible,' he responded airily. 'But I do not know,' he confessed, unable to withstand her direct look. 'I had to think of some way to get you away from the Monkers and provide some rational excuse for bringing you here,' he said coaxingly.

'Do you mean that I do not have permission to be here?' she said in dismay. To be plotting with Marcus in order to win his sister's approval to his marriage to Arabella seemed harmless enough, but to be in the home of Mrs Hastings, without the knowledge and approval of one who was guardian of the house in her absence, seemed quite wrong. She told Marcus so.

'That is nonsensical!' He dismissed her scruples. 'Mrs Hastings would be delighted to think that you lit a few fires and aired her bedding and attended to those domestic matters at which women excel. It would be such a pity to drag the servants from the comfort of their families to attend upon an empty house. It is an ideal excuse for you to be absent from Monker's house. Do you say that you will agree, Crystal? It will only be for a few days, until my sister hears about our little expeditions.'

So strong was her desire to escape from the farmhouse that Crystal reluctantly agreed to the proposal that she should be collected each day and escorted, by Marcus, to spend an hour in Northover Lodge. After Christmas, but one week away, the servants would return. 'Will not Jake Monker discover the deception, for he visits your sister this afternoon?' she asked anxiously.

'Jake Monker? My dear girl, he does not count for anything! If our plan works, Arabella and I will be married in a few weeks and you can come to us directly, I promise.'

The prospect of escape was too strong for Crystal to resist further. Even if Sir James did return to England in the very near future, she could not be sure that he would take her away from Jake Monker's house, and the thought of remaining there indefinitely was unendurable.

The return walk to Monker's farm was not accompanied by the blissful and exhilarating feeling of escape that had marked her walk to Northover Lodge. With lagging footsteps and heavy heart she saw the place and its huddle of attendant buildings before her. 'How much I hate it!' she exclaimed, unable to restrain herself. Self-pity was not an emotion she had experienced before, but now it washed over her and threatened to break down the brave front she had maintained with such calm and dignity.

'It will not be for much much longer, I assure you!' Marcus gathered her into a fraternal embrace, and she was comforted.

Much heartened by the knowledge that she was soon to escape from this dreary house and her unending drudgery, Crystal was able to withstand Lottie's foolish boastings, Caleb's taunts and their father's cruel insults. She discovered that Monker had not been able to see Miss Jackson when he had taken the horse back, since she had been occupied, and had bidden a servant to deal with him. His anger upon receiving this treatment from one whom he considered, in his private daydreams, to be his equal, was dreadful, and it was a consolation for her to be able to escape each day to Northover Lodge with Marcus.

'I wrote to Arabella to explain about our little plan,'

he told her, his eyes twinkling with outrageous merriment. 'And she writes back that it the best joke she has ever heard. She does not think we could be married very quickly, as there is some news of a delay in the return of her parents.' He had spoken carelessly, but she detected some underlying anxiety.

'Delay? I had understood that Sir James had successfully negotiated the ransom for Captain Hastings and that they were on their way back.' Crystal hoped he would assume that her fears were for Captain Hastings.

'It is rather more complicated, I am afraid. It seems that part of the ransom—besides money, of course—is that the Governor of Trinidad must agree to the release of certain villains that he holds prisoner. The Governor will not agree.'

'Do you mean that Captain Hastings is still held hostage?'

'I believe that to be the case. But James is very competent; he is not the man to be afraid of such scum,' he said lightly, and she supposed that the matter could not be serious. 'That is why they particularly requested James to deal, in person, with the matter. I am confident that he can achieve any purpose. You will see them all before long.'

They were sitting before a large fire in the cosy well-furnished room that overlooked the drive. The rain that had melted the snow beat against the window, and the tea they sipped was hot and welcome.

'I have a little surprise for you, Crystal. Tomorrow is Christmas Eve, and it will be our last day here, for we can have no further excuse for coming. Sophia has not mentioned your being in my company, and I must suppose, incredible as it seems, that she has not heard of it, although I have taken every care to ensure that we have been seen together. So I propose taking you to the theatre tonight!' His eyes gleamed triumphantly.

'The theatre?' she exclaimed. 'I have never been to a theatre! I do not think I could possibly go. Jake Monker permits me to come here, for he believes that I do so at Miss Jackson's request, but he would never agree to my visiting the theatre!'

'Now do not say No until I have shown you something. Then, I am convinced that you will permit me to escort you.' He left the room.

The theatre! Crystal had heard Miss Allenwood talk of the Theatre Royal in King Street. She imagined it to be a wonderful place, for it seemed that only the grandest clothes were suitable for such an occasion! When Miss Allenwood had talked of the plays she had seen and the affecting performances given by the young brother and sister, Charles Kemble and Sarah Siddons, she had longed to go. She had revealed only part of her circumstances to Marcus; certainly not of Jake Monker's lustful approaches that made her life so miserable. Why should I not go? she asked herself defiantly. Am I so poor-spirited that I cannot venture six miles to the city? I, who have walked miles over the high plateau?

'Present from Mr Marcus Jackson to Miss Crystal Smith!' Marcus said with military correctness, and saluted, which made Crystal laugh, as he deposited a large brown paper parcel before her.

She removed the wrapping-paper and shook out a rich velvet dress and matching cloak, both in a shade of sapphire blue. They were beautiful, and her work-roughened hands lingered over the soft texture of the luxurious material. Admitting to herself that she longed for an opportunity to wear such lovely clothes, she cast caution to the winds, a mood of recklessness rising in her. 'I'll go with you!' Her eyes sparkled, and a laugh gurgled in her throat. 'But will I be fine enough?'

'Even attired as you are now, you will take the shine out them all.' His gallant response brought a fresh sparkle to Crystal's eyes and a rosy flush to her cheeks. If Marcus wished his sister to hear of the exploit, that meant that Sir James would eventually hear of it also. Excellent! He should discover that she could fend for herself, and that the feelings she had had for him were quite dead. The little book hidden beneath her mattress was temporarily forgotten.

The spirit of adventure urged him to plan the escapade with enthusiasm. 'Creep out of the house at about eight of the clock, when it will be quite dark and you should

not be observed. I shall have a carriage waiting at
the end of the lane. We shall be in Bristol before
nine.'

It seemed as though a thousand candles lit the Theatre
Royal and shed radiance and warmth upon the gaily-clad
crowd who thronged about its elegant pillared foyer.
Many curious looks were cast upon the handsome young
couple, and Crystal was introduced to many of Marcus's
friends, who looked at her with frank admiration. The
sapphire dress clung to the curves of her body exquisitely, moulding them to perfection. It was not as fashionable as those of the other women, but it became her
exceedingly well. The taffeta-lined cloak draped about
her shoulders showed the flawless beauty of her skin to
perfection. She had found a pair of black lace mittens, a
gift from Miss Allenwood, to conceal her roughened
hands. Her only jewellery was the gold cross and chain
that had been Sir James's gift.

'You are wonderful, Crystal!' Marcus whispered excitedly as he helped her to her plush-covered chair in the
box that overlooked the stage. 'Everyone wonders who
you are! How I wish that Arabella were here to share the
jest!'

Later she could scarcely recall what she had seen, for
she drank in the heady perfumed atmosphere of the
theatre and gave herself up to the excitement of watching gorgeously dressed actors and actresses move about
the brightly-lit stage until the final curtain. Much
affected by the play's happy ending, Crystal was obliged
to wipe away a tear, which caused Marcus to laugh with
indulgent and unexpected tenderness.

'Here you are, watering-pot!' He wiped her tears with
a fine cambric kerchief, which he bade her keep for
further use.

After her absorption in the play, she hated the
thought of returning to reality, for there would be no
happy ending for her, no hero to take her in his arms and
protect her with the power of his love. Unwillingly she
allowed herself to be led from that magic place and out
into the frosty night air.

'We are going to dine!' Marcus was laughing, intoxicated by the success of the evening. He was too selfish to give much thought to the plight of another human being, but he had been touched by Crystal's whole-hearted enjoyment. Any punishment Monker might have in store for her after this night's escapade, he pushed to the furthest recess of his shallow mind. The man had always behaved with civil amiability in his presence, and he could not imagine him otherwise. Dinner had not formed part of his plans for this night—he had merely wished to appear in as public a place as possible, certain that Crystal's looks would attract attention. Sophia would hear very soon about the episode! Now he wished to bring some happiness into Crystal's bleak life, for he was aware of her forlorn looks and admired her uncomplaining fortitude.

Champagne! Another bottle was brought. The waiter, who from his elegant, white-gloved appearance Crystal had supposed to be a fellow-guest, moved deftly round the table. Marcus talked nonsense, drank too much champagne, ordered a great many dishes, and entertained Crystal admirably. At this hotel in Clifton, Marcus was a well-known and liked patron, for the staff greeted him by name and made sure that he and Crystal had everything they could possibly desire.

'I have not laughed so much for an age! Are we not attracting too much attention?' Crystal said apprehensively.

'Of course we are! That was my object; that, and to entertain you.'

'I feel we must have succeeded!' she giggled at him.

A pale dawn was struggling through a grey sky when they arrived back at Brentry, and Crystal was alarmed at the hour. She leaped down from the carriage, and Marcus followed her. Catching her in his arms, he kissed her lightly on the mouth. 'I cannot wait to hear my sister's reaction to this night's work. For once in my life, I look forward to one of her scolds!' Imps of mischief danced in his eyes. 'Shall I escort you to your door and thank old Monker for the pleasure of your company?'

The very thought made Crystal run all the way down

the lane to the house. Quietly opening the door, she crossed the kitchen and entered her room, where she stripped off her finery, pulled on her rough cotton work-dress and hastily knotted the large white apron about her waist. With a kerchief over her hair, she went into the kitchen and began to rake out the hot embers from the range, and took out the ashes, before throwing some wood into it. Quickly filling a large pot with water, she set it to boil. How very different were all these activities from those of the past few hours! There had been musicians in the restaurant, and she tried to hum the tunes they had been playing. It had all been so gay, so lively! She added salt and oats to the pot of water, and began to stir it. All the Monkers liked porridge on these cold mornings. She was in the pantry, collecting bread, butter and cheese, when she heard a stealthy sound from the kitchen, and turning quickly, saw that Lottie was trying to cross the kitchen to the stairs.

'Why, Lottie, wherever have you been?' she cried out in surprise.

'Don't act so high and mighty with me, Miss Prim and Proper! I saw you out there with Mr Jackson. Him that is promised to me!' Her face was contorted with rage and animosity. 'And I saw how you were dressed. Did he buy you those clothes? What did you have to do to earn them? Answer me that!'

'I refuse to answer any of your questions, Lottie.' Crystal responded with as much composure as she could. 'It is none of your business.'

'It will be, when pa knows about it! You sly devil!' snapped the girl. Her sudden movement caused her cloak to swing open, revealing her clothes in considerable disorder. Her hair, Crystal now saw, was dishevelled.

'Where have you been, Lottie?' Crystal said, with as much authority as she could muster.

'On the same errand as you, slut! Only I did it in the hayshed, and you did it in some fancy carriage.' Lottie was beside herself with rage and mortification that she had been caught out.

Both girls froze as Jake Monker descended the stairs,

his heavy jowls bearded and his small eyes puffy. He was scratching his stomach and yawning, but his actions were stilled abruptly at the unexpected sight of his daughter, cloaked, in the kitchen so early in the morning. His eyes strayed to the clock at the foot of the stairs; it was not quite seven. 'What's all this?' he growled, his thick brows snapping together and an alert look about his eyes. 'Where you been, girl?'

'Nowhere, Pa,' whined the frightened Lottie, pulling her cloak more firmly about her disordered dress. 'I got to keep an eye on her.' She jerked her head in Crystal's direction. 'She's a sly one! She has that Marcus Jackson hanging around when we're all in bed. So just now I thought I heard a noise, and got up and came down, but she was here getting the breakfast ready.'

'Thought I 'eard the door opening,' he muttered.

'I put the ashes out,' said Crystal quickly. 'Go back to bed, Lottie. There is no need for you to get up yet.'

Lottie shot her a grateful look and sped up the stairs. While Crystal stirred the porridge and cut thick slices of bread and butter, Jake Monker went into her small room and found the clothes that Marcus had given her. He brought them out into the kitchen and flung them across the table.

'That what you wore last night?' he demanded softly, his nostrils flaring and his lips drawn back in a snarl.

'Yes,' she whispered, her heart thudding uncomfortably, for there was menace about that stocky body and softly hissing voice.

''E buy you that—Mr Marcus?' he asked in that soft voice, his eyes measuring her.

'Yes,' she murmured, beginning to feel sick, her joy in last night quickly disappearing.

'So! I got to 'ouse other men's leavings! 'E comes in 'ere, to court my Lottie. Eats my food, drinks my brandy. I got to bow and scrape to 'im. I got to 'ouse the slut 'e buys clothes for and takes out at night under cover of darkness. But I can't 'ave none of the fun myself! 'Ow would you like it if I was to go right over to Miss Jackson and tell 'er just what's going on?'

I should be delighted, thought Crystal, and Marcus

Jackson would probably congratulate you!

Taking the gown and cloak, he stuffed them into the range and watched with vicious satisfaction as they burned. 'I'll tell you this, Crystal: you'll regret rejecting good old Jake Monker! I'll 'ave you, my girl, one of these fine days. I won't tell you when—it'll add to my fun—but 'ave you I will! Then I'll throw you out into the gutter where you belong. I knows what's on your mind: you think you'll run to Sir James Allenwood and whine out your tale of woe. But you won't, my girl. 'Ave you thought that 'e might never return? And even if 'e does, 'ow do you think 'e'll take it when 'e 'ears about you and Mr Jackson?'

If Crystal's life had been miserable before, it now became unendurable. Lottie blamed her without ceasing for stealing Marcus Jackson; Monker watched her all the time, and the air of malevolence about him increased. His sinister threats, coupled with the thought that Sir James might never return, assumed new and more terrifying proportions as he invaded her dreams, turning them to nightmares from which she awoke in trembling perspiration. Marcus had returned to Bath, for Arabella's aunt had summoned him. The absence of news had alarmed the girl, and she needed him to calm her fears.

Crystal was cleaning Jake Monker's room one day in early spring, humming to herself as she put fresh sheets on his bed. It was her first real respite, for there was a difficult lambing at which everyone was in attendance, since several valuable ewes had miscarried. She had the house and yards entirely to herself, and there was a spring in her step as she went about her duties. The door clicked shut behind her, and Monker stood within the room, a lustful smile curving his heavy mouth. He began to unbuckle his belt and tug off the smock he wore over his corduroy trousers. He moved quietly, for he had already removed his boots.

'Got you now, my pretty, good and proper! I told you Jake Monker always gets what 'e wants. Well, now 'e gets you!'

Crystal's mouth was dry, and her stomach churned. She was rooted to the spot and could not escape, for he had locked the door, and the menace and purpose about the stocky powerful frame were unmistakable. He pulled her to him and crushed her in a cruel embrace, but she twisted away from his grasp. When she could feel him pulling at her underclothes, she cried out in terror, but her efforts at escape seemed to excite him, and he laughed gutturally and pulled her to him again.

Then Lottie came clattering up the uncarpeted stairs, calling raucously, 'Pa, Pa, you got to come quickly! Our Caleb . . .' She rattled the locked door, and broke off in evident puzzlement. 'Pa?' she called again, less stridently and with a hint of anxiety in her voice. 'You in there?'

Monker grunted in reply, and tugged at his breeches and clumsily buckled his belt. Lurching to the door, he unlocked it, and Crystal sagged against the bed and almost cried with relief.

Lottie's eyes narrowed speculatively as she measured the occupants of the room. 'You got to come down to the fields right now! Caleb's not too happy about some of the ewes. Says he's not sure what to do, and will you come and tell him.' She cast Crystal a look of pure malice before following her father out.

Crystal spent the time they were out in planning her escape, for to remain was impossible. She would go to Miss Jackson and tell her of Monker's attempted rape, showing her the bruises if necessary. Not another night would she spend in that farmhouse!

She was devasted to receive news at Henbury House that Miss Jackson was from home and not expected to return for at least two days. Returning to the farm across meadows and brooks, she breathed the fresh clean air of spring, and longed to keep going and never to return. But where could she go?

'Reckon you'll have to watch out for yourself, Caleb,' Lottie said at the supper-table. 'Miss Hoity-Toity here is having it with pa. If they get a child between them, who's to say he won't put your nose out of joint?' She laughed gleefully when she saw how this pronouncement affected her dull-witted brother.

When he had recovered from his stupefaction, his face reddened alarmingly, and he stared at Crystal as though trying to visualise how such a despised creature could possibly disinherit him. 'I'll kill 'er first!'

Lottie looked apprehensive, when her father came into the kitchen with blood and mud on his hands and clothes from the lambing.

When he sat down, Crystal cried out involuntarily, 'Are you not going to wash yourself?'

'I'm clean enough for the likes of you!' he barked, hammering on the table for his supper.

Lottie sat back in her chair, a satisfied smile playing about her mouth. 'It's a pity you aren't married to Crystal, Pa.' She looked guilelessly at her father's scowling face. 'I did hear that a man from Felton way sold his wife at the auction, the cattle-auction in Temple Meads —you know, that new one up in Bristol—for five pounds and ten shillings.' She darted a look of spite at Crystal, and then smiled with satisfaction as she observed the effect of her words on him.

Monker attacked his food with energy, and from time to time looked at Crystal with interest as though he were turning over some idea in his mind. He drew his hand across his mouth and, belching, stood up and went to the stone sink. Pumping water, he washed his face and hands, and called over his shoulder, 'Get me a clean shirt and waistcoat. I'm going out.'

Crystal lay wakeful in the dark. Her clothes were prepared in a bundle at the foot of the bed. She planned to go back to Henbury House and demand to be allowed to wait until Miss Jackson returned. If she was denied, she would go to the Reverend Mr Alcott and insist that he give her sanctuary until Sir James returned to settle her future. Terrible confusion raged within her, and she could not even admit her worst fears. Miss Jackson would know certainly that she had spent time with Marcus; that such time was spent in order to make her believe that a love affair was taking place would hardly appeal to his sister's kinder instincts. How was she to explain that it had seemed a good idea at the time? Marcus had promised that, if he was married to Arabella, he would give Crystal some employment. She could not regret those magical hours spent in Northover Lodge—what an oasis of peace and calm they had been! Nagging away at the back of her mind was the fear that Sir James might never return, for the pirates with whom he had been dealing had been exceptionally obstinate in their insistence that the full terms of the ransom be met. The island Governor was equally determined that no prisoners should be released. Sir James had to negotiate alone; there had been no news for almost two months. It had not been kind of Marcus to allow Lottie to believe that he courted her, but Crystal was well aware that her father had given her the idea that she might marry a Marcus Jackson or a Sir James Allenwood. Her vanity and wantonness had been her own downfall. During the day she managed to keep the picture of a tanned face and thick black hair far from her mind, but at night, when her defences were inadequate to protect her, she thought with longing of the time when she had believed that he had returned the feelings she had had for him. The yearning she experienced, however, was always quelled when she thought of the ignominious position in which he had placed her. That he should hear of her supposed love affair with Marcus Jackson was her dearest wish.

A heavy lurching footstep in the kitchen alerted her that Monker had returned and that he had been drinking cider, for she could hear him stumbling about, knocking against tables and chairs. Sweat broke out on her body, and her skin crawled with fear. On the very rare occasions when he went out he did not return until morning, and she had thought herself safe. Violently her door was flung open, and she feared that he might make another assault on her body. She was determined to defend herself, reasonably sure that he would do nothing with Caleb and Lottie in the house.

'Get up!' he snarled, aggressive with drink, 'and put on that dress you came 'ere wearing. That's the one you're leaving in!'

Leaving? Never had Jake Monker given a more welcome order! She pulled on the muslin dress, but he would not allow her to put anything on her feet.

'That's good enough for you, slut!' His voice was thick and his gait unsteady; he was very drunk, and reeked of the rough cider that was known to make men insane.

Wearing only the thin muslin dress, she was pushed through the door of the farmhouse. 'I cannot go to Miss Jackson's wearing only this!' she protested.

'Miss Jackson's?' he jeered. 'I'm not taking you to Miss Jackson's. I'm taking you to Bristol, my bride that never was. I want to see 'ow much you're worth. I'm going to sell you this morning, my pretty, at the Temple Meads auction. You're going into the bride sale!'

'Get along, slut!' Monker pushed her in the back. 'To think that I was prepared to marry you! That takes you by surprise, don't it?' he growled angrily.

Crystal barely heard him, since she was leaving that house where she had endured unhappiness and pain and something more, for Monker inspired a terror in her that was unlike anything she had ever known. She walked barefoot along the road to Bristol with long even strides. If he had hoped to add to her discomfiture, he was mistaken, for she had frequently walked much further distances under greater extremes of weather when she had lived with the tribe. How very far in the past it all seemed now! She discovered to her surprise that her regret in leaving them had been the inevitable feeling of a girl leaving childhood behind. The inexorable movement of time had pushed her into unknown waters. How naive and inexperienced she had been! There was a feeling of freedom and pleasure about walking along a country road in early spring, for the air was mild and sweet, and the song of birds were just beginning as a rose dawn streaked the sky. Beneath her resolve never to think again of the love she had felt for Sir James was the fear that he might never return. If he died at the hands of pirates, she would have no reasc to live, but hate him, she did, for having placed her in the hands of the vile Monker!

Monker rode a small cob behind her, and took vicious

satisfaction in prodding her along if her pace faltered. It did so only rarely, and her proud free carriage and long stride irritated him, for she should be showing fear, not this exultation. Well, he thought, she won't be so happy when she gets to the market and finds herself the object of a public auction! That would soon humble the pride that had driven him almost to the edge of madness.

They crossed the springy turf of Durdham Down and passed by the very spot where Sir James had terminated the wager she had had with Marcus Jackson and she had announced that she might have seduced him. How could I have acted so stupidly? she wondered. Honesty forced her to admit that even if Sir James had held the very highest opinion of her, the outcome would not have been different. The betrothal between himself and Miss Jackson would still exist, and from a worldly point of view, it was desirable. The perfect match of the two personalities was also undoubted. So why could not she accept these facts? He had never given her any real reason to suppose that he felt any more than friendship for her. With her new maturity, and knowledge of life in England, she had to admit that even if Sir James did return her feelings, it would make little material difference to her situation. Men like Sir James did not marry girls like Crystal Smith, no matter what their inclinations were; Marcus had unwittingly made that painfully clear. What were Miss Jackson's feelings upon learning that her brother had been seen with Crystal Smith? Outrage? Crystal chuckled when she thought of the plan they had devised and carried out. How weak Marcus was! Sir James would never have submitted to the tyranny of that will or the dictates of his sister. But Sir James's nature and conduct would never have necessitated the drawing up of a will like that. If her exploits came to his ear, so much the better. He would see that she no longer thought of him with love or dependence. If he chose to regard her in such a poor light, well, she had given him ample justification! The visit to the theatre could never be regretted; she had enjoyed it immensely and it had given her a taste for a life she could learn to love. Had Sir James been her partner that night, it would have completed her happiness. Pushing away the treacherous thoughts, she reminded herself that he was the author of her present unhappiness.

'I'll sell you to the highest bidder!' Monker taunted her, and she could hear the pleasure in his voice. 'Men usually looks about for a kind man to sell a wife to, but, you'll see, I shan't care! I never took no money from Miss Jackson for your keep, so it'll be my little bit of payment.'

They had left the Downs, and as they approached the bottom of the hill, houses became more evident and the distant sounds of a great city clarified into the noise of hundreds of carts and wagons moving over cobbled streets; Crystal could hear the cries of street-vendors. Everywhere was thronged with people anxious for early morning trade or to be at their various occupations.

They crossed a bridge over the river, and inched their way along the congested waterfront. When Monker halted briefly to buy a hot pie from a vendor, it made Crystal realise how very hungry she was, and she became aware that the air smelt of new bread, tasty pies and fruit. Many stalls offered a variety of delicious wares, but Monker urged her to make haste.

'The wife sales 'ave to be 'eld before the cattle are sold, and I don't want to 'ave come all this way to miss me chance of getting rid of you!' His thickened voice told her that he was still feeling the effects of the scrumpy he had drunk. He was unshaven, and there was a wild crazed look in his bloodshot eyes.

Coal was being unloaded from a flat barge on the river on to a dray on the quayside, which blocked their way, and Monker cursed at Crystal. 'Get up there and move that dray! Go on, hussy. Get to the 'orse, and pull 'im to one side so as I can get by.' He accompanied this order with a clout to the side of her head, and she sped to obey, not out of fear, but because she longed for the moment when she would be free of him.

Her feet and the hem of her dress were blackened by the coal over which she had been obliged to climb, and the dust-begrimed horse at first resisted her efforts to coax it to move, even slightly. When the great dray did move, it dragged Crystal with it, so that the flimsy material of her dress tore when it was caught on the harness. In unhappy confusion, she caught up the tattered front of her dress and held it across her bosom, shame flooding over her as she heard the jeers of the onlookers.

The great crowd that filled the market at Temple Meads were dressed, unlike the Bristolians, in home-spuns, smocks and gaiters, and on their heads were broad-brimmed soft hats. They inspected the penned cattle with unsmiling faces. Crystal paused fractionally at the gateway, for she was the only female in the place. She could see a well-dressed man standing beside a large empty circular pen, and guessed that this must be the auctioneer and the auction-ring. He stopped speaking and hurried forward to greet them, a look of displeasure on his open face.

Reginald Tanner took almost as much pride in the new cattle market as did his employers; he ensured that only good cattle were auctioned and that all monies were paid promptly and in full, but wife auctions were a feature of the market that he detested, even though the desperately hard times endured by small farmers forced them to put their children into hiring-fairs and to sell their wives to prevent their having to join the ranks of the prostitutes who plied their lucrative trade on the busy dockside.

He took in the disparate couple in one shrewd glance, and disliked what he saw. They did not bear the marks of poverty that breathed over the countryside like dank fouled air. The fleshy thick-set man and the young girl who walked before him appeared to be in good health, but he looked with belligerence and malice at her. Something was very wrong! The girl was lovely, proud and erect, despite her dirty and dishevelled appearance; her dark hair blew in the breeze like a defiant banner, and those great green eyes flecked with tawny amber looked at him impassively. With a start of surprise, he saw that there was no fear or apprehension in them. What was wrong with her? He became uneasy, sensing trouble from this ill-assorted couple.

Over in the far corner a man was addressing a very interested group of men who listened avidly to his talk of reform. Mr Tanner had sympathy with them, for Parliament needed reform, and badly, if the poor of the countryside were not to starve, but he did not want agitators here! Too serious a mood did not make for a good auction; a mood of rebellion engendered by an inflammatory speech would bring prices down. A wife auction, regarded as a harmless bit of fun, might lighten the atmosphere and restore good humour to the large crowd.

'This is my dear wife, Crystal Smith.' Monker bore all the appearance of a stalwart man driven to despair. 'We've fallen on 'ard times, and it breaks my 'eart to bring 'er 'ere. But I got to find a good 'ome for my wife before I signs up and goes to sea.'

It was a familiar story, and the auctioneer nodded in sympathy and transferred his attention to the girl. 'Do you understand what is happening to you, my dear? Do you realise that any one of these men could buy you?' Snap her up, he thought, for she had a superb figure ill concealed by that flimsy dress, and great beauty. 'And that you will go home with him after the auction?'

For answer, she stepped into the auction ring and stood there without moving or smiling; the wind lifted her hair and skirts. She held the flimsy tatters of her dress across her bosom, and looked into the distance as though she saw neither the men or the cattle.

The auctioneer was surprised by her actions, for he was a good judge of character and saw almost immediately that this man and girl sprang from very different orders of society. This was no farmer's wife! On that he would have staked his considerable reputation. But the crowd were interested, and beginning to drift towards the auction-ring with grins of appreciative amusement. Even the audience of the political agitator were losing interest in him, sensing more sport in the auction. A mood of general good humour permeated the air about the ring, and as the men leaned forward over the rough wooden rail to look their fill at the lovely girl, Tanner felt a fleeting pity, for the men were rough, and those with money either elderly, or extremely hard and shrewd.

His pity was wasted, for none of these rough men held any of the terror that Monker had inspired in Crystal. She had learned from the Indians to mask her feelings and to distance her body from whatever ailed it. In her mind's eye she saw not the market, but instead a far horizon. She was sailing beneath the stars on a great wooden ship, the air was warm and balmy, the sea tranquil and beside her on deck was Sir James Allenwood. He had renounced his betrothed and had asked her, Crystal, to marry him, to sail with him in starlight to Trinidad, where they would begin a new life together, secure in their love for each other. The stern look had left his face and his deep voice whispered endearments against her cheek and neck; all differences and misunderstanding between them were carried away on the salty breeze. Only dimly was she aware that she was the object of the intense and leering scrutiny of many eyes; she heard only faintly the auctioneer describe her many virtues.

'What's she like between the sheets?' called out a wit.

'As good as she looks! And loves it!' Monker called back.

The auctioneer flicked him a look of dislike, as there was a deal more of this than he liked, but the serious men were now guffawing their approval of the two men who were bidding against each other with earnest intent. At one moment the crowd supported the old man who clutched his walking-stick with gnarled hands, then they swung to the side of the big raw-boned man whose unwavering gaze never left Crystal's impassive face. Bidding was brisk and business-like, and as her price rose above that of a prime heifer, the crowd fell silent. She must now command their respect as well as their admiration. The price kept rising, and the auctioneer felt that such entertainment had inspired a mood of reckless spending that could only be good for business later on.

'Fifty pounds!' called the old man. His cracked voice bespoke an intense emotion and excitement.

'That's right, Grandad, you turn the clock back. Do you the world of good!' shouted the wit.

'Fifty-five,' the big man said quietly, and a hush fell.

Crystal turned her head and looked fully at him, and he returned her stare. She knew at once that he was alien here, for although he was dressed like the others, there was an entirely different quality about him. Perhaps because she had been day-dreaming about the sea, she imagined for a brief instant that this man would be more at home on deck than on a farm. She did not care, for freedom from Monker was worth any price she would be required to play. Lottie had once told her, with ghoulish excitement, that girls were often lured on board ship and used for sport by the crew. When they were abandoned, often on foreign soil, they were unfit for any sort of life other than the more degrading forms of prostitution. She shuddered. The protective cloak of her daydream fell away, and she was once more exposed to the harsh light of her present reality.

'Sixty guineas!' shrieked the old man, his rheumy eyes alive with anger at the thought of being cheated of his prize.

The auctioneer looked across at the raw-boned man. This was one day's business he would not recount to his wife and family; his disgust at the proceedings made him want to shout his feelings to them all.

'One hundred guineas,' the big man said with an air of finality.

The crowd gasped, and looked expectantly at the old man, who opened and closed his mouth in silent and futile protest, but eventually he shook his head and turned away to signify that he would bid no more.

The big man stepped into the ring and handed the money to the auctioneer, carefully counting it out from a leather purse. Meticulously the auctioneer counted the money again and handed it to Monker, after taking his own commission. He would have spoken to the girl, for Monker had looked at her with venomous dislike, but the big man was leading her from the ring and she followed without a backward glance.

Crystal felt alive, and longed to question the man who

had bought her, but he was silent and expressionless. She was free! No more Monker! That happy realisation made her confident that she could deal with whatever fate held for her. They hurried through mean dark alleys and into a broader street that seemed familiar; she could not be certain at first, but when they passed the Theatre Royal she knew it was King Street. What happy memories she had of that evening! Dear Marcus! He had been the only bright star in that dreary time she had spent at Monker's.

They halted before a wooden door set in a high stone wall, which the man opened, and bade her enter. Something like trepidation assailed her, for they were in the long back garden of a large and imposing house. She knew instinctively that she had nothing to fear from this man; once the sale had been completed, he had appeared to lose all interest in her. Looking up at the great house with its gleaming windows and trim back lawns, she felt a stirring of apprehension, for she fancied that enmity and hostility were within those walls, and that those forces were about to be directed towards her.

They went up the path, and Crystal noted that small flowers had been planted along the edge bordering the flagstones and a sundial reflected the light of a late spring morning. It was all pleasant and peaceful, and bespoke serenity and comfort, so why should it inspire this feeling of dread? The man opened a back door and invited her to enter a large airy kitchen, which contained a great deal of gleaming copper-ware and a white scrubbed deal table. A hip-bath stood before the range, and several buckets of water were streaming on top of it. On a chair near the tub were soap and a fleecy white towel. Whatever she had expected, it was certainly not this most welcome sight!

'My master told me to tell you that you may wash and change into those clothes.' He nodded towards some clothes on another chair. 'He'll see you later.'

'Who is your master?' Crystal demanded, somewhat reassured, for the big man spoke in a quiet deferential manner.

'He didn't give me orders to disclose that; only to go to the auction and buy you at whatever price. Don't look so anxious! My master is a good man, and he knows all about you. You have no need to fear my master.'

He left before Crystal could question him further. Clearly his master was a man of wealth and importance to have a house of this size, but who could he be? Jake Monker's decision to sell her had been made on the spur of a mad drunken moment. Stripping off her clothes, she poured water into the tub, and stepped into it. Delicious warmth lapped against her tired body and she lay for several moments luxuriating in the water; she noted, drowsily, the bruises and weals on her body caused by Monker's attempted rape. She felt safe for the first time for many months. The identity of her rescuer continued to tease her as she soaped herself; she concluded that it must be Marcus Jackson. He must have returned from Bath and, learning that she had been to see his sister, have called at Monker's farm. Caleb or Lottie had either guessed or overheard their father's plan to take her to Bristol, and told him.

Dear Marcus! She felt a warm glow of gratitude; how he had atoned for his neglect! He had not failed her, after all! He might even be married to Arabella by now, and perhaps this was their home. If so, all her problems were over, for had he not promised that he would engage her as companion to his wife? In this mood of delighted anticipation, she stepped out of the tub and began to towel herself dry.

She had just completed her dressing when the realisation struck her that Monker's extraordinary conduct in selling her at a public auction had stemmed from causes that were not entirely due to his drunkeness. The mere thought that she might report his behaviour to Sir James had always been sufficient deterrent to his worst excesses. That he should have behaved in such a reprehensible way could mean only one thing: Sir James Allenwood must be dead! News must have reached Brentry on that evening when he went out drinking. All her animosity towards Sir James vanished in an instant, to be replaced by the dull ache of despair. Her elation at her escape from Monker disappeared. It no longer mattered what became of her, and she wept unrestrainedly.

CHAPTER ELEVEN

'WHAT DO mean, Pa—run off?' Lottie was fearful and incredulous.

'Good riddance to bad rubbish!' Caleb retorted tersely. He put on his smock, and went out.

'Come back 'ere! I never gave you leave to go out yet,' Monker roared after his son.

'Got work to do, Pa,' Caleb said, puzzled. His father had a frightened look, quite alien, about him.

'Listen 'ere, both of you. Crystal run off with some man. If anyone asks you, that's what you got to say,' Monker said with insistence.

'I'll bet she ran away with Mr Jackson!' Lottie was looking questioningly at her father.

'Ay! More than likely! But we ain't putting that story about. All we know is that she's run off.' Monker applied himself to his belated breakfast.

A firm tap on the door make him jump as though a shot had rung out.

'Who can that be?' Lottie was fearful, and looked at her father for guidance.

'Open it, stupid! And don't forget, neither of you, that Crystal Smith run off in the night.' Monker had pushed his plate away, and now looked at the door with apprehension.

'It's Sir James, Pa,' Lottie breathed, respect mingled with awe.

Monker leapt from the table so quickly that his chair overturned, and tugged wildly at the kerchief round his neck.

Sir James strolled into the kitchen and appeared not to notice either the disorder, or the fact that his appearance had thrown the occupants into varying degrees of uneasiness. 'I see that my safe return had not been expected,' he said pleasantly. Flicking the dust from a chair, he placed his hat and gloves upon it; his riding-crop he kept in his hand.

'Sit you down, Sir James,' blustered Monker.

'Thank you, I prefer to stand,' he replied. 'My business will not occupy many minutes of your valuable time, for I see,' smiling at Caleb, 'that you are anxious to return to your work. Will you be so good as to fetch Miss Crystal Smith? I have been given to understand that she is here, and I wish to relieve you of the charge you so kindly took of her.'

Monker's gaze shifted from Lottie to Caleb, and he passed his tongue over his lips. 'She ain't 'ere. She's run off somewhere.'

'Then I shall await her return. Please be so good as to direct Caleb to find her,' Sir James smiled at the Monkers.

'Can't fetch her. She's run off with Mr Marcus Jackson,' Caleb declared with his customary lack of conversational finesse.

'Run off with Mr Jackson?' Sir James's eyebrows rose at this intelligence, and he directed a keen look at Monker.

'We don't know that for sure. I never said she run off with Mr Jackson,' Monker babbled, the sweat beading his brow. ''E seemed very taken with 'er. Naturally enough, when I discovered she were gone, I took it she 'ad run off with 'im.'

'He was never taken with her, Pa!' Lottie said passionately. 'It was *me* he liked. She stole him from me! She never had any shame!'

'Dear me!' Sir James said mildly, but there was an unpleasant glint in his eyes. 'How came you to be entrusted with the care of Miss Smith, Monker?'

Monker recognised a certain grim intent beneath the pleasantly urbane manner, and fear of retribution took hold of him. 'Miss Jackson didn't know what to do with 'er. She asked me to take 'er in. I only did it to oblige Miss Jackson. Like a father I treated 'er, but she were never satisfied. Out at nights with men. She'd come crawling in 'ere with the dawn. Shamed, I was!'

'It's true, Sir James. Honest! I saw her one morning, Christmas morning, it was. She got out of Mr Jackson's

carriage dressed fine as fivepence. He must have bought
her the clothes, for she never had anything like that
here. Kissing they were, like lovers.' Lottie paused
dramatically, allowing her words to take effect on Sir
James.

'And just what sort of clothes did she wear here, I
wonder? he asked unexpectedly.

'Skivvy's clothes!' Caleb brayed with laughter.

Monker shifted from foot to foot, all the time
watching Sir James's face.

'Be so good as to give me Miss Smith's belongings so
that I may take them with me,' Sir James said, after a
pause.

Caleb had pushed open the door to the little cell-
like room that Crystal had lately occupied, and swiftly
Sir James forestalled Monker's attempts to block
the entrance. He glanced about expressionlessly,
and gathered Crystal's few possessions into a small
bundle.

'I shall return later to deal with the question of your
ownership of this farm, Monker. I take you are still
desirious of buying it from me?'

'I am that, Sir James,' he said eagerly.

'Good. In exchange, I shall expect to find Miss Smith
here on my return. As she was placed in your care, I hold
you responsible for her safety.' The grim intent was
evident, a steely purpose from which he recoiled. Sir
James left without further speech.

Monker's fleshy face whitened, and briefly he told his
children what had happened. 'We got to find 'er, and
quick! That man 'oo bought 'er, I saw 'im once, with
Mr Jackson. You find Mr Jackson, Lottie. Use your
pretty ways, make 'im bring 'er back!' His voice grew
menacing. 'Mind, if she don't come back, don't you
bother coming back neither. And I means that!'

'After luncheon, you must tell me all about Captain and
Mrs Hastings, but pray do not regale me with horrid
deeds, for I have not the inclination to listen.' Thus
prettily did Miss Jackson implore her betrothed. They
were sitting in the dining-room at Henbury House, a

formal room, well furnished although slightly over-heated for Sir James's spartan taste. Miss Jackson was attired in lavender muslin, and a becoming flush mantled her delicate cheeks.

'Then, suffice to say that I effected Captain Hastings' escape, for the pirates proved obdurate in their de-mands, as did the Governor in his refusal. He recovered his health on the voyage home, and both he and Mrs Hastings have gone straight to Bath to be reunited with their daughter.' He watched her with a slight smile on his lips.

She flushed and looked down. He had grown so very handsome! His adventures in the West Indies had added a quality to his austere character that enhanced his masculinity, but she wished he would not watch her so quizzically. That tilting smile had never been there before, and really, it was most disturbing! She might even fall in love with him. How very vulgar!

'I believe that our marriage might be announced quite soon, my love.' His deep voice made her heart thud.

'Oh, no!' She cried involuntarily. 'You must recall the terms of my father's will. We cannot wed until Marcus is married.'

'Nonsense! A court would overset that in no time at all. I am anxious to make you my bride as soon as possible.'

She flushed rosily, and made the entrance of the food her excuse for returning no answer.

'I believe that Marcus is soon to be married,' he continued, when the servants had departed.

She raised a startled look of enquiry to him, her fork suspended half-way to her open mouth. 'I do not think so! I refused him permission to wed Arabella Hastings,' she blurted out.

'I wonder why you did that?' he asked mildly.

'I considered that he could do much better for himself. The Hastings family are well enough in their own way, but hardly of our station.'

'I had not realised that you would be so foolish as to refuse such an eminently suitable match! Or your feck-less brother so unmanly as to approach his sister before requesting the permission of Captain and Mrs Hastings for their daughter's hand in marriage.' He spoke softly, but the smile had quite left his eyes. 'In any case, my love, it is not marriage with Arabella Hastings that your brother has in mind, but rather with Crystal Smith. He has run away with her, you know!'

Sophia was speechless. She could not tell if it was this, or the astonishing intelligence about her brother and that wretched girl, that most suprised her. What on earth had come over him?

'Have you nothing to say? I quite thought that you would be outraged at the thought of his marriage with Miss Smith. In honour, having abducted her from Monker, he can do no less than marry her.'

'I should never consent to such a match!' she declared resolutely.

'How unfortunate! For that means that *we* can never be married. Perhaps you would like me to leave you for a spell, in order to give you some time to think about it. You see, I really am most anxious to be married.' He was smiling again.

'You are unreasonable, James! You surely cannot expect me to consent to so disproportionate a match. I had heard that he was seen about with her a good deal. Why, she even allowed herself to be paraded at the theatre! Do you not think that shocking?'

He flung down his table-napkin and gave up all pretence of eating. 'Yes, Sophia, I do,' he said sternly, and she flinched from the fury in his eyes. 'I left her in your care. You promised me that you would look after her. I understood that she was to remain here, in this house with you. You handed her over to that villain, Monker . . .'

'What grounds have you for calling your most trusted tenant a villain?' she snapped, fast losing her poise.

'I saw the conditions in which she lived! You say that you heard she was seen in your brother's company, and yet you did absolutely nothing to protect her.' He had risen from his seat and came to stand over her.

'I should rather think that *he* needed protection from *her*. I believe her to be a light woman.' Her voice was faint, and she raised a small white hand to cover her eyes.

'I shall find them and bring them here. You are aware that Monker claims that she has run away with Marcus. If they are not yet married, then they shall be, directly I find them. Our wedding can take place immediately afterwards.'

'And if Marcus refuses?' she demanded faintly.

'I shall kill him with my bare hands!' He strode from the room.

So unexpected was all this that Miss Jackson fell back in her chair, shaking, and it was several minutes before she could command herself for action. Rising, she tugged the bell-rope to summon a servant. 'Present my compliments to Mr Monker at his farm, and summon him to my presence, immediately!' She was as composed as ever, and only her quickened breathing betrayed her inner agitation.

Crystal sat for some while a victim to her grief, unable to face the prospect of food. The housekeeper had obviously been delayed, so, to give her thoughts another, perhaps more cheerful, direction, she decided to explore the house and find the room the big man had said had been prepared for her.

A flight of stairs just outside the kitchen door led to a large square, marble-tiled hall, and the ground-floor rooms were furnished with a quiet style and elegance that she liked instinctively. There was such a fragrant aroma of polish and flower petals, and the house felt so cherished and welcoming, that she could not understand her initial feeling of apprehension at its aspect. The library was well furnished with books on every subject, their appearance bearing testimony to much usage. She was surprised, for she had not believed Marcus Jackson to be a great reader; the many pictures of sailing-ships equally surprised her, for he had never spoken of the sea. Longing to stay and pore over some of the many volumes, she decided to return when she had completed her search for her room.

She experienced some hesitation in entering the

rooms upstairs, for while the ground-floor rooms were more public in nature, bedrooms were private, intimate apartments. To her surprise, she found herself in a large-sitting-room with a pianoforte at the further end. The tall windows were draped in rich crimson material, and on the floor was a Persian carpet, the vivid colours winking in the afternoon sun. The sofas and chairs were deep and looked comfortable, and there were one or two magazines on the small tables. Altogether it held a look of pleased expectancy that was absent in the other more formal rooms. The bedrooms were so entirely masculine in style and appearance that she could not doubt that she was in a gentleman's residence. A small room at the very end of the corridor was clearly meant for her, and she was charmed with it. A motif of roses was echoed on the walls, the carpet and delicately embroidered into the snowy counterpane of the bed. On the wash-stand reposed a basin, and the jug was filled with rose-scented water. Some combs and brushes had been placed on the dressing-table, and taking the chair before it, Crystal began the laborious task of disentangling her thick curls. That her recent experiences would have altered her looks, she had expected, but the bleak expression in her eyes reminded her that she had real cause for unhappiness. Certainly she was free from Jake Monker, and for that she must rejoice and be happy, and Marcus Jackson had arranged for her purchase at the auction, so she must be grateful to him. But Sir James Allenwood was dead—he must be! It was inconceivable that Monker would have acted as he had unless he believed that no retribution would follow. She cast aside the hair-brush and went over to the window.

To her amazement, the house overlooked a grassy square, where sheep grazed! She knew herself to be close to the centre of the town, very near the quay, therefore such a rural scene was quite unexpected. A house of superior size and aspect on the opposite side of the square caught her attention, as carriages were drawing up to it, and liveried footmen were either guiding visitors into the house or escorting them from it. Not wishing to attract attention to herself, she withdrew from the window. If Jake Monker were in the vicinity she would not wish him to see her.

Suddenly, weariness overcame her, and she lay on the bed to fall into a deep, dreamless, sleep.

Miss Jackson was prey to a number of unpleasant thoughts and emotions, uppermost of which was the determination that her brother should not be forced into a match with the odious Crystal Smith. The intelligence Sir James had related had come as an unpleasant shock. His changed manner, that steely purpose! She could not doubt that he meant to force her brother into a marriage which must be disastrous for him. It had been an error to place the girl in Monker's keeping, she could see that now. What had James meant when he had referred to the conditions in which she had lived? Surely a girl reared among savage Indians must think herself palatially housed at Monker's farm. She bitterly resented the continuing interest her betrothed showed in the girl; his cousin Vera had wished to adopt her and make provision for her, a procedure to have been arranged during her lifetime. The fact that this had not been done led her to doubt the serious intent of Vera Allenwood. It was grossly unfair that James had been left with the burden of arranging such affairs, and he had behaved quite out of character, quite high-handedly. He would insist that he and she were married as soon as Marcus was married to Crystal Smith! Her civil amiable James had never spoken so autocratically before!

Her frequent sojourns in Gloucester had been enlivened by the company of many of her aunt's friends, one of whom had been the relative of an earl, a charming girl, handsome and reserved, and they had become friends. She had confessed to having met and liked Marcus Jackson in Bath. Miss Jackson had met the widowed earl and was gratified to learn from her friend that he had been much impressed with her. The friendship flourished from then on; the two young women in unspoken but complete accord about their separate matrimonial hopes.

If James had spoken the truth, all her hopes of uniting

the Jacksons' to the nobility would be dashed, and Crystal was the author of this predicament. She would find her and punish her!

Jake Monker had believed that no worse could befall him after the visit of Sir James Allenwood to his farm, so the summons he had just received from Miss Jackson's servant was unwelcome in the extreme. He was sorely tempted to ask the servant to say that he was from home. He had every hope that Lottie would discover Crystal's whereabouts and return her to the farm by any means necessary. He considered his own magnaminity in housing such a girl, reared in such peculiar conditions, without a penny to her name, friendless. Otherwise, Miss Jackson would have taken her in, so he had done her a kindness. Gratitude was what the girl should have shown for his care of her. He would even have married her! By degrees, feeding his anger when he thought of her with Marcus Jackson, he came to think that he had been misled and misused by a scheming hussy. What should he say if it came out that he had taken her to the auction? That would be much more difficult to explain! He would just have to say that it was her own wish, and that the auctioneer had witnessed her willingness to step into the ring. When the effects of the scrumpy had cleared from his brain, he had been aghast at the stupidity of his behaviour. If his suspicions were correct, the man who bought her was known to Marcus Jackson. Supposing *he* had bought her? He shuddered with fear and dread, for his own whole future was in jeopardy. If only Crystal were dead! If he found her, he would kill her!

Always outwardly deferential to Miss Jackson, inwardly he despised her, for he disliked managing women. He was somewhat reassured, for she looked peaceable enough as she sat at her desk in her room of business. He wondered what she wanted of him, for she sat quite still and was looking at him without expression in her eyes, hardly moving, just tapping her foot. He felt uncomfortable in his Sunday coat, despite the fine appearance he knew he presented.

'I understand that Miss Smith is no longer with you,

Monker. I desire a complete explanation. No,' she
signalled to him, 'I did not give you leave to sit. Please
remain standing.'

She was cold as ice. Damn her! Monker recalled that
she had been only too willing for him to take Crystal
Smith into his home, and for no payment. The cause of
her willingness had not been far to seek at the time, for
he had seen Sir James with Crystal at about the time Miss
Allenwood had died. He had shown too much interest in
her, so no wonder Miss Jackson wanted to get rid of her!
Well, she was not pleased at the consequences! So he
would have to brazen things out, sure in his own mind
that she would not want the girl returned. No, he
thought viciously, it was only Sir James who wanted
that. But he must tread warily; he might yet make an ally
out of her.

'I've 'ad a deal of trouble with that girl, Miss Jackson.
A deal of trouble! Like a father to 'er, I was . . .'

'I am not concerned about your relationship with Miss
Smith.' She cut him short. 'I wish to know where she is.'

'I don't know.' He was sullen. The haughty bitch
would not let him explain.

'I think you do, Monker. How were you so sure she
had run away? You told Sir James that she had been
frequently in the company of my brother. I dare say that
you told him the extent to which she had been with Mr
Jackson, and the circumstances surrounding such
meetings?'

'I never told 'im about them going to Northover
Lodge! I thought you must 'ave told 'im that.' He was
affronted.

'Northover Lodge? What are you talking about?
Please be plain with me.' Her voice was sharp now,
interested.

'Them times 'e used to come for 'er. You said I 'ad to
give my permission!' he said indignantly.

'I have only just learnt of this!' She could not hide her
astonishment.

'You knew nothing about it? The scheming 'ussy!
What a fool she made of all of us!' His chagrin was so
unfeigned that she believed him.

'Please be seated, Mr Monker, for it is plain that there is a good deal that I do not understand.'

Much relieved, he sat down awkwardly on a small chair opposite her. 'Every day Mr Jackson used to come and call for 'er. Seemingly you 'ad given orders that she was go over to Northover Lodge and get the place ready for the return of the 'Astings. Hours they'd be gone. Then when 'e took to buying 'er clothes and taking 'er to the theatre—all on your instruction, I understood—I was put out. To say the very least of a very bad matter, I was put out!'

Despite his uneasiness, he sat upright, an honest countryman outraged by the licentiousness he had been forced to witness. She pitied him deeply, but was still not convinced that her brother had taken Crystal away with him.

'Why are you so sure that she has run away? Could she be visiting friends?'

'She didn't 'ave no friends! Only your brother. Begging your leave, Miss Jackson, 'e was always 'anging round 'er.' He was triumphant; knowing that he spoke partly the truth, he felt much surer of himself.

It was clear to Sophia that Monker was unaware of her brother's offer of marriage to Arabella Hastings. That surprised her, for in rural areas everyone's business was common property in no time at all. She was disgusted by the information that her brother had accompanied Crystal Smith to Northover Lodge—the girl must be sunk beneath reproach! Monker had had a great deal to bear. Her brother's part in the disgraceful affair she exonerated immediately. At her express command, he had returned in order to learn something of the management of his estates, and Crystal Smith had lured him into indiscretion. What puzzled her greatly was the knowledge that her brother was in Bath. But could she be sure? If he had conducted a low affair with Crystal while avowing his love for Arabella Hastings, could she be sure that he had ever told her the truth about anything?

'I do not know how you have borne with such shocking conduct.' Thus she addressed Jake Monker. 'I am afraid that I was much to blame in allowing her to go to you. I should have made other arrangements for her.'

Relief almost made Monker giddy, and his confidence was fully restored. 'I wish you would tell Sir James that. Fair berated me, 'e did. Said that 'e would come back later to discuss the sale of the farm. You knows 'ow much I wants to buy that farm. It's me life's work. But 'e said that I 'ad to 'ave Crystal back or 'e wouldn't talk of selling. Flummoxed, I was. I'd only just got back from Bristol . . .' He could have bitten off his tongue. He had not meant to divulge that insane trip to Bristol!

'You were in Bristol this morning?' Sophia's brows arched in surprise. 'How comes this? What took you to Bristol? If you were there, how can you be sure that my brother has run away with Crystal Smith?'

'I'm not sure. I never said I was. Only said I *thought* she 'ad. I got reasons to think she's with 'im. But I'll 'ave 'er back, never fear! I'll track 'er down.' He reddened and assumed a belligerent expression.

Sophia was sure that Monker, tried though he was, was concealing something. She was in a dilemma: if he was sure that Crystal Smith was with her brother at that very moment, he was privy to some information that he had not disclosed. It was imperative for both their sakes that Crystal's whereabouts be discovered. Repugnant though the idea was, she decided that she must admit him to her confidence.

'I do not believe all you have told me; I feel that there is more. I wish you to be absolutely honest with me, for I may tell you that it is to both our advantages that she be found very soon. You wish to purchase your farm, and I wish to prevent a marriage between that person and my brother.' With some reluctance, she recounted Sir James's threat.

'Phew! That puts a different complexion on things.' He mopped his brow with the back of his hand. 'Trouble is, if I tells you where I think she is and you get 'er back 'ere—' he jabbed a thumb at the floor '—then she's out of my control. No saying what she might say! Either way, I can kiss goodbye to my chances of buying my farm. There's a mighty change in Sir James. Begging your pardon, Miss Jackson, but 'e's turning out very like his father. That's only my opinion, of course.'

That unpleasant thought had occurred to Miss Jackson, but she would not admit it to Jake Monker. She had observed the crafty expression that had flitted across his face.

'I can make you a promise, Monker.' She spoke clearly, the flute-like quality of her voice never varying for an instant. 'If you are honest with me, I shall guarantee that you will be the owner of a farm by the end of this quarter. Until my brother marries, an event which must have my approval, I control these estates. If I choose to sell you a farm, one that is not entailed, there will be no objection. If you are sure that that person is with my brother, it means that you must have a reason for this belief, and possibly you know exactly where she is.'

Monker regarded her thoughtfully from beneath lowered brows, rubbing his thumb across his chin. 'Do I take it that it wouldn't suit neither of us to 'ave 'er back?' She nodded, a slight flush staining her cheeks. He drew a breath before continuing, and so much bore that appearance of a man tried beyond endurance that she was moved once more to pity him. 'Fact is, she told me all about 'er capers in Northover Lodge, and she even tried to throw 'erself at me! Naturally enough, I wasn't standing for that nonsense! Seems that she 'ad some arrangement with your brother, or so she told me . . . it might 'ave been a pack of lies! Anyway, she set out for Bristol to meet 'im there, and I followed 'er. Laughed at me, she did! She met some fellow that I once seen your brother talking to.' He described the big raw-boned man, and saw her frown as though in an effort of recollection. He continued, cautiously, 'I don't say the man was a *friend* of your brother, more like a man of business . .'

'Assuredly, if it is the man I think it is, he is not a friend. I believe that I stipulated that you must speak the absolute truth. I do not believe that you have spoken truly, therefore my promise to sell you a farm is not binding. Good-day, Monker. I shall summon a servant to show you out.' She rose, smoothing her skirts with a dainty hand, her expression of the utmost disdain.

'Wait!' He rubbed sweating palms against his knees. 'There *is* more! I couldn't say nothing, for I didn't 'ow you would take it. I sold 'er!' he blurted out. Her expression was arrested, and she remained for several seconds as though turned to stone. Returning to her seat, she motioned him to continue. 'I didn't want to do it! It was 'er idea. She saw this friend of Mr Jackson's —leastways, she declared 'im to be a friend of Mr Jackson's. Stepped into the auction ring of 'er own accord. The auctioneer will tell you that.'

'Auction? What on earth are talking of?' She was startled.

'The wife auction at Temple Meads,' he replied gruffly. 'She was bought by the man I told you about, this morning, for ten pounds. 'E took 'er away. To Mr Jackson, I suppose.'

She did not press him further, because there was much that might provide food for unpleasant speculation. Her first duty must be to find Crystal Smith and forestall the peremptory plans that her betrothed had made for the future.

Her first task upon dismissing Monker was to write a very civil letter of welcome to Captain and Mrs Hastings, in which she apprised them of her brother's wish to marry their daughter, and assured them that so happy an event had her blessing. Then, changing into travelling clothes, she sent word to the stables to bring her light travelling-carriage to the front door immediately. Matters were more serious than she had believed possible. That she had much to answer for, she could not deny, but she would not allow her brother to suffer on that account. It was vital that she discovered the whereabouts of Crystal Smith immediately. If Monker had been so forthcoming with his information to her, it was highly likely that he would divulge all to James, and she was determined to prevent that. Girls like Crystal Smith were wantons. There was a place she knew of, in Bristol, where she could be lodged, a place where she could never again be a menace to the Jacksons or the Allenwoods.

*   *   *

At about the time that Sophia Jackson was setting out for Bristol, Sir James had just ridden into the city. He took his horse to a livery stable in King Street, meaning to walk round the corner into Queen Square where his house was situated. He viewed the prospect of his coming interview with Crystal with the greatest pleasure. When young Ben Hardy had run to him breathlessly that morning, declaring that he had seen her being pushed along the quay by a rough man, he had been astounded. The enterprising Ben had followed the couple and ascertained that the man intended selling her at the wife auction in Temple Meads. Still unwilling to believe so preposterous a yarn, and having much business to transact with the many agents who awaited him, he had sent a trusted man of business to the auction. If the girl really did prove to be Crystal, he was to purchase her, at whatever price, and bring her to his house. The experiences he had recently undergone in the West Indies had changed him completely; they were hideous and had tested the extremes of his courage and endurance. The bearing and demeanour throughout of Mrs Hastings had impressed him vividly. His reserve and cynicism had dropped away, and he viewed the world quite differently. He loved Crystal Smith to distraction. The admission to himself that he could own such feelings had come almost as a relief, and he bitterly regretted that he had thrust her away from him, for in doing so he had been trying to protect himself from the violence of feeling that she invariably aroused in him. He recalled the scene in his cousin's garden when she had clung to him and said: 'Please take me with you. I know that the mission you undertake is fraught with peril. If anything happens to you, I wish to be at your side. If you do not return, I cannot live without you.' Those words had become indelibly printed on his heart.

He would marry Crystal, he was determined; it no longer mattered to him what her background was, or who her previous lovers had been, if indeed she had had previous lovers. She had the intrepid courage that he loved, the vivacity and spirit that he craved, she was the woman with whom he wished to spend the rest of his life. Without her, it would be unbearably empty.

It was beyond his comprehension that Sophia should have sent Crystal to live with the Monkers, although he was uncomfortably aware that Sophia's ill opinion stemmed partly from his own bitter words. The only problem he had foreseen, during his voyage home, was how to break the news that he no longer wished to marry her, but when he learned of her part in placing Crystal, his dearest love, with Monker, he vowed to be revenged. He was filled with the tenderest emotions, so he wished to extract only a small vengeance: the satisfaction of knowing that he had filled the Monkers and Sophia with trepidation was almost enough. He had no serious intention of forcing an admission from Marcus that he would marry Crystal, but had merely wished to provide Sophia with sufficient cause to cry off from their engagement.

The allegation that she had conducted some clandestine affair with Marcus, he dismissed. Mrs Hastings had said sufficient to echo the feelings in his own heart that the two were no more than friends. She had confided her hopes of a match between her daughter and Marcus, when that young man had shown himself settled and responsible enough to undertake the duties of marriage. When he had witnessed the reunion between the middle-aged couple, it convinced him that life could hold no more joy than the felicity of a happy marriage. So with a light step and gladdened heart he strode up King Street.

'Allenwood! Of all the coincidences! You are the very man I have been looking for.' A tall military man was wringing his hand.

'Brereton! How good to see you. How do you go on?' James was pleased to see his friend, a colonel of Dragoons, but wished he could have proceeded without delay to Queen Square.

'Not well, I am afraid,' said the Colonel, grimacing. 'Things are not well in the city, either, which is what I wanted very much to see you about. Now that I have you, I do not mean to let you go easily!' He took his friend's arm and turning him about, walked back down

King Street to an inn situated at the far end. 'I have much to tell. You have been absent from the city, I understand, so you cannot know what is afoot.'

'Could you not dine with me later, and tell me then? I have some pressing business.'

'Sorry, Allenwood, but I am engaged to dine with Major Pinney, that oaf who occupies the house opposite to your own, this evening. Besides, the business I have to relate is of the utmost importance. I would not otherwise delay you,' the Colonel said stiffly.

Hastily disclaiming any wish to hurry away, for he had seen the rather offended look in the man's eyes, Sir James allowed himself to be taken into the inn. Crystal would probably be resting after her ordeal, so an hour or two more could not make a great deal of difference.

'Before I give you my news, let me know what has been happening to you since I last saw you,' demanded Colonel Brereton.

Resigning himself to a lengthy stay, Sir James recounted, in part, his adventures since he had left Bristol.

'You do seem to have been in the wars! I was right in my instinct: you are the very man we need in the coming fray.'

Cutting into a large beefsteak, Sir James realised that he was ravenously hungry. Having despatched Captain and Mrs Hastings, made arrangements for Crystal's reception at Queen Square, and summoned his housekeeper to return to the house, he had had little time to think about food. Anger had been uppermost during his luncheon at Henbury, and he had barely been able to swallow a morsel. 'In what way may I be of service to you?'

'As you know, there has been much unrest in the city since the Reform Bill was defeated,' began the Colonel.

'Yes, I do know. I cannot say that I blame the agitators, for they have much to complain of. Parliament and the electoral system are badly in need of reform.'

'The unrest has mainly been confined to speechifying and pamphleteering, but that is not our concern. What is very much our concern is the intelligence we have received indicating that there will be a concerted effort to overthrow the authorities.'

'I do not foresee such an event; Englishmen are too fond of law and order.' Sir James was amused. 'Do you fear a revolution after the French style?' He grinned at his friend.

'That is just what we do fear. It is rumoured in legal and political circles that the new legal officer for Bristol is to be Sir Charles Wetherall.'

Brereton had the grim satisfaction of seeing Sir James's look of amusement disappear, to be replaced by a look of foreboding. 'The very worst appointment,' he said tersely. 'If I recall correctly, Wetherall is bigoted, vicious and vehemently opposed to reform. Are you sure that what you have heard is not merely rumour?'

'One can never be sure of these things until the appointment has been confirmed. But, yes, I have been told, in confidence, that the appointment will be confirmed very shortly.'

'Then I take it that your concern is ensure that riots, revolutions, or any similar events, do not take place.' Sir James dabbed a napkin against his mouth, and swallowed some coffee.

'I wish it were as simple as that! We have received the most conflicting instructions. Your Lord Mayor, that pompous, vacillating old fool Pinney, does not like to make any decisions at all; not at this stage, at all events. If we were prepared, we could avert a catastrophe. For you can be sure that this appointment will act like tinder to the political powder-keg that Bristol has fast become.' The Colonel looked grave.

'Does the Mayor not realise that open confrontation may lead to bloodshed!' Sir James was aghast.

'Mayor Pinney knows nothing of military affairs, and cares even less. The only orders he seems prepared to give are for his dinner. We shall be caught in the middle! Can you imagine? Our soldiers, who acquitted themselves so nobly against Napoleon, to be turned against their own countrymen?' Brereton was disgusted. 'It hardly bears thought!'

He did not say so, but Sir James was deeply disturbed by the Colonel's disclosures; he knew very well that

Bristol and the surrounding countryside had been in a foment of unrest for several years. War, unemployment and the high price of corn had all made their contribution. The arrival of a known enemy of reform to the judiciary, one who was famed for the savagery of his sentences and who seemed to delight in ordering hanging and transportation, would be fuel to the fire of the political agitators. No man of reason or sense could welcome such an appointment. Frowning, he stirred his coffee abstractedly for several moments, then said quietly, 'You mentioned that you particularly wished to see me. If there is some way in which I can be of service to you, please do not hesitate to ask.'

Colonel Brereton leaned across the table, his face eager. 'I believe that if I can recruit, privately, enough men of substance and standing, we can alleviate the worst of the problem.'

He continued for some while to outline his plans, the gist of which were that each land- or factory-owner would be responsible for his own men. In the event of a riot, or worse, the men of peace would mingle with the agitators, thus preventing a gathering turning into a mob. There was much in this vein, and Sir James listened quietly and attentively.

In a remarkably short space of time, the redoubtable Miss Jackson had established that Crystal had been taken to a house in Queen Square. The auctioneer, a most respectable man, had been willing to reassure the gracious lady who questioned him that he, too, had been uneasy about the purchase, but his fears had been allayed when he had followed the couple and seen them enter the house of Sir James Allenwood. Surely, she must agree, the girl could come to no harm in the home of such a well-known and well-respected member of the community? Sophia was furious. That wanton person must have persuaded Marcus to use the house in Queen Square as they had used the home of Captain and Mrs Hastings; it was disgraceful! It could not be unknown to many people that the Jacksons had free access to the house during the frequent absences of the owner.

Crystal awoke from a deeply refreshing sleep; she had slept very little on the previous night. Someone was in the house! She heard the light tap-tapping of a woman's feet in the corridor, but moving quickly, and with agitation! It must be the housekeeper. The door of the bedroom was flung open, and Sophia Jackson trembled on the threshold, every bone in her small delicate body rigid with wrath.

'Is Mr Jackson with you?' said Crystal, starting up from her slumber. She wanted very much to see her benefactor, but was surprised to see his sister.

'No, he is not. And I do not want you to see him. You shameless hussy, get up at once! I am taking you to a place where he will not be able to find you. You will never again be able to exercise your wiles on unwary young men.'

Crystal was so astonished that she wondered whether Miss Jackson had taken leave of her senses. What had she done to merit such terrible words? 'I fear that I do not understand you, Miss Jackson. I have no designs on your brother.'

'Do you deny that you await him at this very moment?' demanded Miss Jackson, her flute-like voice punctuated with tiny gasps of rage.

'Yes,' admitted Crystal reluctantly. 'I wanted to . . .'

'I have no desire to be admitted to your shameless confidence! Go down immediately, and await me in the hall.'

Crystal ran from the room in the greatest perturbation, for she had never seen a person so much enraged. Surely Miss Jackson could not hold her responsible for that dreadful auction? Yet her presence in the house must mean that she knew of it, unless she was frequently in the habit of visiting her brother's house, and had chanced upon her. Believing this to be the case, Crystal determined to make her listen, for clearly she had a duty to disabuse Miss Jackson's mind of the notion that she had been guilty of any improper behaviour with Mr Jackson.

'Miss Jackson,' she began, when that lady descended into the hall. 'You must listen to me . . .'

'I am neither going to listen,' she interrupted, 'nor to answer any questions about my brother or Sir James Allenwood!' She bit her lip when she saw the look of amazement spread across the lovely face. Could it be possible, she wondered, that the girl did not know who owned this house?

Misinterpreting the look on Miss Jackson's face, Crystal felt her blood turn to ice. 'Then it is true,' she said in a small, quiet, voice. 'Sir James is dead?'

Sophia Jackson disliked lies, finding them unnecessary, but she felt compelled by some force she barely recognised to acquiesce in the girl's mistaken belief. She was a wanton hussy who did not merit the consideration of decent people. She nodded, and saw to her relief that all the spirit had gone out of Crystal. Her proud form drooped, and there was a look of infinite sadness in her eyes. She was shepherded, unresisting, into the carriage that awaited them at the front door.

It rumbled away over the cobblestones just as Sir James, having made his escape from Colonel Brereton, turned into the Square. Whistling, he made his way to his house, and with a look of pleased anticipation took a key from pocket and inserted it into the front door.

CHAPTER TWELVE

THE HOME for Fallen Women and Wayward Girls, of which Miss Sophia Jackson was a patroness, was situated at the very top of a steep hill and overlooked the busy dockland and the life that teemed about it. Not that the inmates had much leisure to observe much of this, for their strict routine occupied them from early morning until evening prayers. Agatha Pennington, the Superintendent, was thirty when she had first encountered one of the trustees of the Home, who was bemoaning the fact that they were shortly to lose their Superintendent. Would she herself consider such a post? It was not well paid, but the work was a reward in itself, for such women were rehabilitated and returned to society with useful domestic skills. Would she accept? She leapt at the chance to prove herself worthy of such a task.

Her early crusading zeal quickly wore itself out. Few of the inmates responded with enthusiasm to the Christian principles with which she attempted to imbue them and were ungrateful—all of them!—that they had been rescued from the degradations of a life of vice or poverty and were fed, clothed and instructed in domestic skills. Prospective employers were personally vetted by her, so that there could be no chance that any dishonest person might lure one of the inmates back into a world of wickedness. Did they love or thank her? Not they! Disillusionment quickly followed. It was her practice to retain her father's custom of taking a glass of port in her own sitting-room every evening. But what had begun as a pleasurable relaxation—for neither the twittering Miss Roberts nor her other assistant, Miss Evans, could be deemed fit company for her—had developed into an entirely necessary habit. Her meagre allowance for her labours was insufficient to fund her little indulgence, so she accepted from prospective employers a small financial token of their gratitude. Part of this money was spent on port, the rest she wisely lodged into a bank account in her own name.

Miss Jackson, for all her beauty, was endowed with the same Christian spirit—she had recognised that immediately, and consequently accorded her affection as well as respect. Miss Pennington was somewhat surprised and greatly flattered that Miss Jackson should personally escort a new inmate to the institution.

'We are honoured, Miss Jackson. Please be seated.' She hurried forward with a chair for her favourite patroness.

'I do not have time to stay, Miss Pennington. This person,' she flicked a disdainful hand in Crystal's direction, 'is to lodge with you. I warn you in advance that she is extremely difficult and devious. She has been associating with men. You will hardly credit it, but she has attempted to inveigle my unfortunate brother into marriage with her.

Crystal was astounded. She had remained mute while being admitted through the heavy oak door into the institution. Her heavy heart could register very little emotion, and she had glanced without interest at the fine oak panelling and highly polished floorboards that reflected a quantity of furniture that had received equal attention. But these words startled her from her sad reverie.

'Indeed, Miss Jackson, you do me a great injustice! I never attempted to inveigle your brother into marriage. We have been nothing more than friends!'

Miss Pennington's frame quivered in mountainous wrath, and she stared at her diminutive patroness as though scarcely able to believe her ears. Sunlight danced over her crimped grey locks, was reflected in her steel-rimmed glasses. She enunciated her words in a deep stentorian voice. 'You will be silent! Inmates are not given permission to speak unless directly invited to do so by myself.'

Miss Jackson continued as though no one had spoken. 'I would be very gratified, Miss Pennington, if you would ensure that she is kept away from the other inmates. Perhaps you could arrange some special duties for her.'

'Naturally, Miss Jackson, you will not wish her to be in contact with others whom she might corrupt.'

Miss Jackson smiled graciously. 'Exactly so! I am so glad we understand each other. There is one other thing . . .' She drew a roll of notes from her reticule. 'Miss Smith is of foreign extraction.' The Superintendent stared at Crystal as though she were a snake. 'I feel sure that she would be happier out of England. If perchance some prospective employer, leaving the country, would wish for her services, I am sure that you would be able to arrange it.' She paused delicately, allowing her words to penetrate Miss Pennington's mind. With only the slightest hesitation, she handed over the roll of notes. 'A small donation, to aid you in your work here,' she murmured.

Miss Pennington's eyes glistened as she accepted the notes. 'Everything will be just as you command, dear Miss Jackson,' she whispered fervently.

There was some doubt as to whether any employer could be found who would be prepared to take an inmate out of the country, but the roll of notes settled so comfortably and so naturally in her pocket that she would quite happily have taken Crystal to Japan, if necessary. This girl must have behaved very badly for her dear, dear Miss Jackson to have had recourse to such an action. Already Miss Pennington could detect the light of Jezebel in those green eyes. Would the task be beyond even her more than adequate powers? No! Grimly, she accepted her duty.

When Miss Jackson had left the Home, Crystal felt as though her last link with Sir James had been severed. She cared little what befell her here, but it had not taken her long to see that Miss Pennington was a bully—and bullies had their weak points! Doubtless she would be unkind for a time, but soon she would find other prey. Miss Jackson had given orders that she was to associate with no one. So much the better! She had little desire for company, being far too weary and sad. If the Superintendent chose to give her plenty of work, she would be doing her a service. She wished to be so much occupied that she had no leisure to think, to dwell upon what might have been. That would be fatal, for she would be sure to give in to her wretched feelings of self-pity.

Pinned across the Superintendent's grey serge ample bosom was a gold watch; at her waist she carried a bunch of keys; and suspended from a leather thong was a long thin cane. Fingering the cane, she watched Crystal's face for signs of rebellion. She rang a small brass hand-bell on her desk, and the clanging brought a fussy little woman with wispy grey hair and a thin anxious face hurrying into the room.

'Miss Roberts, this is a new inmate, Smith, who is to be lodged alone. Perhaps her first duty could be to clear out that small room next to the laundry-room. It will be most suitable for her occupation.'

'In the cellar?' Miss Roberts had a high thin voice that exactly matched her appearance.

'Basement, Miss Roberts, basement.' Thus did Miss Pennington gently correct her assistant. The roll of notes nudging her thigh had mellowed her.

'Could she not be lodged with the other new inmate? She could . . .'

Miss Robert's twitterings were cut short by her superior. 'Miss Smith is foreign,' she said repressively. If this pronouncement was meant to be explanatory, it fell wide of its mark, for Miss Roberts once more opened her thin lips to speak. 'I do not expect to have to explain myself, Miss Roberts. This person is of a particularly vicious and unreliable disposition. Her work is to be confined exclusively to the laundry-room. She will not mix with the other inmates.'

'Meals?' Miss Roberts squeaked timidly.

Miss Pennington hesitated, and appeared to give the matter profound thought. The word 'meals' had conjured up visions of a really good bottle of port, which she would drink alone in the comfort and privacy of her own room. She was in such high good humour that she could almost wish for some company tonight. Mentally shaking herself, she forced her pleasantly dazed mind to contemplate the vexed question of where Smith should eat. 'Oh, she might as well eat with the others. As she will be constantly under my eye in the dining-room,

I do not suppose she would be able to do much harm.'

Crystal was never to forget the next few hours—they remained imprinted on her mind for what seemed an eternity. Her haze of misery was pierced effectively by the initiation ceremony customary for all the inmates of the Home for Fallen Women and Wayward Girls. Her hair was chopped off—to prevent the spread of head-lice, Miss Roberts explained. She was bathed in cold water and soaped with foul-smelling carbolic—how very different from the bath she had enjoyed only hours earlier! She was dressed in the rough grey serge common to all. A drab hessian apron covered the dress, and an enormous calico bonnet covered her shorn head. Miss Roberts accompanied her ministrations with a constant prattle of praise of Miss Pennington, and a tinkling laugh that irritated Crystal. Reverently she handed her a thick grey cloak, starched apron and some stout boots, which she obtained from a closet lined with such garments.

'These are to be worn on Sundays only,' she told Crystal brightly. 'You must be very careful not to let them become soiled, or we shall have our dear Miss Pennington in a very bad mood.' She put her head to one side and playfully wagged a finger under Crystal's nose.

'Do you mean that she is now in a good mood?' Crystal could not help asking.

'Dear me! I should have supposed that from her demeanour you were already quite a favourite!' It would have been wrong to have said that Miss Roberts shrieked, but her voice had risen several tones, and her indeterminate eyes had widened in astonishment.

'If this is a good mood, I should dread to be in her presence when she is in a bad one!' Crystal responded with tartness and a wry expression.

Pulling her into the closet and partially closing the door, Miss Roberts dropped some of her fussy, twittering manner. 'Listen, my dear, and be guided by me. Miss Pennington is, for the most part, a good woman. But if her wrath is roused, the miscreant suffers, and so do we. Do you understand?' She had been whispering.

'Yes. I will remember that we must do nothing to anger her.'

'Just so!'

Miss Evans, calm and placid, adopted a practical attitude to her life and her immediate relationships. If a person chose to be difficult, it mattered very little to Miss Evans, unless, that is, such behaviour directly affected her own life or work. 'So you see, Smith, it will not be in your own interests to shirk. I supervise the laundry, while Miss Roberts supervises the kitchens and dormitories. Our work is of the utmost importance, for people from the outside world send in their washing, ironing and mending. We perform all those tasks, and the recompense we receive goes some way to defraying the many expenses of such an establishment as this.' Her neat form moved ahead of Crystal as she inspected the laundry-rooms in the cellar.

'How on earth am I to manage all this alone?' Crystal cried out in despair.

The cellar consisted of a series of adjoining rooms, stone-walled and stone-floored; light entered from grilles set in the roof, which also formed part of the pavement of the street outside. In one room was an enormous wooden washing-tub and a huge iron mangle, another housed labelled sacks of dirty laundry. The ironing-room would provide Crystal's only respite, being brightly lit and containing a tiny stove for heating the two flat-irons. Everywhere was the stench of damp and carbolic.

'I dare say that Miss Pennington wishes you to become proficient in all aspects of the work here. Doubtless it is her intention that you should eventually supervise these rooms. As soon as is practicable, I shall try to arrange for you to have assistance.' Miss Evans's calm tone reassured Crystal.

The dining-room was a surprise. It was high-ceilinged and panelled with oak carved in patterns of birds and fruit. An enormous fire burned brightly. Crystal had not imagined, from her inspection of her own quarters, that the institution held any degree of comfort. How wrong she was! The room was dominated by a dining-table that ran its entire length. A row of grey-clad figures stood, heads bent, hands folded, along one side, facing a dais. Here Miss Pennington took her meals with her two assistants. Beside the staff dining-table was a great oak lectern whose slender column was surmounted by a book-rest, the front of which was shaped like an eagle with outspread wings. Crystal was fascinated by the eagle—its head to one side afforded a view of a cruelly curved beak, and a small vigilant eye that seemed to watch the inmates constantly. A Bible reposed on the lectern, and from it Miss Pennington read at some length each morning and evening; the inmates were forced to watch their small portions of food congeal on the plates while interminable passages were read to them.

'I have an unpleasant duty to perform,' boomed Miss Pennington on Crystal's first evening. 'We have among us a foreigner. She does not speak English, so there will be no point in communicating with her, for she will not understand.'

Miss Roberts had put a thin hand to her mouth and looked as though she might speak; Miss Evans continued to watch the Superintendent with her customary calm.

'I have personally discovered viciousness in this person, and wishing to protect your morals, I urgently entreat you to keep away from her. You may remember her in your prayers, for, despite all, she has a soul. We must never forget that.'

The wickedness that Miss Pennington had found had been the bruises on Crystal's body. She had stepped from her cold bath and was drying herself with the coarse towel when Miss Pennington entered the washing-room.

'Miss Jackson, before she left, told me a little of your adventures. They are unsavoury in the extreme. You have been guilty of gross ingratitude. We do not tolerate ingratitude here; it is repugnant to me. How did you come by those?' She pointed her thin cane at the bruises.

'A man in whose house I lived attempted to rape me,'

Crystal said sharply, for she disliked the way the woman looked at her, and felt more humiliated than she had at the auction.

'Do not lie!' The cane swished against her thighs. 'That man was good enough to offer you a home, and you repaid him with ingratitude and lies.'

When Miss Pennington had departed, Miss Roberts betrayed her pity. Clasping her hands across an emaciated bosom and casting her eyes heavenward, she said sympathetically, 'You poor dear! How you girls suffer at the hands of your menfolk! Yet you are all so loyal to them. But believe me, Smith, you are far better off here.'

These surprising sentiments were uttered, some weeks later, by the first of the inmates with whom Crystal was allowed contact. The woman who followed her to the cellar was of scrawny build, with the thin withered cheeks of the chronically underfed, and she sniffed constantly, and drooped all the time. Crystal wondered if she would be capable of the extremely heavy work of the laundry.

'Nice little number I had up in the sewing-room! Can't see what I did that was wrong!' she said in a low mumbling whine so it was difficult for Crystal to distinguish her words.

'Do you mean that being sent down here is a punishment?' Crystal blurted out without thinking.

'Gawd! You do speak English, then! I—we all thought you was a heathen. What did you do, anyway, that was so wicked?'

'Nothing.' Crystal responded with dignity.

'That's what they all say,' the woman growled.

'Is it very terrible for you here?' Crystal could see the deep furrows on the woman's brow and the look of wariness in her sharp eyes.

'Terrible?' she cackled, a dry unpleasant sound. 'Are you making a jest? I was near dead from starvation when they brought me in here. My man was pressed, so I stole some cloth so as I could sell it and buy food for my kiddies. They'd have transported or hanged me, but this place,' she jerked her chin at the ceiling, 'took me in and saved me. I eat every day, and sleep alone at night. What more could any woman want?'

Much, much more, said Crystal to herself. To walk the high plains in freedom, to eat, talk, laugh and communicate freely with others. There were many sorts of poverty, she had discovered, but the poverty of the closed mind was the worst of all.

'Who was talking down here?' They had not heard Miss Pennington approach, and jumped with fear.

'I was saying my prayers,' the woman said.

'Good!' the Superintendent snapped, while her eyes glittered dangerously behind her spectacles. 'But there is no need for two of you to be ironing. You, Smith, will not enter this room, but you will be responsible for any pressing that is undertaken.'

'That is not fair, Miss Pennington! How can I be responsible for work I do not undertake?'

The woman hunched her drooping shoulders and tried to efface herself; her cropped head, visible beneath the voluminous bonnet, moved from side to side as though seeking a way out, her eyes more wary than ever. No one ever talked that way to Miss Pennington without suffering the direst consequences! The cane swished through the air, and Miss Pennington stood swaying slightly, her nostrils dilating and a look of intense astonishment on her face.

'I have been too lenient with you, Smith! From now on you will . . . What are you about, Mary Brown?' Miss Pennington rounded on the sagging form of the scrawny woman, for she had started to snivel and sniff.

'I were thinking of my man and what he must be suffering,' moaned Mary Brown distractedly.

'Nonsense! You should be glad he had a chance to serve his country!'

'And my three lovely children, worked to death in the basement of that tailor.' She sounded anguished.

Miss Pennington snapped at her, 'That worthy man was goodness itself, for he could have had your children put on the parish. You stole from him . . . Remember that. He housed your brats. Have you no gratitude?'

'My poor mind wanders . . .' Mary Brown's voice and

demeanour were fast becoming demented. 'Down here all day, in the cellar . . .'

'Laundry-room!' snapped Miss Pennington. 'I shall have you moved back upstairs and put someone else down here. We must deliver this laundry by tomorrow.' She turned her gimlet eyes back to Crystal. 'You will join us for prayers this evening, but you will not eat. The mortification of the flesh is the salvation of the spirit.'

Mary Brown gave her the merest wink as she followed Miss Pennington from the nether regions.

Crystal wondered if Mary Brown had staged the scene deliberately to save her from Miss Pennington's ire, or whether she merely wished to have herself removed from the laundry duties. Duties, it seemed, that were considered a punishment!

By the following afternoon, Crystal felt light-headed with hunger and fatigue. A bleary-eyed Miss Pennington had decided that she had escaped too lightly by missing one meal. She would not be allowed any breakfast. In a matter-of-fact voice Miss Roberts observed that it was a pity, for she would not have the laundry ready on time, and this made the Superintendent think. The kitchen girl, a cheerful willing girl whom Miss Pennington liked very much, had been acting strangely all day: she had dropped things and responded cheekily to her reprimand.

'I am astonished at your behaviour, Monker! I must maintain the high standard of discipline upon which we pride ourselves. Regrettably, I am obliged to punish you. You must spend some time each day in the laundry-room, but you may return each evening to your cooking duties. We shall miss your food, otherwise!' Miss Pennington had attempted a smile, but the effort was too much for the little-used muscles of her face and she succeeded only in grimacing. 'But take this warning *very* seriously. You are on no account to communicate with the person who is in the laundry-room. If you do, you will be punished with the utmost severity.'

Lottie nodded mutely. 'The 'utmost severity' was a public caning, with the miscreant stripped to the waist.

She had never witnessed this herself, but had heard it spoken of, fearfully, by the others. As soon as she had heard from Mary Brown that a 'real lady', with a slightly foreign accent, green eyes and brown hair, was down in the cellar, she formed the conclusion that it might be Crystal. Determining to get into the laundry-room, she had behaved as badly as she dared all day. Her ruse had succeeded!

Moving ghost-like across the floor of the laundry, she laid a finger to her lips and drew Crystal into a shadowed corner. 'Is it you, Crystal?' she whispered.

'Good heavens, Lottie!' Crystal exclaimed.

'Ssh! Keep your voice down! We won't have much time to talk, so just listen. Old Pennington's got it in for you, so mind yourself!'

'You do not need to tell me that! But how did you come to be here?' All emnity gone, Crystal was sincerely glad to see Lottie, but greatly puzzled by her presence in the Home.

'I'll tell you all about that, later. Here!' She delved into the pocket of her apron. 'I brought you something to eat. It's only some bread, and a few bits of meat, but it's better than nothing. I'll bring you what I can every day. I got a job in the kitchens; good little cook, I am. Seems I learnt something from you, after all!'

A slight sound on the stairs down to the cellar alerted the girls that someone approached. Gliding noiselessly in her bare feet, for she had removed the clumsy, noisy wooden pattens, Lottie sped into the ironing-room, and placing the iron on the stove, began to smooth damp sheets with her hands on the wooden table.

Crystal went about her duties with a lighter heart. It was welcome to know that there was someone here who would talk to her, and allow her to answer!

Since Miss Pennington kept a constant attendance on the cellar while Lottie was there, it made conversation very difficult.

'I'll creep down tonight, after supper,' Lottie whispered before departing.

Crystal had completed her after-supper duties and was going to bed. It was still quite light, for it was midsummer, and many of the terrifying night shadows were held at bay. She hoped that Lottie would come, for she longed to question her about so many things, and an instant later, she materialised through the gloom.

'Quick! Over here, behind the wash-tub. We shan't be seen there.' Lottie pulled Crystal after her. 'Here, you will have to make do with this.' She handed her some candied fruit, which Crystal put into the pocket of her apron. 'I couldn't get nothing else. I think they're watching me.'

'Thank you, Lottie, but I do not want you to take risks on my account. Do tell me how you come to be here.'

'Pa sent me to find you and bring you back . . .'

'You mean he regretted what he did?'

Some obscure loyalty to Monker prompted Lottie to nod agreement. She would tell Crystal later about Sir James, but only if she had to. It might still be possible to get Crystal to return with her to the farm. Then her father would be able to buy the farm, and everything would be all right.

'Then how did *you* end up here?' Crystal asked.

'I asked some geezer in an inn if he knew how I might find you, but he had plans for me.' She shuddered. 'Ooh, Crystal! He was really horrible. It was one of those places near the quay, where the roughest sailors find their sport. He wanted me to . . .'

'. . . to become a prostitute.' Crystal ended her sentence quietly for her.

'I was scared, Crystal, really scared! He was clouting me, and I was shouting, and then along comes this lady and asks me if I'm all right. No, I tells her, I'm *not* all right! This geezer's trying to get me into the game, and I don't want none of that. So she says, "Don't you have no ma and pa, then?" I couldn't say anything, because they might have found out what pa did to you and he could have been punished. So I said I was an orphan. She brought me here.'

Lottie had begun to cry childishly throughout this recital, and Crystal realised that life in the city must be fraught with dangers for young girls like herself.

'I did think of running away. That door there in

garden, where you hang the washing, it leads out into Lodge Street.'

'Yes, I know about the door, it's frequently unlocked. But is it worth attempting to escape? Surely, without money, you would find yourself in the same position again?'

'No fear! But everyone knows these clothes. I wouldn't get beyond the bottom of the hill.'

The unmistakable tread on the stairs warned the girls that Miss Pennington was almost upon them. So absorbed in their talk were they that they had forgotten to listen out for footsteps.

'Quick, Lottie, hide!' she entreated, and helped her to scramble into one of the wash-tubs. She herself tried to shrink into a corner, but a cursory search would reveal her presence. She stood rooted to the spot, and could only gaze with fascinated horror as Miss Pennington's vast bulk filled the doorway.

'So I find you here, Smith, idling away your time!' Her voice did not hold its usual rasp, but was slightly slurred. 'To whom were you talking?' she asked.

'You mistake, Miss Pennington. I was checking the duties I have for tomorrow. Perhaps I was talking aloud.' She envinced a composure she was far from feeling.

'Who is with you?' Miss Pennington swayed, but rapped out the question so quickly that Crystal was in danger of blurting out the truth.

'No one. I like being alone.'

'So, Madam likes this privacy, does she?' Miss Pennington sneered, and fingered the cane suspended from her waist.

Much as Crystal was afraid of the rod, she feared much more that Lottie would be discovered, and punished. 'Yes, I like this privacy. I would like to remain, if you do not object.' She gambled desperately that this contrary woman would take exception to her words and contradict her.

'Get above stairs at once, you insolent slut! I shall teach you to dictate your preferences to me.'

Crystal ran clumsily up the stairs on her wooden

pattens, and was followed by the panting and wheezing Superintendent.

The inmates were brought down from their dormitories and assembled in the dining-room. Several looks of sympathy were directed at Crystal as she stood passively at the lectern. Her stomach churned with sick fear, for she sensed that this was the prelude to a punishment. The Superintendent's steely glare settled on the inmates, and they shuffled into a straight line. The silence was uneasy.

'You will pray while Smith is being chastised.' Miss Pennington now slurred her words quite noticeably. 'She is lazy as well as wanton, and we will not tolerate such vices in our midst.' She glanced down, noticing that Crystal had something in her apron pocket, and swooped to seize the piece of candied fruit. 'A thief as well! This passes all bounds! Your punishment is doubled, you wicked girl!'

As the blows fell about her shoulders with sickening regularity, Crystal resolved that she would not give this sadistic woman the pleasure of hearing her cry out. Never had she been so glad of the stoic lessons she had learned from the patient Indian people. When she saw Lottie's white agonised face, she willed her to stay silent. It would be pointless for them both to suffer.

'It is only through pain that we can truly appreciate goodness,' grunted Miss Pennington.

Crystal's world was coloured with pain, and she began to lose consciousness.

'Stop it! Stop it! I done it, ma'am! I done it!' Lottie shrieked, and ran forward. She was on her knees before Miss Pennington. 'Please don't hit her again! I stole the sweet, and gave to her. She's hungry.'

Lottie's action seemed to drag Miss Pennington from her frenzy, and she regarded her through a sweat-drenched haze. 'How noble of you, child, to try to protect this miscreant! But I know she is guilty, and even out of such generous motives, you must never lie.' She looked at the kneeling Lottie and then out at the assembled company, aware that she had punished Crystal with unwonted severity. There was a mutinous look about the shorn heads, bowed with accustomed deference, and the staff wore gently entreating looks, for they knew that even a deserved punishment was followed by a period of difficult behaviour. Miss Pennington's anger towards Crystal flared anew, for she felt that the evil girl had placed her in this position.

Crystal endured many lonely weeks as a consequence of that punishment. Her days became a monotonous round of work unalleviated by the exercise the inmates were allowed every Sunday afternoon after church. If Miss Pennington could have denied her the attendance at church, she would have done, but Miss Roberts had wondered what the trustees would have to say if they found out. It was Miss Roberts who insisted that Crystal be allowed to take some exercise in the garden, on Sunday afternoons, with the others.

'I cannot think it right that Smith should be confined exclusively to the laundry-rooms,' she told the Superintendent. 'She is beginning to look ill, and I am wondering what we should tell the trustees if she were to die.'

Miss Pennington was much impressed by this, and it occurred to her that she had better attempt to find an employer for Crystal. She knew of several families who were going abroad, and decided to make some enquiries among them.

October was unusually cold, with the chill winds carrying tiny flakes of snow. But despite the need to huddle into thick cloaks, the inmates breathed more deeply and freely when the door clanged behind them. The short walk to church, in pairs, was an opportunity for prospective employers to vet the women and girls discreetly. Then they would sit with the Superintendent in her sitting-room overlooking the back garden, and when they had satisfied her as to the honesty of their intentions, she would summon up the chosen girl from the garden, who would go quickly and quietly to freedom and a new life. Goodbyes were never exchanged.

The sermon, this Sunday, had dealt with the terrors of revolution and the need to accept gracefully the decisions made by the authorities. Many glances of trepidation were cast back and forth among the sombre congregation, and anxious murmurs arose from the crowd who streamed out into the cold bright day.

They were waiting to cross the road, when their attention was distracted by the sound of many tramping feet and the chanting of rough male voices. There was a grim determined quality about the men who marched in an endless procession from every alley and side street and joined the main body of marchers in the broad thoroughfare of Park Row. An excitement ran among the inmates as the men began to chant of reform, for any diversion was welcome in their monotonous world. These ragged men bore no arms, Crystal observed, nothing except a bitter resolve to reform Parliament. They would be annihilated!

'Do not be afraid, Lottie!' The girl was shivering, and pressed close to Crystal. 'We shall be indoors and safe in a few minutes.'

'It's him! That man I told you about. You remember!' She sounded impatient, and more like her old self. 'The man with the inn who wanted me to work for him.'

'What of it?' Crystal tried to sound casual, but the well-dressed man who was regarding Lottie was doing so with such a fixed expression that there was little doubt that he recognised her.

'Help me, Crystal! Don't let him take me away!' Lottie sounded desperate.

'I cannot understand why he should wish to force an unwilling girl into prostitution, when there must be dozens of willing girls!'

Lottie spoke with the wisdom of the streets. 'Because I'm young and plump and healthy. And, being up from the country, he reckons I'm a virgin.'

Crystal did not seriously suppose that such a man, for all his smart appearance, would have the temerity to approach the morally upright Superintendent.

The afternoon was drawing to a close, and the light was fading as the inmates continued their walk in the garden. They were silent, only raising a head from time to time as distant rumbles echoed about their enclosed world. They sounded like the floundering of a great

wooden ship in a storm. Crystal thought, as she frequently did, of that journey to England with Sir James
Allenwood. How she missed him! Miss Jackson must
have been unhinged by grief, she thought, otherwise she
would not have acted in the extraordinary way she had in
bringing here to this place. Little could she know that a
world without Sir James was not one in which she cared
to live. The Home for Fallen Women and Wayward
Girls was a haven of sorts: she disliked the monotony
and the isolation of her work, but she did not want to
communicate with anyone. Sooner or later Miss Pennington must find her an employer, for no one stayed in
the institution indefinitely.

A tap on the window caused all heads to look up, and,
to their horror, Crystal and Lottie saw that the well-
dressed man was beside the Superintendent, who was
beckoning with a crooked finger to Lottie.

'I can't, Crystal! I just can't!' Lottie was almost
incoherent with fear.

The lethargy and depression that had held Crystal in
its grip for almost seven months, making her the passive
victim of fate, fell away in seconds, and her brain worked
swiftly. The door in the wall was close to the house, so it
was possible that the Superintendent might not see if it
was opened. Indeed, so certain was she that her summons would be obeyed that she had withdrawn from the
window. Praying that the door would be open, Crystal
fumbled with the latch, but her hands were so cold that
her movements were stiff and clumsy. Miraculously the
door swung inwards, and Crystal bundled Lottie out.

'You must hurry down the street, over the bridge and
into Queen Square. Find the house of Mr Jackson, it is
number . . . Oh! I cannot recollect, but it is about five or
six houses along, on the first side of the square as you
enter. It has a black front door with a brass knocker. He
will help you.'

Lottie was gone in an instant, her grey cloak merging
with the dusky light. There was every chance that she
would reach her destination before the alarm was raised,
and with so much unrest in the city, she would be
unnoticed. In the meantime, Crystal planned to take her

place. If she were to go upstairs as slowly as possible, perhaps she could pretend that she thought *she* had been summoned, talk to the man, anything that would gain time for Lottie. If she ran all the way, and she was certain to do that, she could be in Queen Square in fifteen minutes. If they had both run away together, they would certainly be noticed. It was doubtful if they would get to the bottom of the hill without being returned. Miss Jackson might be in Queen Square, and while she would certainly repulse Crystal and bring her back to the institution, she must help Lottie. In any case, unlike Crystal, Lottie had a home to go to and someone who cared about her welfare. It had been a source of great disappointment to Crystal that Marcus Jackson had not attempted to find her. He could have done so quite easily, she convinced herself. Having taken the trouble to purchase her, lodge her in his house, arrange for the housekeeper to return, it seemed very strange that he had accepted her disappearance without a murmur. Unless his sister Sophia, anxious to prevent Crystal ever seeing him again, had told him that she had gone away.

She could delay no longer, and pulling the hood of her cloak about her face, she went slowly up the stairs.

CHAPTER THIRTEEN

BY THE TIME Crystal knocked on the door of Miss Pennington's sitting-room, she judged that Lottie should have reached the quay and be on her way to the bridge. From there on it ought to be easier for her to escape notice, for as well as the growing darkness, there would be many more people in the centre of the city. The sitting-room was small, over-furnished, but very cosy; deep armchairs stood before a cheerful fire, and on the small table by Miss Pennington's chair was a bottle of port and a half-full glass. Her companion, the well-dressed man, lay back in his chair, feet crossed at the ankles, holding his glass and eagerly watching the door.

'This is not the one!' he spluttered, and rose from the chair, his carefully cultivated accent deserting him. 'It's the little plump fair one I want. Bring up the other one.'

Miss Pennington's lips thinned ominously. 'What foolishness is this, Smith? You know very well I meant Lottie Monker to come up here. This man is prepared to offer her employment as a cook.'

Frantic to gain time for Lottie, Crystal pushed back her hood and adopted a coquettish air. 'Take me instead, sir. I can do most things better than Lottie! You would find me a very willing girl, sir.' She achieved a wink.

Setting down his glass, he clasped his hands behind his back, a smile spreading across his florid face. 'You have the looks, my dear, I'll grant you that, but you are a trifle tall, and too old.' Seeing that Miss Pennington was regarding him with some astonishment, he hastened to explain. 'The kitchen is very small, and the lady with whom she would be working has a preference for young girls, as they are easier to train. Older girls are too proud and headstrong.'

Crystal flashed him her most radiant smile, and swung her hips provocatively as she ran her fingers through her thick curls. The man smirked in involuntary appreciation as she dimpled at him and pirouetted about the room. It was a pity she was so refined and well spoken, he thought with regret; she was bound to have connections somewhere who could make life very difficult for him if they chose. Now the other one—a nice plump little blond with no family to bother him!

'This girl would never do for your needs,' Miss Pennington said sharply. 'She is of unsavoury morals and would be a bad influence on others. I cannot understand her extraordinary behaviour now, although it saddens me to say that I am not surprised.'

'I don't know that I couldn't find a place for her.' He smiled, beginning to respond to Crystal, who judged that Lottie must have reached Queen Square, so that she could now end her little charade.

'Go down and fetch up Lottie,' snapped the Superintendent. But before Crystal could obey, she frowned suspiciously and moved to the window. 'Where is she?'

'Gone!' Crystal was triumphant and felt more alive than she had done for many months. 'She is gone to lay information with the magistrate that you are attempting to sell her into prostitution with this man.' She had endured months of torment at the hands of this woman, and now had ample revenge when she saw her jaw drop and a look of ludicrous dismay replace the habitual frown.

The innkeeper shifted uneasily, and glanced furtively at Miss Pennington. In the normal run of things, no magistrate would believe any tale told him by an inmate from here, but this tall, beautiful girl with the manners and speech of some high-born lady was a different proposition. She might have friends in high places . . . He could feel trouble in his bones. He made a handy few guineas from sailors, by selling them girls who were taken on board ship and never seen again. One like this would wreck his lucrative trade! Regretfully, he decided to cross the Home for Fallen Women and Wayward Girls off his recruiting-list. Old Pennington was a greedy fool, but she would never let him purchase girls if she knew what he did to them!

'I think I'll leave you now, Miss Pennington, and let you resolve your domestic problems.' He bowed himself, hat in hand, urbanely from the room.

A dreadful fear overcame the Superintendent: what if there should be something in the girl's tale? She had not missed the furtive expression on the swift departure of the man. It was preposterous, of course! She had seen the way the slut had paraded herself and attempted to entice him, but he, good soul, had not given in to her lures. The city was in turmoil, so if Lottie Monker had gone out alone and unattended, she would be in danger; what bothered Miss Pennington much more was the thought that a magistrate might arrive at any moment to investigate her activities. Her books and her actions were all above reproach, but Smith, the author of this misfortune, would not escape her just deserts.

A tense calm filled Crystal as she walked the length of the dining-room to the dais where Miss Pennington awaited her. Many of the inmates looked fearfully at her as they carried their bowls of gruel to the long wooden table. She recalled that Lottie had told her that the staff ate roast beef, rich puddings and wholesome bread. Poor little Lottie! Had she reached Queen Square?

Miss Pennington surveyed her flock with a benign expression, and lightly swished the birch cane against the skirts of her gown. It was the only sound in the room: no one moved, not even to smooth down an apron. 'There is one who cannot be with us, for, as you know, she left us today,' she said pleasantly, softly even, but her words reverberated around the oak-panelled room. 'We have word that riotous mobs are roaming the streets, beating up decent people, some of whom have been murdered. Many of our finer buildings have been set on fire, and carriages attacked. We very much fear that our poor Lottie Monker is dead.' She paused, and did nothing to check the horrified murmuring that ran about the room. Crystal felt an almost crippling wave of nausea. Then Miss Pennington pointed her cane at her. 'I denounce this viper, for she sent poor foolish Lottie to her death! Even now the child might be safe among us. This agent of Satan who, not content with her own wicked ways, sought the destruction of another, shall be punished.'

Miss Pennington did not say how she had come by her information concerning Lottie, or offer any prayers for the repose of her soul. If Lottie was dead, Crystal must accept some responsibility; they had received the most incoherent reports from Miss Roberts and Miss Evans, both of whom had gone out to look for the missing girl. A drunken mob had harangued passers-by in Park Street, and large gangs rampaged in Queen Square, where the new Recorder was lodging with the Lord Mayor.

'Take off your apron and unbutton your bodice, Smith, and approach the lectern.' The Superintendent tapped the lectern with its spreading eagle wings. 'Pull down her dress, Miss Roberts, and bind her wrists to the lectern.' Miss Pennington's acolyte ran to obey these commands, but with a look of such acute distress on her indeterminate features that Crystal pitied her.

Crystal was glad that her back was turned to the inmates, for their wretched looks pained her unbearably. Above the hammering of her heart she thought she could hear the regular thud of hammering on the outside door, but it was distant, as distant as the fading rumbles of the mob in retreat. Miss Evans had said that Dragoons had been called in to patrol the streets and keep order.

'Do not move,' Miss Pennington warned the half-naked and bound girl. 'Stay quiet, all of you.' For there was a restless shuffling in the neat grey ranks.

'Superintendent, I believe that there is someone at the door. It may be news of Lottie, or of the riot!' Miss Roberts was flustered.

'The riot is no concern of ours!' boomed Miss Pennington majestically. 'We must conduct this business first; then we shall deal with the riot.' She was not going to be cheated of this moment, for this girl had richly earned her punishment and she, Agatha Pennington, was going to make sure that she was justly punished. She was sorry for Lottie, but relieved that she had not laid information against the institution. She had seen the excitement in the faces of the sluts when they had been told that rampaging mobs were behaving disgracefully: they had thought that their hour of easy freedom had come! Disgust was her chief emotion when she learned that women had been among the militant riff-raff who roared their vile abuse at the new Recorder when he has arrived in Bristol.

In some obscure way, she was punishing the rabble when she punished Crystal. As she looked at her pale back, still marred by marks of the earlier chastisement, she could see the stupid ugly faces of the mob, and that the same rebellious spirit that fortified the rabble was sustaining this girl. Silly Miss Roberts had run from the room.

Crystal noticed with revulsion that Miss Pennington appeared to be enjoying herself, for her eyes gleamed and sweat beaded her upper lip. A whiff of heavy body-odour mingled with the aroma of port exuded from her body, and Crystal heard the woman's corset creak as she raised a stout arm to bring the cane across her naked back. She clenched her bound wrists and willed herself not to cry out. When Indian women gave birth, they were trained for months beforehand not to cry out. They entered a trance-like state so that the mind was in control of the body; the belief was that if the child was born to the sound of its mother weeping and wailing, it would learn that life was not a joyful business and would have no desire to overcome the trauma of birth. Crystal firmly believed that she would overcome this ordeal safely if she controlled herself and did not cry out. A great pounding in her head, sorrow for Lottie, her humiliation, all combined almost to overset her. A clamouring at the door reminded her of another clamouring many years ago when the soldiers had come to her home. It seemed as though every noise and sensation of her entire life had compounded in that moment to bind her physically and emotionally to that spot.

The commotion at the door increased, and she could clearly distinguish Miss Roberts' reedy voice squawking in protest as the handle rattled loudly. Booted feet came pounding the length of the dining-room.

'Touch her, and I will kill you with my bare hands!' Crystal dared not turn round, for she knew that voice —knew it and loved it—but was afraid it was an illusion that had come to taunt her. She had believed that Sir James Allenwood was dead, and Miss Jackson had confirmed her belief! Had she induced a trance so deep that she could imagine the voice of her love?

The birch was torn from Miss Pennington's nerveless fingers by the tall dark man who seemed to dwarf even that great room. For a moment, she thought that Lottie must have indeed informed against her, and that retribution had arrived in the shape of this angry man. Never had she witnessed such cold fury in any eyes before, or felt so close to being physically assaulted.

'I am perfectly entitled to chastise any inmate,' she had started to babble, but he was not listening. He was untying the girl, and kissing her and caressing her in the most abandoned fashion! He cradled her in his arms, her curly head pressed close to his chest, while he buttoned up her dress. Miss Pennington's confidence began to return, and she decided to reassert her temporarily lost authority. 'Smith is an inmate of this institution, and, whoever you are, get out and leave her to me, for she is . . .'

Miss Pennington's speech was cut short in mid-sentence, for the madman—he must be a madman! —had rounded on her with dangerously glittering eyes, his face a mask of fury.

'This lady is my future wife. I shall take her from here this instant!' He picked up the birch cane and snapped it in one swift movement. 'You are a disgusting old harpy, and I can promise you that you will be relieved of your duties within twenty-four hours. I do not advise you to be within the city boundaries then, for I shall make it my personal business to hound you from Bristol and ensure that you never hold such an office again!'

Miss Pennington's mouth slackened with dismay as she saw how these words were greeted with looks of unholy joy by the inmates. Even Miss Roberts and Miss

Evans looked primly relieved. When Sir James picked the girl up in his arms and strode to the door, they ran ahead to hold it open for him. Crystal and Sir James left amid the deafening cheers of the assembled women.

Crystal was with Sir James in the library of his house in Queen Square, sitting before an enormous fire. Warmth and happiness made her giddy, and she barely felt the wound dealt by the single blow of the cane. He had asked her to marry him!

'Promise me that you will never leave me again.' He was serious, although he caressed her with increasing urgency.

'It is you who must promise not to leave *me*!' she implored him.

His grip tightened. 'When I learned of your ordeals in the home of that man Monker, I could have whipped *him*! But he fell from the roof of one of his barns and will never again walk. I could not turn him out, even though I privately thought that fate had served him well for his treatment of you. He had entered into some sort of agreement with Sophia . . .' He spoke with reluctance, for his pride had been wounded when he learned of the way in which Sophia had been prepared to deceive him.

'Do not speak of these things if they give you pain.' Love had made Crystal perceptive.

'No, I wish you to know everything. She would not admit that she had any part in your disappearance. I searched everywhere, put notices in the paper!' Crystal could imagine the depths of his love, and was thrilled. Any sort of notoriety would be repugnant to a man of his proud reserve. 'Sophie told me that she had given you a sum of money, at your request, to return to Brazil. I thought that you had returned to the mission at São Paulo, and went there.'

'You saw Father Superior?'

'Yes. He told me that my love for you would be the salvation of my soul,' he said drily, but chuckled. 'Damned impertinence! That swain of yours, Brother

Michael, was no better, and I was glad to escape the pair of them. They promised me that they would pray for your safe keeping! Oh, Crystal, you cannot imagine my suffering, thinking that you might be dead, or, worse still, trying to survive alone. The Stewarts were kindness itself, and . . .'

'You went to Port-of-Spain?' she said wonderingly.

'I seemed to have searched the whole world! And to think that all the time you were a mile away! Why did you not come to me? Did you think I would cast you off?' There was anger in his voice, but she could sense the anguish beneath his words.

'Miss Jackson told me you were dead. I did not care what happened to me after that!' she was stung into retorting.

'I hope her earl turns out to be pot-bellied and cross-eyed!'

'Is she married to an earl? Mr Jackson did mention something about . . .' she paused delicately, not wishing to give him further pain.

'Not yet. She is hoping to be married within the month. We had decided that we should not suit. I had already given her ample cause to believe that! If only I had gone to you that morning, and not to Henbury, we should both have been spared this pain. I knew then, oh, for months before that, that you were the only woman for me, that life with you was the life I wanted above all other things.'

'When Miss Jackson told me you were dead, I went with her without resistance, for I did not care what befell me. She had some idea that I wished to marry her brother.'

'Such nonsense! It seems that she wrote to Captain Hastings, giving her consent to the match, but, by that time, he had discovered some correspondence between Arabella and Marcus, and was vastly displeased, I can tell you!'

Crystal turned to look more fully at him, easing herself slightly away from the curve of his arm. 'I do hope that they are allowed to marry, for I believe that Arabella exercises a most desirable effect on him.'

He threw back his head and laughed. 'You are behind the times, my love! They *are* married, and their first child will be born before our own!' He pulled her back to him, and began to kiss her cheek and neck.

A light tap on the door preceded the entrance of Mrs Hennessy. If she had found anything odd in the appearance of a shabby girl in a rough grey dress and with cropped hair presented to her as the future Lady Allenwood, she had not shown it. Until the arrival of Lottie Monker earlier that evening, she had never known her master in such despair: he had become haggard in his obsessive search for Crystal. Many times she had heard his friends implore him to give up the search—the girl must be dead, or not wanting to be discovered, they told him. Would he let the matter rest? Not he! Lottie Monker she wrote off as a trollop; she knew her sort! But the news she had relayed to Sir James had caused him to kiss the trollop and present her with a purse! He had then ridden off immediately, only pausing to give orders that Lottie be restored to her reprobate father at once. Such goings-on! And with the city on the point of rebellion, and that nice colonel with the smart blue and yellow uniform—such a real handsome gentleman!— haunting the house day and night. What does Sir James do? Nothing! Only sit on the sofa with the girl with a radiant face, talking and murmuring as though he had not a care in the world! Anyone who could bring that change to her beloved master could be sure of being loved by Mrs Hennessy, although neither of them had done more than nibble at the delicious dinner she had taken such pains over. That, too, would be put right tomorrow, for she was not going to stand for that sort of nonsense! No world was ever won on an empty stomach.

'I beg your pardon, Sir James, but Colonel Brereton is here again. Says he is very sorry to insist, but he must speak with you urgently.'

Reluctantly Sir James withdrew his arm, and got to his feet after dropping a kiss on Crystal's head. 'What can he want at this hour?'

'I'm sure I couldn't say, sir. It may have something to do with the crowd that's gathered outside Mayor

Pinney's house.' There was only the suggestion of tartness in her voice.

'Right. I had better go and speak to him. Crystal, will you wait up for me?' He had looked down at her with longing in his face, as though he begrudged even a few minutes away from her.

'She'll not be able to do that, sir, for you can see that she's near dropping with fatigue. Whatever it is you wish to say to Miss Smith can wait till morning.' Purposefully assisting Crystal to rise from the sofa, Mrs Hennessy bore her from the room before Sir James could protest.

She had slept deeply, and awoke refreshed, her body tingling with memories of the evening before. Pushing back the bedcovers, she ran to the window and looked down into a now empty square. Thank goodness! The crowd had evidently dispersed, there would be no further trouble. The water in the jug was warm and a small fire burned bright in the grate; she must have slept very well indeed not to have heard the sound of Mrs Hennessy making these preparations! Pulling on the grey serge dress, she made a hasty toilet, anxious to find Sir James. Mrs Hennessy had thoughtfully provided a pair of slippers for her, as her clumsy pattens had been removed the previous evening.

Disappointment almost made her cry out when she was told that Sir James had left the house hours earlier.

'And I don't know when he'll return, miss. There's bad trouble brewing. This'll be a black Monday, unless I'm much mistaken.' These grim words from the housekeeper accompanied the mundane task of serving Crystal with a belated but excellent breakfast.

'But the crowd have gone! There is no one in the Square. Look for yourself.'

'They haven't dispersed, but have gone to the Assize Court. The new Recorder goes there this morning to open the Assize.'

'Will that mean trouble?' Crystal was instantly fearful that something might happen to Sir James; she could not bear the thought that something might occur to destroy her new-found happiness.

'They were drunk and belligerent, for they have no

cause to love him. The Dragoons are standing by. Yes, there'll be trouble.'

Crystal said eagerly, 'Surely, if the Dragoons are present, they will prevent any trouble?'

'They would, if they were allowed to act! It seems, from what the Colonel was telling Sir James—not that I was listening, mind you!' She coloured, and looked away from Crystal's twinkling gaze. 'Anyway . . . it seems that Mayor Pinney won't give any orders, not any orders that the Colonel can act on! I ask you! If there *is* trouble, the first thing folks will say is: "And why didn't the army do anything?" Poor young man! My heart goes out to him.'

Trouble or no trouble, Mrs Hennessy was not to be deterred from her visit to the market, and Crystal wandered disconsolately round the house, bored and anxious by turns. Every time she fancied she heard a step or a carriage, she ran to the window. The very quiet seemed ominous: a pale sun struggled through a gradually lowering sky, but by twelve o'clock gave up the unequal effort and retired behind grey clouds.

A sharp rapping on the front door sent her spirits soaring and her feet flying to obey that summons. It must be Sir James. How much she had to say to him! Patting her curls into order and smoothing down her skirts, she opened the door. The happy smile of welcome froze on her lips, for there, trim and elegant, clad in a sable cloak, carrying a huge sable muff and with a martial light sparkling in her violet eyes, was Miss Jackson.

'Is Sir James at home? Pray tell him that I am here.' She stepped past a bemused Crystal into the hall, where she cast off her cloak and muff.

'No, he has had to go out, but I expect him to return directly. What is your business with him?' Crystal said faintly, terrified of the answer.

'Under normal circumstances I should deplore that impertinence, but as my being here is to do with your presence in this house, I shall tell you.'

Sophia went into the small sitting-room at the back of the house, where Mrs Hennessy had lit a fire. With every appearance that she was the mistress of the establishment, she sat down by the fire. Wonderingly, Crystal looked at her, for she seemed more beautiful and self-possessed than ever, and doubt began to stab her happy bubble of self-confidence. How on earth could Sir James prefer her to this lovely woman, so much his equal?

'I have heard from Miss Pennington all that transpired last evening,' began Miss Jackson in her clear voice. 'I am grievously shocked that he should behaved so ill towards one who is a pillar of the community. James has told me his opinion of my behaviour towards yourself. I cannot share it.' She eyed Crystal coldly, and did not invite her to sit. 'I can only say that I have no regrets about the way I behaved. My sole aim when I placed you in the Home for Fallen Women and Wayward Girls, a place where you belong, was to protect the interests of those I loved. Today I have come to entreat him to give up all association with you before he is ruined. He has already made himself a laughing-stock with his pursuit of you. Doubtless his adventures in the West Indies unhinged his mind—that is how his friends have accounted for his extraordinary behaviour. I am prepared to reconsider my decision, and marry him.'

'But he has asked *me* to marry him,' Crystal blurted out.

'*You!* I knew that he was temporarily besotted, but this passes all bounds!' Sophia said with disgust.

'We love each other!' Crystal was desperate to make her understand.

'Love? You do not know the meaning of the word! If you did, you would assuredly give him up at once.'

Sophia's tone of pity rather than the contempt she had shown moments earlier alarmed her anxious listener. Rising gracefully, she crossed to stand before Crystal and took her trembling hand. 'You think me very cruel, but indeed I am prompted by affection for Sir James when I speak. You *must* end your association with him. You can do nothing but harm to him. If you love him, truly love him, do you wish to see him ostracised by his equals?

'He loves me,' persisted Crystal, but she was less sure of herself.

'He thinks he does, that is all. How long do you think such love lasts? For I take it that, by love, he means that he desires you? What happens when he no longer physically desires you? He would be quite alone; no person of birth or breeding would dare to befriend him. His love would then turn to loathing, for you would be to blame.'

These words of reason fell like a cold rain. Could they be true? 'I recall that Miss Allenwood once told me that all these barriers could be overcome with a little resolution.' The thought of her friend warmed Crystal and lent her courage.

'Oh, *you* may be as resolute as you please! If it makes you happy to pursue such a course, then do so, but we are speaking of Sir James. And Miss Allenwood, as you recall, had no friends.'

'That is not true!' Crystal was stung in defence.

'How many callers did she have?' The quiet question gave Crystal pause. 'There might have been many who professed to admire her conduct, but she stepped outside the boundaries of her own station, and she died alone and friendless.'

Everything she said was true! With dismay, Crystal was forced to acknowledge the reason in her words. Her love would never be enough to sustain her husband through the years to come.

Seeing the unhappiness in Crystal's eyes, Sophia squeezed her trembling hands. 'Do not think that I do not sincerely pity you, for I do. You love Sir James, and for the time being he believes he loves you, but it will not suffice. There cannot be many who do not know of your unhappy history; while they may feign sympathy, they would be grievously shocked if Sir James were to ally himself with such a one as you. Can you bear to think of his pride humbled?'

So sincerely did she speak that Crystal could feel tears coming to her eyes. 'I recall, once, that my foster-mother told me I should cross water, and marry and find happiness,' she murmured.

Abruptly releasing her hands, Sophia turned away in

scorn. 'The prophecy of a savage! Is that what you would base your happiness upon? How very foolish! The Allenwoods are a very old and proud family. Sir James might be immensely rich, but his wealth would not be a sufficient cloak for your adventures, Miss Smith. Even if you were the most innocent victim of circumstance, how do you think the world would regard an Allenwood bride who had been reared among savages? Would they be amused to discover that you had been the subject of a public auction? Would they tolerate in their midst an ex-inmate of the Home for Fallen Women and Wayward Girls? If you think that Sir James does not value the affection and respect of his friends, you do not know him.'

Crystal's brain was in a whirl: she could not deny the truth of Sophia's words, whatever might have motivated her to speak thus.

'I am sure you will know how to answer Sir James, for I believe you value his happiness as much as I do. I am sorry for any pain that I must have given you, but I am persuaded that, given time for reflection, you must arrive at the same conclusion. No, do not move. I shall see myself out. You may mention that I called, if you wish. But perhaps you would prefer James to think that you took the right and noble course of action of your own volition.'

For long after Miss Jackson had departed, Crystal remained in the small sitting-room, her mind numb, her feelings in chaos. She loved Sir James! That was the crux of the matter. If she really loved him and cared about his welfare, she must give him up. Had he not said that he would never help her to enter English society? Had he not questioned her motives? His love might blind him to the realities of her situation, but he had not always loved her, and when he had not loved her, he had spoken the truth. She would go away—far away. When he had thought her quite disappeared, he had searched for her at the mission at São Paulo, so she would return there, certain that she would find a haven. She wanted no more of England!

There came a hasty step in the hall, and Sir James

flung open the door. A light blazed in his eyes as they
rested on her, and with a hoarse, inarticulate cry he
gathered her into his arms and began to kiss her hungri-
ly. Fearing that the treacherous response of her undis-
ciplined body might betray her and weaken her resolve,
she pushed him away. 'Please do not touch me! I cannot
bear it!' She broke off in distress and turned away. How
could she explain that she no longer wished to marry
him, when his merest touch turned her blood to flame?

Mistaking her action for disgust, he dropped his
hands, and regarded her back with consternation. What
on earth had occurred to change the vital loving creature
of yesterday?

Clasping her hands, and not daring to face him, she
spoke with constraint. 'I am sorry if I misled you last
evening, but I cannot marry you. I have no wish to be
married at all. Truly, I am grateful to you for rescuing
me, but I mistook gratitude for love.'

'To hell with your gratitude!' He turned her to face
him, and grasping her roughly by the shoulders,
demanded an explanation.

Willing herself to find the right words, words that
would permanently repulse him, she closed her eyes and
made ineffectual efforts to push him away. His proximity almost overcame her resolve, but she loved him, and
must spare him the consequences of his own misguided
actions.

'It is not kind of you to use me so. You take advantage
of my defenceless position in your house to force your
attentions on me. I had to endure such attentions from
Jake Monker, but I did not expect you to behave in a like
manner.' She had the satisfaction of seeing her words
strike home, for his hands fell to his sides, clasped in fists
of helpless rage. With whitened face and bewildered
eyes he watched her. How she longed to comfort him, to
tell him how much this sacrifice was costing her! In a few
seconds she had thrown away her hopes of happiness.
No other man would ever win her heart, for it was
irretrievably lost to the man who confronted her.

'I wish I could relieve you of my presence, madam. I
have no wish to remind you of Monker. If you believe

that we are similar in some way, you have only yourself to blame. He said that you had led him to believe that you had some affection for him, and that caused him to behave in the way he did. Do you realise that I almost killed him for that? Thank heaven that fate intervened to prevent my carrying out a gross act of injustice.' The haggard look had returned to his face and the lines about his mouth were deeply etched; the light in his eyes had dulled, and she felt her heart contract with pain. She must keep up her resolve, for one day he would thank her for her present action.

'If it could be arranged, I would like to leave as soon as possible.' She walked away from him, terrified that her feelings would show in her face. He must never guess that she still loved him!

'Before we settle anything, you must explain yourself. You cannot tell me that you will not marry me. I *cannot* accept it.' There was such a note of pleading beneath the harshness that her defences all but crumbled. Why could he not accept what she said? Why did he insist on explanations? Drawing a deep breath, she spoke heedlessly. 'My recent experience has left me with a distaste for any physical contact with you. I could never be a wife . . .'

In a few swift strides he was at her side. 'What a brute I have been, my darling! Of course, I should have realised! I shall be tender with you, for you are more precious to me than anything else. Consider! You have had the most vile experiences, you are frightened. Do you think that I, above all others, would wish to frighten you more?' He attempted to take her in his arms, convinced of the power of his own love to overcome her alarm.

Stiffening, she removed herself from his reach. 'You have not understood. It is you who cause this revulsion in me! It will never change, I am convinced of that.'

'I see,' he said without expression. A muscle twitched at the side of his face, and his eyes held an odd blank look that frightened her. 'Then there is nothing left to say. I respect your decision, and we shall not refer to this matter again.' Sighing deeply as though to expel something unpleasant from his system, he strove to resume his more normal manner. 'You spoke of wishing to leave, but that is impossible.'

'But I must!' She was aghast, and raised a hand to her breast, consternation on her face. How could she remain another instant in this house, having just made that most final of pronouncements?

'The city is in riot. The mob stoned the Recorder when he went to open the Assize, and the troops are being mobilised. It would not be safe for you to venture out.'

It would be more unsafe for her to remain! What a stupid moment she had chosen to tell him that she would not marry him! What on earth was she to do?

Misreading her consternation, he laughed, a short bitter sound. 'Oh, don't fear that I shall force my unwilling attentions on you, Crystal. Nothing would disgust me more! You are perfectly safe.'

Mrs Hennessy bustled into the room in great agitation. 'Sir James! There is a terrible to-do in the city! The mob has gone mad! They are looting shops and burning buildings, and now they are going to burn down Bishop Grey's Palace! I heard them planning it!'

With a muffled oath, Sir James strode for the door, turning only to issue curt instructions. 'I must find Brereton, and warn him. You are to admit no one, do you understand? And you are not to venture out at all. Remain here until I return!'

CHAPTER FOURTEEN

By TEN o'clock that night, Mrs Hennessy confessed her alarm because Sir James had not returned, and she was sure that something dreadful must have befallen him. All day she had been receiving reports from a young soldier of the Third Dragoons posted outside the house. In exchange for mugs of ale and hot pasties which she thoughtfully provided, Private Arthur Brittan had told her of the plight of the Dragoons. What could they do when faced with a bunch of men and women hell-bent on the destruction of their own city? Mrs Hennessy had been dismayed to learn that the mob had stormed Bishop Grey's Palace, dragging out furniture, precious manuscripts and rare books, and burning them in a huge bonfire. After raiding the Bishop's excellent cellar, they had drunk themselves into a stupor and were consequently in an even more dangerous mood. The lack of opposition to their actions had engendered such a false courage and bravado that they talked of revolution. Colonel Brereton had seemed to think that the presence of the Dragoons only inflamed them more!

Crystal believed that Sir James had not returned because he wished to avoid her company. The more she thought of Miss Jackson's advice to her, and her own subsequent decision, the more convinced she was that she had acted rightly. She was more in love with him than ever, and therefore could not bear the prospect that marriage to her would mean that his own kind would ostracise him. Long ago, he had made his feelings quite plain: he might like Crystal, but he could never accept her as an equal. The barriers he had perceived had not ceased to exist because he now admitted that he loved her. Miss Jackson had to be acquitted of any ulterior motive, for she was to marry her earl within the month. Crystal was convinced that she had announced her own change of heart only to strengthen her argument. She

must have believed Crystal to be ignorant of the proposed alliance with an earl! Calmly Crystal tried to
consider a future without Sir James, but it caused her
almost unbearable heartache.

'Will you not go up to bed, Miss Smith? The hour is
late, and I do not think that Sir James will return now.
Perhaps he will lodge with Colonel Brereton tonight.'
Mrs Hennessy had come into the library, where Crystal
was attempting to read a book.

'I shall go up in a few minutes. I would like to . . .' She
had been going to say that she wished to read for a little
longer, to postpone the moment when she would be
alone in her room, a victim of her unhappy thoughts and
emotions.

'You want to wait up for him. How thoughtless of me!
Oh, do I hear him now? That's the Colonel's voice as
well! Good gracious me! They'll be wanting to eat. I
must go and prepare something.' She almost collided
with Sir James in the doorway. 'You must give Miss
Smith all your news, Sir James. I'll have something laid
out in the dining-room in ten minutes!'

Sir James and Colonel Brereton looked fatigued and
dejected, but despite this, the Colonel professed himself
delighted to meet Miss Smith, asked her to accept
felicitations on her future happiness, and begged her not
to think of removing herself. 'For I am certain that you
must wish to hear some news of today's events.'

In the face of such courtesy, Crystal felt it would be
boorish to hurry from the room. Secretly, she was so
relieved to see that Mrs Hennessy's fears had been
groundless that she had almost run to Sir James, but the
presence of Colonel Brereton prevented her from be-
traying herself. Besides, after her words of the morning,
it would have been unfair and inappropriate for her to
have expressed her joy. How she longed to smooth away
those lines from his face! But she flinched from the hard
angry look in his his eyes when they rested on her.

'It is all over!' She tried hard to concentrate on what
the Colonel was saying to her. 'But the fury of the mob! I
never thought to see the like of it in England.'

'You did well, Brereton, for I feared that there would

be much more bloodshed,' Sir James said with his customary reserve, as though he had once more re-treated behind a barrier of icy politeness. Crystal was distressed, knowing that she had caused this. 'When the mob charged your company, I very much feared that they might overcome them.'

'Overcome the Dragoons? Never!' The Colonel laughed at the idea. 'Most of the rioters were too drunk to stand, let alone to charge. I never felt there was much danger. Still, I shall send them out of the city in the morning.'

'Is that wise?' Sir James said, his brows snapping together.

'I think so,' the Colonel responded easily. 'If there is any lingering discontent, it will only inflame people to feel that the city is under martial law. The sooner things return to normal, the better. This day's madness will soon be forgotten.'

'I dare say you are right.'

Mrs Hennessy came to announce that she had pre-pared a dinner, of sorts, and that she would be glad if Sir James and Colonel Brereton would come and eat.

'I shall be delighted, for I am famished,' declared the Colonel, with a promptitude that delighted her.

'I shall bid you good night, Colonel Brereton,' Crystal said, rising to take her leave.

'I shall beg Allenwood for the pleasure of your com-pany for dinner tomorrow night. We have much to celebrate, and very little time. I fear that the Dragoons will have to move out of the city altogether quite soon. We have duties elsewhere.'

'That will not be possible,' Sir James said sharply, and the Colonel stared at him. 'Miss Smith leaves Bristol in the morning, and will not be returning. So you must bid her goodbye now.'

Crystal knew this must happen—she had instigated the event—but her heart was leaden as Colonel Brereton said his farewells. There was so much genuine regret in his voice that she longed to assure him that nothing would give her more pleasure than to dine with him. Preceding the men from the room, she went straight to her bedroom, and was both relieved and disappointed when Sir James made no effort to detain her.

She passed a wretched night: her few sleeping hours were pervaded by nightmares; her waking hours were made worse when she contemplated her lonely future. Although Sir James had told her that he could not live without her, there might come a time when he no longer loved her. Physical feelings could diminish. Then what? Crystal had already experienced the disgusted look on Sir James's face, and were it not for the fact that she must be thrown constantly into his company, she would have gone to Marcus and Arabella and begged them to give her a home. Now, above all times, Arabella would probably love to have some company.

Profoundly depressed and heavy-eyed, she presented a woebegone appearance at the breakfast-table. Sir James, too, looked as though he had slept badly. Crystal found herself with little appetite, yet she wished to prolong what must be their last time together. In the small hours of dawn she had formed a resolve about her future and had to discuss it with him. He would not refuse her simple request, she was sure.

'You mentioned, last night, that I am to leave this morning, Sir James.' She had summoned up courage to speak. 'Do you have any plans for me?'

'I would prefer to finish my breakfast before addressing myself to the question of your future. Besides, I am tolerably certain that you have plans of your own that you merely wish me to endorse,' he said cuttingly, and thus snubbed, she had no desire to speak further. 'I have some business to attend to, but I should be able to see you in an hour. You may come to the library then.'

His humour was no better when Crystal entered the library. Absorbed in some papers, he appeared not to notice her arrival, but the bleak expression in his eyes when he eventually raised them to her face told her that he felt equally desolate.

Throughout the harrowing events of the day before, he had gone over her extraordinary behaviour again and again. He concluded that she spoke the truth when she said that he repelled her, for no other explanation offered itself, yet he was sure that she returned his love—her delighted response to him had been so natural and spontaneous. Cursing himself for his precipitate declaration, he knew that he could not have acted otherwise. Obviously he must have frightened her, but how? Had he been too sure of himself? Had her experiences damaged her in some way? All his wealth and position could never compensate for a life without Crystal Smith. The empty loneliness that he had endured in the years after the deaths of his mother and brother would be his again. Like many proud and reserved men, he had been slow to fall in love, but when he had, it was an emotion so deep and strong that it threatened to consume him. When Crystal had rebuffed him he had been thunderstruck; a man with more experience of women might have taken her in his arms and kissed away her fears. But Sir James was too sensitive to ignore Crystal's words. Once more he must learn to hide his feelings behind a mask of cool indifference. That he must be an object of disgust to her hurt him deeply, but when she had likened him to Jake Monker, she had dealt his pride a blow from which it would be slow to recover.

Twisting her hands and looking absurdly beautiful with her fine eyes sparkling with tears, she addressed him. 'If you would give me some of Miss Allenwood's money, I should like to be sent back to the mission at São Paulo.'

'So that you can be with that damned friar?' He had never experienced jealousy until this moment; it was a powerful and hurtful emotion.

'Presumably you mean Brother Michael? Yes, I should like to go to him, for he was a good friend.' Her dignified response reproached him.

'He does not repel you, does he? When you slept in his arms, were you not afraid? Or perhaps he has some quality that I lack.' Privately he was appalled at his own words, but a demon was driving him beyond the edge of reason. Brazil! He might never see her again!

'You mistake me. I want to start an orphanage there like the one Miss Allenwood had in Westbury-on-Trym.

If I work hard, I believe I can be successful. Will you assist me?'

'Assist you to leave me? Never!'

'You must, Sir James, for I cannot marry you.' Her voice was low and troubled. 'It is not pleasant for me to have to beg from you, but I am penniless, and have no choice.'

He pushed his hand through his hair in a familiar gesture. 'Forgive me, Crystal. I cannot think why I am behaving so boorishly. Of course I will help you. It will take a day or two to sort out Vera's affairs, but her fortune is certainly yours. Also . . .'

'No, I do not want Miss Allenwood's fortune. I require only a small sum to enable me to get to Brazil and start my orphange!' she cried.

'Let us not wrangle about it. In the meantime, you could go to stay with Marcus and Arabella. I am sure that they would like that, for they have expressed a desire to see you. The carriage can be here in a few minutes. There is nothing more to say, other than that the sentiments I expressed last night have not changed, nor will they ever. It is not in my nature to pester you with declarations of love that you find unwelcome. Suffice to say that if you ever change your mind, you will find me waiting for you.'

These simply expressed words so powerfully affected Crystal that she was quite unable to reply, and with swimming eyes, she fled from the room.

In little less than an hour later, just before noon, Crystal was being warmly welcomed by a radiant Arabella and a grinning Marcus Jackson.

'Crystal! How charmingly your hair looks! Is it all the rage now? Should I have my hair cut, Marcus?'

'I love you just the way you are, silly goose!' Marcus was all love and pride.

Loath to talk of her disappointment, Crystal allowed the couple to think that she intended to marry Sir James. Later she would tell them that she was going to Brazil, but for the present she was content to be shown all the redecoration that had been carried out in Henbury

House. It was not quite the happy reunion that she had anticipated, for the evident affection that existed between the Jacksons was a constant reminder to her of what might have been. Arabella's constant references to her joy in marriage, her delight in her expectation of a happy event, all combined to lower Crystal's spirits. It was only by the exercise of iron self-control that she schooled her features into an expression of interest.

'When do you propose to marry?' Arabella demanded, as they made a tour of the garden. She was beginning to be puzzled by Crystal's lack of response to her questions. Surely it was natural for one friend to be interested in the affairs of another? This reserve was abnormal. 'Heavens! Do not tell me that Sir James did not ask you marry him?'

She blurted this out with such a look of comic dismay that Crystal laughed affectionately. 'Do not worry! He did indeed ask me.' Plucking away some leaves from a bush close at hand, she debated whether to tell Arabella about her decision. The longing to confide in someone overcame her scruples about divulging her most intimate affairs, so without relating Sophia Jackson's part, she gave Arabella her reasons for not wishing to marry Sir James.

'So please do not ask me any more questions about it, for there is nothing more to say,' Crystal ended sadly.

Private Brittan saluted Sir James Allenwood as he emerged from his house just after noon.

'Still here? I thought that the trouble was over,' Sir James said pleasantly.

'Don't reckon so, sir. I've got a feeling.' Private Brittan considered that he had said enough: he knew that this man was a friend of his Colonel. It was said that the fury of the mob had spent itself last night, but he had a soldier's instinct of impending danger. Holding his musket lightly, he glanced warily in the direction of King Street, whence came the tramp of marching feet.

'More soldiers?' Sir James raised an enquiring eyebrow.

'Don't think so, sir. Colonel didn't say nothing about soldiers coming into the city.'

'Perhaps it is some workmen to clear up the destruction.'

But the large body of men who darkened the entrance to the Square were not bent upon any such errand. The very silence with which they bore themselves was somehow more deadly than the erratic excited shouting of other mobs. There was purpose and determination on every face, and all carried iron bars or cudgels.

'Where are the other Dragoons?' asked Sir James.

'What's left of them are deployed about the entrances to this Square.'

'Gather them up, and tell them that the Recorder has fled. Instruct them to go among the mob with that story. I am going to summon the other Dragoons and the Gloucesters. In the meantime, I shall advise Mayor Pinney to seek other lodgings.'

'That lot's bent on destruction, sir! If you'll pardon me speaking my mind.'

'I know it. Tell them that they would better be employed in breaking down the doors of the prisons and relapsing their comrades.'

'Break down the doors of the prisons? That's treason, sir!'

'Perhaps. But a good deal less harmful than their present mission.' Sir James nodded at their purposeful descent on the Mayor's mansion.

His air of confident command reassured Private Brittan, who sped away to ensure that his commands were carried out. The Dragoons were pushed and jostled by the humourless crowd, who paid not the slightest attention to their pacific requests to move away.

Sir James marched into the Mayor's mansion, and demanded to see him. Upon being told that he was unwell and could receive no one, Sir James bounded up the stairs two at a time and, flinging open door after door, eventually was successful in finding his quarry. Rousing Mayor Pinney with little ceremony, he thrust a piece of paper under his nose. 'Sign this,' he commanded.

'I am unwell; my heart is not strong. I really cannot be disturbed. What is this, anyway?' demanded the flabby older man in a querulous voice. There was nothing wrong with him other than an inability to face any unpleasant reality.

'An order for reinforcements to be sent here immediately. I shall personally deliver the order, and upon my return I expect that you will have summoned the magistrates, who will give the command that the riot be put down with all speed.'

'I cannot. I will not. We are not at war! Colonel Brereton must . . .'

He got no further, for he was dragged from his bed, nightcap askew, to the window. Ruthlessly Sir James forced him to look out at the sullen men who were staring at the house with murderous intent in their eyes.

'We *are* at war,' Sir James told him.

'They are scum, riff-raff!' the Mayor exclaimed viciously. But, hand shaking, he signed the order, unable to resist the force of the dominating personality of the man who stood over him.

'And now,' Sir James said, pocketing the order, 'I want you to climb out over the rooftop and leave your house that way.'

'What?' the Mayor shrieked, outraged by such impertinence.

'If the mob can see you leaving, they will not take any action. With luck, I should be back with a company of troops within two hours. It is possible that an impressive show of military strength will be sufficient to disperse the mob without any bloodshed.'

The Mayor saw the force of these arguments, and with a pathetic attempt at dignity, said, 'Very well, but I am not going out on the roof in my nightshirt.'

Turning his head in the act of leaving the room, Sir James, lips twitching, said, 'I do not think the idea would appeal to me, either.'

When the mob glimpsed the frightened face of the Mayor at the window, they were inflamed to a collective anger. Private Brittan, struggling through a great press of bodies, was attempting to reach a huge man who appeared to be one of the leaders. If he could only persuade him to take his fellows down to the prison, it might give their thoughts another direction. There must be five or six hundred men and women gathered now, and the handful of Dragoons would be quite incapable of controlling them.

When they saw Mayor Pinney scrambling over the rooftops, they roared with laughter, and Private Brittan sighed with relief as he could feel some of the tension evaporating. But the huge man, his face grim, would not allow his efforts at revolution to peter out in the mood of hilarity that was fast taking over the mob.

Helplessly the Dragoons watched as he advanced towards the house and, pushing in the door, bade his fellows to follow him. Inside the Mayor's mansion they began an orgy of destruction that culminated in the house being set on fire. In a frenzy of excitement, the mob followed their leader to the prisons, where they proposed to follow, belatedly, the advice given them.

Returning to his home some hours later, Sir James was appalled at the scenes of destruction he had witnessed. His mission had been successful, but subject to so many delays and frustrations that he was in no humour to appreciate the difficulties surrounding the mobilisation of an army in peacetime. Himself a man of decisive action, he found the attitude prevailing among the magistrates intolerable. All the looting, burning and destruction of life and property could have been prevented by prompt action.

He turned the key in the lock, but the front door would not open. Guessing, rightly, that Mrs Hennessy must have barricaded herself in, he was obliged to call to her several times before gaining admission.

'Terrible it was, Sir James! Like madmen they were. Thank the Lord they did all their burning on that other side of the Square, for I'm sure I don't know what I'd have done if they had come here.'

Sir James was packing up important papers and

documents relating to his shipping interests, and had almost finished. 'I should have made arrangements for you to leave with Miss Smith.'

'We should all have gone with Miss Jackson.' Mrs Hennessy shuddered.

'Miss Jackson?' Sir James paused to direct a puzzled look at his housekeeper. 'What has Miss Jackson to do with all this?'

'Nothing, I should hope, Sir James, but she was here yesterday morning. You must know of it, for surely Miss Smith told you. She was just leaving in her carriage when I was on my way back with the shopping. You came to say that we couldn't leave the house. You had news —you must remember—and it went out of my head! I did not see that it was so important.'

Sir James stayed silent for several moments to digest her information: so much was now clear to him. *Sophia* must have said something to Crystal to cause her to change her mind! Silently cursing her managing ways, he vowed that he would end her interference in his affairs once and for all!

'I must despatch you to a place of safety, for you cannot remain here.' He was sitting behind his desk now, writing on a large sheet of paper.

'I'm not deserting you! No one shall make me budge from my post.' She stood before him, arms akimbo.

'I must insist, Mrs Hennessy. These papers are of the utmost importance, and I wish you to take them with you. I expect you would like to go down the coast to your sister's house?' He was relieved to see that she wavered. The trouble was much worse than he expected, and he did not wish to alarm her by telling her that the authorities feared the revolution was imminent. 'I am directing my ships to leave the port. One of them will sail down the coast, and you may board her.' He continued writing as he talked. Now that he had finished, he sanded the paper and then handed it to her. 'This is my will. You must keep it for me. I have left you a comfortable independence, and everything else I wish to become the property of Miss Crystal Smith.'

Her face quivered. 'Don't talk so, Sir James! You

sound as though you expect to be killed! Come with me!'
she entreated.

'Run away? I could not! We must stay to ensure that
this riot turns to nothing worse. Do not worry! I am quite
capable of dealing with any trouble.' Seeing the alarm in
her eyes, he grinned. 'I shall hide under the table if need
be! There, does that satisfy you?'

It did not, but she allowed herself to be escorted to the
ship, and was soon on her way.

It was not to be supposed that there could be any secrets
between such a husband and wife, and Crystal was displeased but not surprised to find that Arabella had
confided in her husband. They were sitting in the with-
drawing-room after an excellent dinner, Marcus loung-
ing at his ease before an enormous fire, Arabella and
Crystal sitting on a pretty sofa.

'You are a ninny, Crystal! Do you seriously suppose
that James did not consider all that before asking you to
marry him? Men do, you know,' Marcus said with
unwonted gravity.

'It is just as Marcus says,' interpolated Arabella. 'He
was in a dreadful way when you disappeared. Marcus
said all along that Sir James was in love with you. I am
married to the cleverest man in the world!' She
accompanied these words with looks of tenderness.

No one had ever spoken of, or thought of, Marcus
Jackson as moderately intelligent, let alone the cleverest
man in the world; he blushed, but looked gratified by his
wife's opinion. 'It was obvious by the way he looked at
you that day when you both landed in Bristol. Never saw
him smile that way at my sister.'

The mention of Miss Jackson caused Crystal to flush
and look down. Perceptively, Marcus cocked an eyebrow at his wife, who responded with a tiny nod.

'Dearest Crystal, we should not wish to pry, although
I must confess I am dying of curiosity! Marcus feels that,
perhaps, his sister might have had something to do
with your decision not to accept Sir James. Is that
so?'

Crystal became flustered; she did not wish to give the

couple any cause to think ill of their relative, but when asked directly like this, how was she to respond? Bitterly did she regret having said anything to Arabella, for it seemed that Miss Jackson must then bear all the blame for her decision to change her mind concerning her marriage to Sir James. The truth was that Miss Jackson had only put into words the thoughts that had nagged persistently at the back of Crystal's mind since Sir James's proposal. She had no name, or any clear idea of who her parents were. Until now, she had given little thought to the question; it had not seemed important. The Indian people had given her an identity, a name, a place among them. At the mission, she had been groomed to begin a new life in England, and her lack of knowledge rather than her lack of name had been of the utmost importance. It was not until she had met Sir James that she had even begun to appreciate the significance of a name and partenage. Without consulting her, he had given her the name 'Smith'; through her reading of Miss Austen's novel, she discovered that the English considered lack of parentage as sufficient grounds to preclude, absolutely, the possibility of entering into a marriage with such a person as Sir James Allenwood. Had he not endorsed that himself? She could not suppose that he had changed so completely that he was prepared to contradict the code by which he had been brought up. At first he had seemed so very much older than herself, but she had matured since she had first met him. He was reserved, which made him seem much older than his twenty-four years, but she felt that Miss Jackson could be right: what he felt now was not love, merely desire. Would he, when he was older, still be prepared to contradict the code of his own society? Would he be prepared to live with the consequences of his own rash actions? She feared not. She loved him too much to put him in that position.

'Miss Jackson did come to see me,' she began with some hesitation, trying vainly to seek the right words. 'But do not, I beg you, think that she attempted to change my mind.'

'Rubbish! I know my sister! She must have control of

everyone's life. Even though she is to marry her earl, she cannot resist interfering. I would ignore anything she said to you.'

Arabella had risen to pour the tea, which had just been brought into the room. 'I am sure that if you were to go to Bristol tomorrow and tell Sir James all you have told us, he would reassure you. I vow that I would love the expedition, and mean to accompany you.'

Arabella had her back to Crystal and her husband, and did not see the warning look Marcus directed at Crystal. It was accompanied by a shake of the head, which she was at a loss to understand until some minutes later, when Arabella was obliged to leave the room, and Marcus explained.

'Do not allow Arabella to make any plans to go to Bristol, for I would be obliged to forbid any such expedition. I do not like to tease her with anything that might be damaging in her present delicate condition, and I have had the most serious news from the city.' Rising, he went to the window and pulled back the curtain, to reveal a sky, not dark as betokened the late hour, but bright orange.

'What is this? I do not understand.'

'The city of Bristol has been put to the torch! It is out of the question for you to go there.' Marcus looked unusually grim for one of his sunny temper.

'But the riot is over!' she stammered.

'Over! It has only just begun! If the reports I have received are accurate, and I believe them,' he jerked his head at that violent orange sky, 'we might be on the point of revolution.'

Crystal's dismay turned to the deepest anxiety. 'Then Sir James might be in danger! I must go to him at once! You must provide me with a horse.'

'Provide you with a horse!' He allowed the curtain to fall back into place, and resumed his place at the fire. 'A pretty fellow I should look, allowing a girl to go alone into that!' Seeing that she was about to argue with him, he forestalled her. 'Do not even think of it, Crystal. In fact, first thing in the morning I intend to give orders that no horse or carriage is to be taken from the stables.

Careless of your reputation I might have been, but of your life I am most certainly not.' A few seconds later he somewhat undermined the nobility of these sentiments by grinning outrageously, and adding, 'Besides, James would kill me if he came here to collect you and found you gone. Mind!' he admonished, as Arabella could be heard returning, 'not a word more of this! I do not wish my wife to be troubled in any way. The whole thing will probably be over in a day or two, and you can be quite sure that James will come to no harm.'

With these comfortable thoughts he was able to resume conversation with them for the remainder of the evening. But Crystal was not reassured. Her attempts to appear unconcerned were almost tested to their limits as she strove to join in the conversation of her kindhearted hosts, and it was with relief that she greeted the suggestion that they all retire to bed.

She had no intention of sleeping: her determination to exclude Sir James from her life was at an end. If he was in danger, she wished to be at his side. How unkind she had been to tell him that he was like Jake Monker! No two men could be less alike. She wanted desperately to tell Sir James that she loved him, and that she was sorry for the cruel and stupid things she had said. If he were to die! Covering her face with her hands, she watched the glowing sky through her fingers. No! She would will him to live! But he had a dauntless courage that had already led him into danger!

She planned to wait until the house was quiet and all the occupants asleep; then she would go down to the stables and take a horse and ride to Bristol.

It seemed as though she sat at the window for several hours, for someone, possibly a restless servant, moved about downstairs for a long while. Eventually silence reigned, and she crept down as quietly as she could. The front door was chained and bolted! She halted in dismay, for the sounds that she would make opening the door must surely rouse the household. Going into the break-fast-parlour that overlooked the front drive, she carefully raised a window and, holding up the skirt of her riding-habit, climbed out over the sill. The night air was

cold and clear, and the orange glow in the sky seemed
brighter than ever as she ran to the stables. It was the
work of a few minutes to saddle a horse, but she feared
that the stable-hands must hear her if she took it out into
the yard. A stertorous snoring and strong odour of cider
told her that they were beyond hearing a cannon, even if
it were to go off in these very stables! Murmuring
quietly to the horse, she walked it to the iron gates,
and a few minutes later she had mounted and was
riding furiously, by the light of that ominous sky, for
Bristol.

Private Brittan remained impassively at his post, staring
woodenly ahead. He had had only a few hours off duty,
and precious little sleep had he been able to get! His
Colonel had given him strict orders to guard this house
and to let no one in. Although why anyone should want
to come into the house of Sir James Allenwood he was
sure he did not know, but then he did not know why the
mob had razed all those houses and buildings. He looked
about the Square with abhorrence, for they had torn
down all the railings and pulled up the paving-stones.
The furniture from the looted houses was piled in the
middle as though ready for a huge bonfire. The stench of
fire and a pall of smoke hung over the Square, giving it
an evil aspect. The faces of the great horde who filled it
were sullen, their clothes ragged and charred, their spirit
dangerous. As they stared silently at the lines of
mounted Dragoons, a tense, uneasy silence reigned: no
one seemed to move, and imperceptibly there was a
stirring among the crowd. A change of mood turned a
crowd into a mob, and if they were bent upon more
damage, the Dragoons, now backed by the Gloucesters,
would have to move in force against them. Private
Brittan groaned inwardly. Had they not had enough of
riot? Besides, what use was their collective anger against
muskets and swords?

   He saw Sir James Allenwood talking to Colonel
Brereton on the other side of the Square: much good
talking was at this stage! Nodding to the Colonel, he was
making his way back to his house. A great shout went

up, and torches were raised and put to the bonfire.
Simultaneously, on the order to charge, rifles cracked
and confusion reigned. Private Brittan saw Sir James
disappear into the mob. Pity! He could not survive that
onslaught, for in their terror to escape the relentless
onward movement of the Dragoons, the people ran in
every direction. What on earth had made a cool-headed
man like Sir James suddenly walk into the very heart of
that mob? Private Brittan was caught in an agony of
indecision. His orders were to guard the house, but its
owner had fallen in the thick of the affray. Should he go
to him? Turning his head, he saw a girl with wild green
eyes and a smudged face, mounted on a sweating terrified horse, bearing down on him. She was trying to
urge her mount through a group of men and women who
were fighting the soldiers. Recognising her as the girl
living in the house he was guarding, he ran to her and
assisting her to dismount, attempted to push her to
safety.

Crystal struggled away from him. On her arrival at the
entrance to the Square, it had taken her only a moment
to comprehend what was about to happen. Her eyes
sought out and found Sir James immediately, for there
was no mistaking that dark head or those broad shoulders. Some instinct had made him turn in her direction,
for an instant their eyes met and locked, and a message
seemed to pass between them. Then, to her horror, she
had seen him plunge into the crowd, as though by force
of will he would part that sullen company to be at her
side.

'Sir James is in there! You must help me to find him!'
she gasped at a bemused Private Brittan.

'I've got orders to guard the house, miss. I daren't
disobey!'

'Then I shall go alone!'

From the corner of her eye Crystal could see a line of
blue and yellow as the horsemen continued their progress, great swords flashing up and down to cut a way
through the wall of bodies. It evoked an older and more
terrifying memory, and she put her hands to her ears to
blot out the hoarsely shouted orders to rioters—or

soldiers—she did not know or care. She had to reach Sir James before that remorseless line of blades hacked him to pieces, as it hacked all those who impeded its implacable progress. Pray God that he was still alive! Miraculously the crowd dispersed for a moment, scattering like chaff before the soldiers, and she saw him on the ground. With a hand to his head, he was looking about him dazedly.

'James! James, my darling!' She rushed forward and, dropping to her knees, gathered him into her arms. It was impossible to escape the carnage; they would both die, but at least they would die together. Hooves flashed perilously close to her head, and she held her arms round her man to protect him.

She could not tell how it happened, but one moment she was kneeling on the grass with the man she loved, and the next she was torn from him by rough arms, her screams of protest merging with the shrieks and cries of the dying around her. Someone was dragging her backwards, back, it seemed, into the oncoming soldiery. Her last glimpse of the man dearer to her than all others was obscured by a black horse with upraised front quarters that threatened to crush him to death. Then a blow to the side of her head forced her down into a painful black quagmire.

Someone was moving quietly around the room, but Crystal remained very still and allowed consciousness to return slowly. With a great effort she recalled that she had been in the middle of the riot. There was some disturbing scene that she was trying to blot out—some dreadful spectacle from which she kept shying away. Suddenly across her mind's eye flashed the image of Sir James Allenwood in that moment when he had lain helplessly beneath the upraised hooves of the black horse.

'James!' she tried to cry out, but her voice was no more than a whisper.

'Now don't you fret, for he is downstairs and quite anxious to see you.' Mrs Hennessy bustled forward, a branch of candles in her hand. Firelight flickered over the rose-coloured bedroom.

'Do you mean that he is alive?' Crystal feared that she had misheard.

'Of course he is alive! That brave Colonel Brereton rescued him when he saw him go down in that brutish mob. He brought him here. It's you that was injured! If it hadn't been for Private Brittan, you would have been dead. He dragged you away from the others and in here. Nearly two weeks you've been in that bed. But, I must say, you look quite well now.'

'You have nursed me for two weeks? How kind of you! Thank you.'

'Don't thank me; I only got here a couple of days ago. It was Sir James who nursed you.' Mrs Hennessy allowed her gaze to travel over Crystal, then, colouring, she looked away, and said quickly, 'Not that it signifies, as you two are to be married.'

'Where is he? I must go to him!' Crystal sat up, and pushing back the covers, swung her legs to the floor.

'I don't know if that's advisable. You've been ill.' The housekeeper attempted to restrain her, but one look at the radiant face of the girl who was anxiously pulling off her nightgown and attempting to struggle into her gown silenced her protests, and she helped her to finish dressing. 'Mind you don't stay downstairs for too long. You still need your rest.' But her admonishments had fallen into empty space, for Crystal was already on her way.

Gently pushing open the door of the library, she saw Sir James sitting before the fire, a book open on his lap. A moment later the book was on the floor and, with eyes blazing with love, he had crossed the space that divided them. Gathering her into his arms, he scanned her face as though he would devour her with his eyes; he would have bent to kiss her, but she pushed him gently away.

'You are not obliged to marry me because we have been alone for almost two weeks!' She had meant to say so much to him, but what foolish words with which to greet the man she loved!

'I am obliged to marry you, or rather you are obliged

to marry me, for I cannot live without you, as I have told you already.' His grip on her tightened, and he bent once more to kiss her.

Moving her head back, she averted her face and felt his warm breath on her cheek and neck and a langorous flame of desire to begin its heady course through her body. 'You must consider your position, Sir James. You cannot marry one with no name! Although . . . I think I recall that my name is Maria; it came to me when I was in the Square. The sight of those soldiers caused some early memory to return . . .'

'And your mother's name was Margaret Fry; she was an Englishwoman. Your father was Luis Manoel Delgado, a Portuguese. They were killed in one of the Brazilian revolutions, and you may have some family members, both here and in Portugal.' He grinned down at her startled face.

'But how do you know all this? Are you sure?' Crystal could hardly assimilate what he was saying. Was she dreaming?

'I'm not absolutely sure. Vernon Marshall made enquiries on your behalf when you first arrived at the mission, then months later, at the time I arrived seeking you, word arrived that a family of that name had perished. They had had a daughter, but her body was never found. No relatives ever came seeking the Delgados, so no enquiry as to the whereabouts of the child were ever set in motion.'

'But why did you not tell me?'

'I forgot! It seems stupid, but it did not seem important at the time. Recall, we spent only one evening together before you told me that you would not marry me. Fortunately I discovered that Sophia had been to see you, and could then guess whence stemmed your foolish objections. Likening me to Jake Monker! I shall punish you for that, my girl!'

She could not resist returning to the original subject. 'But, if you thought that names were so important, how on earth could you forget?'

'They *are* unimportant! Only you are important to me, so stop talking, because I am longing to kiss you.' Gently at first, then with increasing hunger, he kissed her until she could not help but respond.

Vainly she tried to make him see that he did not have to marry her, and she might be relieved to discover that she did have some identity, but still that would not gainsay that she had been the subject of a public auction and the inmate of the Home for Fallen Women and Wayward Girls. 'You think you must marry me only because we have been alone in this house. It is my reputation that you are considering.'

'Nonsense!' He grinned at her before resuming his pleasurable exploration. 'It is *my* reputation that I am considering!'

BRIGHT SMILES, *DARK* SECRETS.

Model Kristi Johanssen moves in a glittering world, a far cry from her small town upbringing.

She carries with her the horrific secret of physical abuse in childhood. Engaged to Philip, a top plastic surgeon, Kristi finds her secret a barrier between them.

Gareth, Philip's reclusive ex-film star brother, has the magnetism to overcome her fears.

But doesn't he possess a secret darker than her own?

Available July. Price £3.50

W⬤RLDWIDE

Pack this alongside the suntan lotion

The lazy days of summer are evoked in 4 special new romances, set in warm, sunny countries.

Stories like Kerry Allyne's **"Carpentaria Moon"**, Penny Jordan's **"A new relationship"**, Roberta Leigh's **"A racy affair"**, and Jeneth Murrey's **"Bittersweet marriage"**.

Make sure the Holiday Romance Pack is top of your holiday list this summer.

AVAILABLE IN JUNE, PRICE £4.80

Available from Boots, Martins, John Menzies, W. H. Smith, Woolworth's, and other paperback stockists.

SPOT THE COUPLE

AND WIN A

£1,000

REAL PEARL NECKLACE

PLUS 10 PAIRS OF REAL PEARL EAR STUDS WORTH OVER £100 EACH

No piece of jewellery is more romantic than the soft glow and lustre of a real pearl necklace, pearls that grow mysteriously from a grain of sand to a jewel that has a romantic history that can be traced back to Cleopatra and beyond.

To enter just study Photograph A showing a young couple. Then look carefully at Photograph B showing the same section of the river. Decide where you think the couple are standing and mark their position with a cross in pen.

Complete the entry form below and mail your entry PLUS TWO OTHER "SPOT THE COUPLE" Competition Pages from June, July or August Mills and Boon paperbacks, to Spot the Couple, Mills and Boon Limited, Eton House, 18/24 Paradise Road, Richmond, Surrey, TW9 1SR, England. All entries must be received by December 31st 1988.

RULES

1. This competition is open to all Mills & Boon readers with the exception of those living in countries where such a promotion is illegal and employees of Mills & Boon Limited, their agents, anyone else directly connected with the competition and their families.
2. This competition applies only to books purchased outside the U.K. and Eire.
3. All entries must be received by December 31st 1988.
4. The first prize will be awarded to the competitor who most nearly identifies the position of the couple as determined by a panel of judges. Runner-up prizes will be awarded to the next ten most accurate entries.
5. Competitors may enter as often as they wish as long as each entry is accompanied by two additional proofs of purchase. Only one prize per household is permitted.
6. Winners will be notified during February 1989 and a list of winners may be obtained by sending a stamped addressed envelope marked "Winners" to the competition address.
7. Responsibility cannot be accepted for entries lost, damaged or delayed in transit. Illegible or altered entries will be disqualified.

ENTRY FORM

Name ⎯⎯⎯⎯⎯⎯⎯⎯⎯⎯⎯⎯⎯⎯⎯⎯⎯⎯⎯⎯⎯⎯⎯⎯⎯⎯⎯

Address ⎯⎯⎯⎯⎯⎯⎯⎯⎯⎯⎯⎯⎯⎯⎯⎯⎯⎯⎯⎯⎯⎯⎯⎯

⎯⎯⎯⎯⎯⎯⎯⎯⎯⎯⎯⎯⎯⎯⎯⎯⎯⎯⎯⎯⎯⎯⎯⎯⎯⎯⎯⎯⎯⎯

I bought this book in TOWN ⎯⎯⎯⎯⎯⎯⎯⎯⎯⎯ COUNTRY ⎯⎯⎯⎯⎯⎯⎯⎯

This offer applies only to books purchased outside the UK & Eire.
You may be mailed with other offers as a result of this application.